The Billionaire Bodyguard Next Door

ERIKA LYNN

Acknowledgments

I'm so grateful to have people in my life who will read my books and give me honest feedback. It's their feedback and ideas that help give the book more depth and more heart.

Thank you Hannah and Dina for reading early versions of this book - even when I only had half of it written.

And thanks to you, my readers, for allowing me into your homes and your imaginations. I appreciate you more than you will ever know.

Enjoy!

Dear reader

While I don't normally put content warnings in the beginning of my books, if you do have triggers, I recommend quickly jumping to the back of the book to read about a specific potential trigger.

Prologue

LUNA

The night was a total bust.

I'd spent all this time on my hair and makeup and picked out a killer outfit, and for what? Nothing.

There were absolutely no prospects at this damn party. Trust me, I did a lap.

And then I did another lap, just to double-check my work.

I was thorough like that.

Paige promised this party was going to be riddled with hot guys. She was wrong. *Very* wrong.

Speaking of friends, where *was* Paige?

I scanned the room, which was bustling with people. I knew some of them from college and others must have been friends of Paige's roommate since I didn't recognize them.

My best friend was likely playing hostess with the mostest, making the rounds with her roommate. Besides, there were a lot of nooks and crannies in this ritzy apartment that made it damn near impossible to get a good vantage point.

Ohh there she is. I spotted her across the room, making out with some guy with a mullet.

Hmm. Not who I would have picked for her. But then again, our tastes—especially in the opposite sex—were night and day. She went for grungy guys, and I went for the bad boys.

At least it meant we were never vying for the same guy's attention.

While I contemplated extracting her, someone bumped into me with a thud, my vodka soda nearly spilling over the rim of the glass.

"Hey, watch it." I turned to glare at the culprit to find a man with warm brown eyes, a wide smile, and a sleeve full of tattoos cascading down his arm.

Well, hello there.

This night was looking up.

My mystery man must have just arrived, because I certainly wouldn't have missed him during my earlier rounds. He wore a black t-shirt that molded to his chiseled chest, and he'd paired it with dark skinny jeans and some shit-kicker boots.

This good girl needed a bad boy and the man in front of me fit the bill perfectly. I was sure of it.

"Sorry about that." He grinned, reaching out to make sure I was steady. "Someone thought flailing their limbs was a good idea." He glanced over his shoulder, and I followed his gaze.

Sure enough, someone was dancing—if you could even call it that—on the dance floor.

I sank into my hip, accentuating my curves, and nodded at the real offender. "Well, that's a hazard."

"Hence my bumping into you," the tattoo guy said as he scanned my body, and I couldn't help but notice the look of appreciation on his face while he did. "Any injuries I should be aware of?"

I bit my lip playfully. "Are you a doctor?"

"Yes," he said, eyes alight.

I reached out, casually running my hand down his arm. "I've never seen a doctor with tattoos like that."

He leaned into the touch. "And why can't doctors have tattoos?"

I shrugged. "I'm not saying they *can't*. I'm just saying I haven't seen it before. Maybe I should take a closer look."

A broad smile broke across his face. "I think that's a fantastic idea."

He grabbed my hand and led me to the kitchen where the drinks were laid out on the counter. He snagged two beers and then led us through the living room and out onto the small rooftop garden.

If anyone glanced our way, I didn't notice. I was too focused on the man in front of me. We hadn't even exchanged names yet, and I wanted to know everything about him— who he was, and what he did for a living because this man was not a doctor. For one, I could feel the calluses on his palm. I'm pretty sure doctors didn't have time for the manual labor required to carve those into his hands.

Second, he had a mysterious glint in his eyes. One that made me think he was joking and wanted to run with this ridiculous ruse.

The man was so scrumptious I had no qualms about letting him do just that.

My kitty was certainly in agreement. It had been two long months since I'd gotten laid, and I was practically in heat.

If this gorgeous man had a working dick, he'd suit my needs just fine.

As long as he wasn't a serial killer.

That would be a hard pass for me, which should go without saying, but I feel like I should mention it, nonetheless. I do have *some* standards.

But pending that, it was game on. While he sat down, I took a quick second to smooth my hair.

I had spent a considerable amount of time styling it,

perfecting the 1950s movie starlet look I'd been going for. Earlier this week, I'd found a gorgeous dress at a thrift store and the whole vision practically formed in front of my eyes. It was frankly the only reason I dared to venture out tonight. I should be spending time working on my business plans. It was my only day off from Veuve where I worked as the assistant manager under my mentor Gigi Holstein.

But the lure of hot men and some much-needed me time tipped the scales.

The sizzling specimen in front of me patted the spot next to him. The terrace only had room for a small loveseat, which I planned to take full advantage of.

I sidled right next to him, our thighs touching. My bare leg against his tight black slacks.

In a swift—and frankly presumptuous move—he lifted my feet off the ground, turning my legs so they were in his lap. The gesture was reserved for an intimate partnership between two people who were completely comfortable with one another.

And us.

He grinned. "What's your name?"

I wasn't distracted at all by his large hand right above my knee. Nope. Not even a little. "Luna, and yours?"

"Beckett, although all my friends call me Beck."

I reached out and palmed the scruff lining his cheeks. "And do I get the honor of calling you my friend?"

He leaned over, his scent infiltrating my senses. Beck smelled of pine and mint. Fresh and clean, and for some reason a startling contrast to the way he looked. Although I should know by now not to judge a book by its cover, we all do it. His breath was warm as it hit the shell of my ear. "You can call me whatever you'd like, gorgeous."

A shiver slithered down my spine. "Flattery will get you everywhere."

He smirked. "There's more where that came from."

"I'm sure of it. Although I have to tell you, that was one cheesy line." The man's tongue was made of honey and if anyone could pull off cheesy, it was him. "How do you know Paige?"

He frowned. "Who's Paige?"

That made me laugh. "She lives here with her roommate." I pointed to the glass partition that separated us from the inside of the vast apartment most people would kill to have. "You know, the party you're at. She's the host. Bubbly brunette with a streak of pink in her hair, nose piercing."

He nodded. "Ahh, Paige and Kristina, right? I just moved in on nine. I met some women in the elevators, and they insisted I come tonight. Apparently, they were worried there wouldn't be enough hot guys." He narrowed his eyes. "You wouldn't know anything about that, would you? I think they mentioned a certain friend demanding hot men in attendance."

I shook my head, the picture of innocence. My friends knew they could lure me here with the promise of good-looking men that could help me scratch my itch.

"Doesn't ring a bell, and that definitely doesn't sound like me." Then I sat up straighter, leaning back to take him in. This man was what wet dreams are made of. Like hot book boyfriend material. Those men were just works of fiction.

That could only mean... "You're not some sort of gigolo, are you?"

The man was *that* good-looking. It was a genuine question. There was a very real possibility women paid good money for this man to fuck them senseless.

So that's a third thing we could add to my list of requirements to break my dry spell: a working dick, not a murderer, and not a gigolo.

That's a solid list.

I waited for his response with bated breath.

Finally, Beck threw back his head and released a rumbling

laugh, his deep voice rattling his chest. Tears sprung in his eyes.

I swiped them away, wanting to soak up as much of this time with him as possible before sending him on his way, because again, gigolos were not on my list. A noble profession, if done consensually. Just not for me. "Sooo, yes?"

He winked. "I'm a doctor, remember?"

I pointed at his face. "You did that little wink there, and it undermines everything you said after that."

Beck captured my hands and glanced down. His thumb rubbed against my inner wrist. "What's this?"

I didn't need to look down to know exactly what he was asking about. The soft spot between my palm and my wrist was home to a "c" shaped scar. It had been there since I was seven when I'd accidentally tugged the cord of my grandma's ancient curling iron, only to have it fall on my arm, leaving behind a permanent mark.

I used my free hand to cover it as I shared the story with him.

His brows furrowed. "Did it hurt?"

"Yes. I sobbed so hard I gave myself a headache. My grandma felt terrible, so she sent my grandpa out to get us both Dairy Queen sundaes. That's when I learned I could cry and get ice cream. Gotta love a silver lining."

"And you have a badass scar."

I rolled my eyes. "Yes, that's definitely what mattered to seven-year-old Luna."

He smirked. "No doubt."

Beck squeezed my hand one more time before letting go, breaking that physical connection.

But I couldn't *not* touch him. I poked him gently in his firm chest. "Now that you know my scar, I want one of yours."

He splayed a hand in front of him. "There are so many to choose from."

My eyes darted to his bare skin, searching for hints of scars. I used the opportunity to run my fingers down his tattoo-covered arm, mesmerized by the intricate patterns I found there. "Did you cover any—" I gasped, my fingers finding the mark.

If I didn't know better.

"Is that a gunshot wound?" My voice was barely a whisper.

He nodded solemnly. "I got that one in Afghanistan while trying to evacuate a hospital from enemy fire."

"Did it hurt?" I asked, my lungs seizing as my finger glided over the spot that he'd covered in intricate waves that reminded me of a famous Japanese artist. The design was dizzying. Gorgeous and rough. Rugged.

"Yes."

"Did you cry?"

His thumb reached out and swiped a thumb across my lips. "I cried like a baby."

My head tilted into his palm, like a cat seeking comfort. "Brave of you to admit it."

"Men shouldn't be afraid to show pain or feelings. Shouldn't be afraid to be human." He sounded like he meant it.

How might our world look different—look better and safer—if men were strong enough to show their emotions, to let them breathe? "I couldn't agree more."

Sitting here, string lights casting a glow across his face and the darkness of night surrounding us, I felt I knew this man. Somehow, the stars aligned and sent him straight to me. Some cosmic forces at work.

I wondered if he could feel it too, as his hand covered mine, holding it right around his upper arm.

He stared deeply into my eyes. "It doesn't hurt anymore."

I peered at him from beneath my lashes. "Are you sure?"

His Adam's apple bobbed. "Positive."

Before I could second guess myself, I bent forward and kissed the scar, a million follow-up questions sitting on the tip of my tongue.

Beck growled in response, immediately threading a hand through my hair, drawing my mouth to his.

One thing was certain: this outfit wasn't going to waste, and my dry spell would finally come to a satisfying end.

CHAPTER 1

Luna

"WHAT DO YOU MEAN, it's going to take six more months? You said three months, and that was two months ago. The math isn't mathing."

I adjusted my hard hat. They were required on all job sites, although it really ruined my look. My red bob would be a frizzy mess by the time I was done here, but I'd gladly sacrifice my usual put-together look to ensure this latest venture was a success.

Unfortunately, the second I set my stiletto-clad foot out of my car, I knew it was bad news. My contractor hadn't told me the whole truth, and I'd gone too long between site visits. I should've been personally checking in on the progress every other day to keep them on their toes.

Jordan Weber, my lead contractor on the project, proceeded to spin some bullshit web of confusing, circular arguments without ever really explaining explicitly why my project was months behind. I should be walking around a building with some completed walls and a semblance of the casino it would become. As it stood now, the space was basically a blank slate. There were slabs of concrete and not much else…

A sharp pain jabbed behind my eyes. "Dammit."

I knew this feeling all too well. My migraines had been getting worse lately. The late nights at the club combined with early mornings checking on my new project were running me ragged.

Pivot, Marks. Make a new plan.

"I want to see all your emails on this project within two hours. I'm going to make some calls."

I turned on my heel and went back to my black sedan. Luckily, my driver, Darnell, hadn't left. He knew the drill and would stick around until I gave him a solid ETA on when I'd need him to return.

As I opened the car door, I turned over my shoulder. "Get me those emails, Jordan. I'll be back tomorrow to talk to you and the crew."

Then I slid into the car and shut the door, wincing at the loud noise.

Fuuuuuck.

I searched my purse to find my medication. If I took it early enough, I could avoid the worst of it.

My hand slid over the familiar cylindrical container. "Gotcha."

I popped the lid and threw back the little white pill, unscrewing the top of my water bottle and sipping some water to help the pill reach its destination.

My sunglasses provided some protection against the glaring summer sun. The tinted windows added another layer.

Still, it wasn't enough.

I groaned, pinching my eyes closed and tipping my head against the leather headrest.

"I'll turn the music off, ma'am," said Darnell.

"Thanks, D."

He turned off the light jazz music he loved to play.

I willed the migraine to go away.

There were so many things I'd have to do.

First, hire a new contractor—perhaps a woman this time. I should have done that from the jump. Second, I needed to follow up to see if we had an issue procuring the resources for the project or if it was a result of failed leadership. Contemplating these necessary next steps did nothing to help the metaphorical icepick currently lodged between my eyeballs.

"We're going to have to make trips out to the worksite every other day, Darnell."

"We can do that," Darnell assured me.

"Remind me to give you a raise when my head doesn't feel like someone ran a spike between my eyes." My stomach roiled.

That was *not* a good sign.

Please work, medicine. It would totally ruin my day to have to pay for Darnell's car to get detailed because I couldn't keep my breakfast down.

"Just ten more minutes," Darnell said, as he pressed the turn signal.

"Thank God." I didn't think I could manage much longer in this car. With my eyes closed, I dug into my bag, searching for my little blue sea bands. I'd purchased them for a flight long ago and they were frayed from overuse. The little bands were supposed to hit pressure points in my wrist to naturally alleviate nausea.

I could use all the help I could get. Even if I was half convinced it was just a placebo effect.

By some miracle, I made it to my brownstone without spewing my guts all over the nice leather seats. I waved off Darnell, insisting I was well enough to get myself in bed.

I managed to enter my sixteen-digit code that Sebastian Steele, a friend and confidant, made me set up. It only took three tries.

The door clicked open as something caught my eye in the periphery. A *for-sale* sign, next door.

Hmm, that wasn't there this morning.

But that was the least of my worries. I stumbled inside, kicking off my heels, and landing on the chaise lounge near the door. Despite what I told Darnell, there was no way I'd make it up the stairs.

My phone beeped, and the high-pitched chime rattled in my ears.

It didn't work. The medicine didn't work. The nausea worsened. The spike through my brain stayed firmly in place.

I wanted to curl up and cry. Instead, I glanced at my watch. It was still early, but there was a good chance I couldn't get off this chaise lounge today.

"Hey, Siri. Call Monroe." I had to let someone on my team know I was incapacitated and unlikely to come in today.

The phone rang. I curled up in a ball, the phone lying in front of me on the plush chaise.

"What's up, boss?" Monroe answered.

I'd hired Monroe last year, and it was one of the best business decisions I'd ever made. Trust was hard for me to come by, but Monroe earned that trust every day.

"Monroe," I groaned.

"Shit, it happened again, didn't it?"

I hummed. "It's bad this time."

"Did you take your meds?"

"Yes but not working." Great, I couldn't even speak in full sentences. "Fort, hold down."

Annnnd now I'm Yoda.

"Aye aye, Captain. You can count on me," Monroe said, as if eager for the challenge. "Do you need us to drop anything off?"

"Fine," I insisted before hanging up, even though I was far from *fine*. I couldn't spend even ten more seconds on the line.

I sighed. Blissful silence… Until I succumbed to the pain, and soon the lure of sleep pulled me in.

CHAPTER 2

Beck

"CONGRATULATIONS, Mr. Bennet. The house is officially yours." Gabby Espinoza, my real estate agent, shook my hand after I signed on the dotted line. The last of the dotted lines, if we were being precise.

Purchasing a house was akin to signing your life away.

In this case, that turned out to be a good thing because Alice and I were getting our very own brownstone.

A place with an actual backyard, just a stone's throw away from her new school. I wouldn't have to worry about her on the terrace of the skyscraper we'd called home for the past seven years.

Maybe we could even get that dog she'd asked for every day since she was three.

I dragged a hand through my hair. *I should have done this sooner.*

The guilt pooled low in my gut and I tossed it to the side.

Better late than never. At least that's what I told myself.

"Daddy, when do we move in?" Alice asked from her chair beside me in the real estate office in Brooklyn. The stark white office looked nothing like those real estate shows on television.

Gabby lined up all the papers in front of her. "You can move in as soon as the ink is dry."

"Wonderful." I picked up my phone and texted my assistant, Miles, to make the arrangements with the moving company. I planned to get new furniture for the new place, so it was mostly Alice's toys and our clothes that would make the trek from Manhattan to Brooklyn.

Alice had created a Pinterest board a month ago in anticipation of us finding the perfect family home. I hadn't even known about Pinterest until she pulled it up on my computer in the middle of a work call.

I turned to my daughter, her shock of curls obstructing some of her face. "Should we go out to celebrate?"

"Can we do pizza *and* ice cream?" Her earnest expression reminded me that this little girl held the key to my heart.

"Absolutely." I stood, reaching for her hand. I figured I had a year or two tops before she started protesting. We waved goodbye to Gabby. She'd be in touch within the hour, making sure I had copies of everything. The woman was efficient, which was one of the many things I appreciated about her.

Alice pressed the call button on the elevator that took us down ten stories to the ground floor.

"Want to walk by the new place first? Then we can time it to see how long it takes to get from our new home to the nearest pizzeria." I palmed my phone in my other hand, navigating Yelp to see that there were a couple of pizza places and ice cream options nearby.

Alice tugged my hand, glancing up at me. "Daddy, maybe we could get ice cream *first*." She batted her eyelashes and brought her hands into a prayer pose. "Please. Pretty please."

I shook my head. "You know my stance."

"But—"

"No buts about it."

"Dad, don't be so cringe." She rolled her eyes and in that

moment, I caught a glimpse into the very near future. My feisty little girl would turn into a teenager, and I was not mentally prepared for that.

I should probably start reading some books. Not that I had free time on my hands. All my time was devoted to my daughter and my business, as it should be.

The business boomed. Damn, did it boom.

Turns out, our country wasn't the best at taking care of its veterans. That was where I came in. I offered good, meaningful work and employed retirees from all arms of the military.

Protection was big business. Especially when those doing the protecting had as much training as my people had.

I employed the best, the brightest, the boldest. My clients paid well for that. Everyone from professional athletes, to pop singers, to elected officials. There were a few billionaire clients on the roster too, including my friends Sebastian Steele and Dominic Waters. I charged them double since they usually pushed the boundaries of our friendship and what was expected of bodyguards. Plus, they intentionally withheld information to fuck with me.

If they called, I answered. They might not have served with me overseas, but that didn't make them any less my brothers.

"Daddy, look," my daughter shouted, pointing across the street. "Ice cream shop."

She gave me the biggest eyes, silently pleading for me to reconsider.

"No." I held firm, even though her smile fell. I'd give myself gold stars for sticking to my guns. Just then we came upon a pizzeria. The smell of yeast and melted cheese permeated onto the busy street.

My stomach grumbled. "Come on, Al. Let's eat."

"Fiiine," she said, full of sass, all the while beaming at me, the expression tugging on my heartstrings even more.

CHAPTER 3

Luna

"CALL IF ANYTHING COMES UP. I appreciate you getting a handle on the procurement process." I hung up on the new contractor leading my team, having fired Jordan and a few of his top guys.

It had only taken a few calls to realize why we didn't have the materials for the job site: Jordan never ordered them.

After that horrendous day at the job site, I'd called in the big guns. Having a cyber security expert as one of my best friends really came in clutch.

Within an hour, Sebastian tracked down all the ammunition I needed to fire Jordan's ass and not pay out the healthy sum he would have gotten if I'd breached the contract. As it was, he lucked out because I decided *not* to sue him.

Though, the idea did tempt me.

Now that Parvati led the project, things were already turning around. She sent daily photo evidence of the progress, including images of the shipments, and the team working hard.

Thank goodness for that. Women get shit done. I should have known that from the beginning.

Thankfully, that pesky headache of mine hadn't returned.

Having Parvati onboard significantly reduced my stress levels.

As long as I had a strong team around me, I could keep my businesses booming.

Speaking of businesses, I was due at Club Deux in thirty minutes.

Hair and makeup flawless, I put on a skin-tight blood-red bodysuit and a leather mini-skirt.

I was serving sex kitten, which felt ironic given that I'd been celibate for years now. As a club owner, it was exactly the look I was going for because, let's face it, sex sells.

Then I paired it with some killer heels that would be swapped out for unicorn slippers once I made it safely behind my massive desk at Club Deux. The club was my headquarters—the place where I ran all of my business ventures.

While I didn't have meetings until later in the day, I wanted to catch up on paperwork. That's what Sundays were for. The boutique casino resort I'd fondly named The Chateau required an ungodly number of permits, and I was double checking everything with my lawyer before submitting them to the city.

Then I'd meet with the interior designer and go over her latest sketches for the club at the casino. My new friend Faith Waters lent me her design expertise to improve the plans, and now they were infinitely better.

One final check on my hallway mirror and I was out the door. I had just stepped out of my brownstone when someone swore.

Wait, I knew that voice.

The deep timber. Voice like gravel.

I knew that voice. *Intimately.*

I'd gone years without hearing it and now it seemed to be popping up in the most inconvenient times. Like now.

Sure enough, my eyes bounced up from the lock pad to find Beck Bennet in front of me. Leather jacket, tight pants that molded to an ass that looked like it belonged to a base-ball player, and a mouth like a sailor. That filthy, dirty mouth that made me come harder than I ever had in my entire life.

"What the hell are you doing here?" I hissed quietly.

It was bad enough that the best one-night stand of my life disappeared eight years ago without a word. Then he popped up a few months ago while spending time with one of my good friends, Sebastian Steele. And now this?

This had officially gone too far.

Beck's gaze lifted to mine, a cell phone glued to his ear. "I understand. Focus on getting healthy and don't think about coming back until you're one hundred percent. I've got it handled."

While he spoke to whoever was on the other end of the line, he kept his eyes firmly on mine. "I'll check on you later."

My hand landed firmly on my hip.

"You're pretty," said a young voice.

That's when I noticed big bad Beck was not alone. There was an adorable little girl with outrageous curls at his side.

I softened. "Thanks, sweetheart. I'm Luna, and you are?"

"Alice!" she shouted with enthusiasm.

My gaze reluctantly returned to her father. Somehow, having a kid made this man even more attractive than any man had any right to be. Besides, he didn't look surprised to see me. If anything, that little smirk on his face made me think he *expected* to see me.

Wait…did they just come out of the house next door?

I glanced from the door to Beck to the door again, realization sinking in.

"You moved in next door?!" I sputtered.

I lied before; it hadn't been too far. This, this now, this was too far.

Beck seemed to take pleasure in this observation. A wide grin split across his face, almost as if he'd been anticipating my reaction. Then the smile fell, his attention turning back to his phone. He glanced between me and his daughter as if forming a plan.

Beck's attention darted between me and Alice. The line of his brow furrowed.

I didn't like this thinking face. Not one bit.

"Listen, I need you to watch Alice for a few hours. My nanny is out sick, and I have a work emergency I need to take care of."

I glanced at his daughter like she was an alien with two heads. Had I ever babysat a child? No, no I hadn't. I didn't know the first thing about kids.

"I don't know anything about kids. You need to find a grown-up to do this. Besides, I have work."

He held up his phone. "My nanny is severely ill. And if there was anyone else who could handle the work issue, I would send them. I wouldn't ask you otherwise."

"But you *didn't* ask!" I wagged my finger at him. "No. Bad, Beck."

Beck dragged a hand down his face. "I don't have a lot of options and if I know Sebastian, he's decked out your house. It's safe. You're a trusted adult. You can handle this. You *have* to handle this."

He was saying it to me, but part of me wondered if it was more to convince himself.

"Uh, but," I stuttered. "It's not baby proof."

We both glanced at his daughter who was now looking at me like *I* was the alien with two heads.

I gestured to my mouth. "As I was saying it, I realized how ridiculous it sounded." I shook my head. "But that doesn't matter because I don't know about babies or kids. And she definitely falls into the latter category."

Beck stepped forward, and I shifted back, fresh pine invading my senses. He shook my shoulders. "You're the grown up. You're a grown-ass woman with a growing busi-

unceremoniously re-entered my life a few months ago when Sebastian hired Beck to watch Faith who was getting accosted by paparazzi. We'd verbally battled those few times I'd seen him since, and his presence brought up a lot of old feelings…

My phone buzzed again.

BECK

Order the damn pizza, Luna.

I rolled my eyes at the command. The man was a first-class prick, and he knew it.

"Nobody even likes Hawaiian pizza," I muttered.

Alice's hand shot into the air. "I do. It's actually very popular."

I now felt personally responsible for making sure this kid knew there were better pizza options out there.

Yet my feet remained planted in the foyer, just like Beck knew they would be.

And with that little mental mind fuck, I got my ass in gear.

———

The pizza arrived twenty minutes later.

I'd called my team and told them I'd be working from home. This set Monroe on high alert. "Is it another migraine? Are you okay? Are you a fall risk?"

"I'm fine. Just working from here. Maybe the designer can make a house call instead. I'll text and see if she's flexible."

Monroe hummed in agreement. "And I'll hold down the fort at Club Deux. You know it's a slow night. We have a couple VIP booths reserved and Dean is set to work his magic."

Dean was one of the strongest VIP managers at the club. He was cute and flirty, and all the straight women and gay men fell in love with him. The man raked in the tips.

"Good, good." My eyes shifted to the couch. The *empty* couch.

Shit. "I've got to go."

I ended the call and started moving. "Alice, where are you?"

My palms began to sweat.

Oh God, I lost his daughter.

I was officially not to be trusted with children. I *told* Beck we needed a grown-up to supervise.

Panic rose in my throat as I dashed around the kitchen. The pizza remained in place, the box open on the marble island.

She was just here. Where could she have gone?

The pantry? *No.*

Bathroom? *No.*

The closet under the stairs? Also *no.*

The only thing saving my sanity was that my door would have beeped had she gone outside. I sent a mental thanks to Sebastian for the impeccable work he did designing his security app.

Something crashed upstairs.

Fuck.

I took the stairs two at a time, stopping abruptly at the adorable landing between floors. It was a gorgeous little alcove I used when I had a chance to read, and it occasionally served as my friend Faith's ersatz painting room.

And there's my floral vase from Oaxaca broken into a million little pieces on the ground.

Tears pooled in Alice's eyes. "I'm so sorry. I wanted to grab that." She pointed to a wooden princess doll I'd gotten from Magical Moments twenty years ago. My grandmother had taken me to this adorable little town called Christmas Cove, and the visit was filled with love, cookies, and celebrations that included the whole town. My grandmother died the following year, and those memories became imprinted on me as the last holiday before her passing.

At least it wasn't the doll.

The vase was expensive, but the doll was priceless.

"It's okay," I promised her. "Are *you* okay?" I scanned her body for any obvious injury.

Her tears threatened to spill over.

Ohhh, no. I don't think I could handle tears.

"I have an idea. Come get the dustbin with me and help me clean this up. Then we will go back downstairs—*where we will stay*—until your dad picks you up. Capiche?"

"What's capiche?"

I blinked. *Riiiight*, she's seven, not twenty-seven.

"Sound good?" I clarified.

She nodded earnestly. "Yes, let me help clean up."

So we set to our task. I obviously kept her away from the shards and had even insisted she get shoes before helping. Gold star to me.

After we finished, my stomach growled. "You ready for pizza, Alice? Because I'm starving."

"Let's go!" She raced down the stairs with the energy of a... well, a seven-year-old.

"Oh, boy..." I muttered.

CHAPTER 4

Beck

SOMEONE HANDED me the briefing document the second I walked into the office.

I needed the space as a command center where I could meet with prospective clients, manage operations, and onboard new employees.

Today, my team called me in because someone actually got shot on the job. It didn't happen often, because my people made sure it didn't. They performed background checks on everyone surrounding the clients they managed, learned their itineraries, and figured out the most secure ways in and out of a location.

Sometimes, however, things went wrong. We were in the business of protecting some of the most high-profile people in the world from politicians to diplomats and celebrities, it made the work interesting enough for my team of ex Marines and Navy Seals whose highly specialized talents were wasted otherwise.

Still, I didn't appreciate my people getting shot. Margot Madison was one of my most decorated employees and lived for the most dangerous assignments. The diplomat she was assigned to protect had traveled out of the country.

The details were written on the document in my hands. I squinted, the words blurring together, morphing on the page. I handed it back to Miles as we headed to my office. "Read it to me."

I couldn't afford to get the information wrong. We didn't need to get involved in an international incident because I mixed up a few letters, fucking up the details. Dyslexia did that to you.

"Sure," Miles said, clearing his throat. "Margot Madison, age twenty-nine, sustained a bullet wound to the upper arm. She was immediately transported to the local hospital and treated on site. Her client, Ambassador Armando Herandez, was unhurt in the incident."

We made it to my corner office and took our usual seats. "Do we know why she was shot at?"

Miles' brow furrowed as he read the report. "Initial reports consider it a freak accident."

I lifted my laptop and pulled up Margot's work phone. She'd have it on her like other employees. With a few taps, I initiated the video call.

Margot's disappointed face filled the screen. "Boss, I have it covered. I'll be out of here in an hour. Two tops."

I watched as she tugged at the various tubes and IVs connected to her.

"Stop doing that. You'll hurt yourself," I said immediately, putting on my best boss voice. It worked on the grown-ups I employed. It failed me when it came to my own seven-year-old.

Margot stopped picking at herself. "Fine. But I am perfectly okay over here. It was practically a graze."

I heard someone guffaw from Margot's side of the line.

"Who's in the room with you?" I asked, haunches raised. She better be in a secure location. I paid well for international insurance so that my people were protected in situations like this. The one thing about international deployments was that it made it harder to extract employees when they were compromised.

"It's Armando," Margot said, staring at something—or more likely *someone*—off screen.

I swiped my face, trying to hide my smile. "Margot, hand the phone to Armando."

"Do I have to?" she replied, sounding just like Alice. Sometimes managing people was just like parenting. Freakishly similar, really.

As if knowing she was going to lose this battle, Margot handed the phone to Armando.

The portly ambassador dabbed the sweat from his brow as he greeted me.

"Nice to see you again, Ambassador Hernandez. Are you okay? Were you injured at all?"

He continued to dab his face using his monogrammed handkerchief. "I'm perfectly fine. Just shaken up for poor Ms. Madison here."

I appreciated the sentiment. At least someone in that room was worried about Margot's condition.

Elbows on the table, I leaned forward. "Can you tell me what happened?"

"Boss, I'll have the full report for you in sixty," Margot said offscreen.

"I'm not asking for the report right now, Margot. I'm asking the ambassador a question."

I decided to ignore a few muttered expletives and suppressed a smile as I watched Armando turn beet red.

"Ambassador," I said, refocusing his attention on me. "Tell me what happened."

I listened as he recounted walking out of a government building after connecting with the local economic advisor. Given the political unrest in the country, we wanted to have coverage. It didn't sound like a targeted attack. If anything, it seemed like Margot and Armando got caught up in some local gang activity that had absolutely nothing to do with them.

"God, this is so embarrassing," Margot said once I finally let Armando pass the phone back to her.

"Nothing embarrassing about being shot," I firmly let her know.

"They weren't even trying to shoot at us! And I got hit anyway. I feel like this is amateur hour starring me in the lead role."

I frowned, knowing I'd probably feel similarly. And still, I didn't like her beating herself up. "You could be amazing at your job and still not know the local climate as well as you'd wish. This would have happened to anyone. This could have happened to me."

Margot was incredulous.

I ignored her. "The team is already figuring out transportation home. Miles is on the phone right now talking to the hospital administrators. We aren't going to let you out until you're cleared."

"But—" Margot started.

"The last thing we need is a medical incident mid-flight."

Margot leaned back in the hospital bed, trying to cross her arms, and failing, because of the IV line. "Understood."

"The Ambassador will go home with you, and you'll be grounded until you've fully healed," I explained.

Margot didn't like that. I watched amused as she bit her tongue, and probably not just metaphorically.

"Excellent. I need to go take care of a few things but if you need anything day or night, you call me. I want you both on US soil ASAP." My people came first, and I wouldn't feel fully settled until she was back home and taken care of by the doctor we had on retainer.

"Yes, sir," Margot replied, resigned.

I hung up and turned to Miles, rattling off at least a dozen other things we needed to do to plan the extraction.

I scrubbed a hand down my face. This was going to take a little longer than I anticipated.

Especially considering Alice was nearing hour three at Luna's house.

What the fuck had I been thinking?

Oh, yeah, I didn't have a lot of options.

The face Luna had made when I forced her to watch my daughter: you'd think I'd just told her she had to sit down to take a final exam for a class she'd never been to.

I dragged a hand through my hair, then remembered I'd cropped it short again, just like in my marine days.

Finding any semblance of balance between my responsibilities felt damn near impossible especially under circumstances like this where I had few backup options for watching Alice. So much had changed in the last few years and it was like my mind was still playing catch up. Finding out I was a dad, becoming a one-parent household with a new child I had no idea how to care for, all the while growing my company into something I could be immensely proud of, it was a lot. Sometimes it felt too much to bear.

But then I got to go home to Alice, and all was right in the world.

I needed to find out how my girl was.

BECK

How's Alice? Everything okay over there?

LUNA

Just teaching her about world domination.

Despite myself, I chuckled as I entered the cab that would bring me back to the townhouse.

BECK

And she still has all her limbs and is otherwise unhurt after that masterclass you undoubtedly led?

LUNA

> Maybe.

Not comforting. But she was a responsible adult, and I knew she could handle my daughter. I trusted her with that even if she didn't trust herself.

I finished up a few calls and reviewed Margot's extraction plan, making sure I'd have Margot's replacement in country within the next few hours. With that in as good of a place as it was going to get, I finally left the office.

Ping.

Speaking of…

Luna sent a photo. I opened my text messages to find a photo of Alice sound asleep on the couch even though it was still early afternoon. Her curly hair was a mess across her face, and a plush black-and-white checkered blanket covered her body.

LUNA

> She crashed after eating her bodyweight in chocolate. That's what you're supposed to serve kids that aren't your own, right? Lots of sugary goodness so that they're great for their parents.

BECK

> I doubt you keep enough sugar in your house to make her crash. But thanks for the proof-of-life photo. I appreciate that.

LUNA

> I made her watch Persuasion with me. I think the British accent is what did her in.

BECK

> Undoubtedly.

My fingers hovered over the send button. I tapped it,

closing the phone and tossing it on the seat next to me. I wanted to ask so many more questions of the woman that left me hanging after that perfect night together.

When she had reappeared in my life a few months ago, it felt like a sign. Like we were drawn back together for a reason after all these years.

And now the perfect one-night stand was now my next-door neighbor.

Before I knew what I was doing, my phone was back in my hands, our text thread on my screen.

I typed and deleted and retyped half a dozen variations of the questions that had haunted me over these past eight years.

Maybe I wasn't the only one, because when I paused my typing the dots danced. Bouncing up and down before disappearing. Then they'd start their dance again.

Again, they stopped.

It was a fucking tease.

BECK

I'm ten minutes away.

LUNA

Good.

BECK

Good.

CHAPTER 5

Luna

I CHECKED ON ALICE AGAIN, adjusting the blanket that had slipped down her little body as she tossed and turned on the couch.

The little girl had been a total surprise. Once we finally cleaned up the mess upstairs, we sat on the couch and ate our pizza. She suggested we watch some show I'd never heard of, and I insisted I introduce her to the world of Austen.

Turns out, seven-year-olds aren't too interested in second-chance romances. Her little snores started up within fifteen minutes of me pressing play.

I paused the television and pulled out my laptop to take care of some emails. If Beck came back soon, I'd still be able to make the meeting with my designer. We agreed to meet at a coffee shop a block over, so it would be easy for me to slip out as long as the tiny human had some adult supervision.

Again, I checked the time. How much longer would he be?

Just then my phone chimed.

Speak of the devil.

Beck was checking in, asking about Alice. My goal was to give him heart palpitations.

Finally, he mentioned he was about ten minutes away.

I felt an odd catch in my chest. In the shock and confusion of being put in charge of his daughter, I hadn't fully processed the new reality:

Beck Bennet lived next door.

When the hell was he planning on telling me this? Sure, it's not like we didn't bicker like an old married couple whenever we were together. Or that he conveniently never called me after the best sex of my life even though I deliberately gave him my number.

I *never* gave out my number.

One-night stands were one-night stands for a reason.

Except with Beck, it had felt different from the jump. From the second he knocked into me at that party, there was the invisible string tying us together.

But then invisible strings were the stuff of fairytales.

After that night with Beck, I swore off bad boys. Turned off the neon sign on my forehead that drew guys like Beck to me like a moth to the flame. Unfortunately, it didn't stop that *other* man from trying to…

I pushed thoughts of *that* night to the side. *That* night that made me avoid intimacy

Since then, I've dated *nice* guys. Clean cut, polo shirt and khaki wearing guys who'd fit in seamlessly at a country club. There was a string of them: Connor, Noah, Daniel, Carter.

Ohh Carter. He was the most recent of my failed relationships.

All part of my attempt to erase the best night of my life from my memory.

A motion detector alert flashed on my phone, bringing me back to the present.

Beck was back.

I set my laptop on the coffee table and got to my feet. I smoothed out the skirt I'd kept on despite the change of plans.

Beck knocked on the door. I opened the door quickly, not bothering to greet him, before turning on my heel back to the living room.

"You have some nerve just dropping your daughter off." I glanced over my shoulder to glare at him.

"It's not like I had a lot of options, trust me," he grumbled.

I lowered my voice, Alice still sleeping soundly on the couch. "Well, you trusted me with your child. Which seems like terrible parenting in my book."

Beck's face softened as he spotted his daughter. "Did she give you any trouble?"

I shrugged. "Broke a vase, but she helped clean it up. Otherwise she was good, minus the fact she spent the afternoon with a perfect stranger. She was much easier to spend time with than her dad." I gave him a pointed look.

"You're not a stranger." Then a deep v formed between his brows, and he did a little motion with his fingers. "Let's rewind. What do you mean she broke a vase?"

Alice stirred. Our conversation paused as our attention swayed to her.

"Daddy?" she said sleepily, rubbing her eyes.

"Yes, sweetheart. I'm here." Beck bent down and picked up his daughter, cradling her against his chest.

It made my heart tumble, the reaction foreign to me.

Beck brushed the hair out of her face and kissed Alice's forehead. "Let's get you home."

He carried her to the front door, turning before he made his exit. "Thanks for watching my baby."

I nodded, unsure what to say.

Then, just as he was leaving I called out, "Don't think we won't talk about this new neighbor thing."

He chuckled softly, his good-natured laugh ringing like bells in my ears. "I expect nothing less."

———

Beck hadn't followed up. Hadn't come over to explain why he was suddenly my new neighbor.

"The audacity!" I bellowed, filling Faith in on everything.

We were at her place in the city, and I was busy petting her dog, Willow, behind her ears. Willow usually stayed at the home upstate, but occasionally Sebastian and Faith brought her to the city for their quick twenty-four-hour visits.

Willow *loved* the city. There were so many new smells and places to explore. But the city wasn't the best place for a pup who was used to wandering around.

Faith leaned forward, hands planted firmly on the blanket around her as we faced each other on her gray sectional. "He didn't tell you he moved next door?"

I shook my head. Faith's expression was appropriately incredulous, just as it should be.

"Nope. Just one day, out of absolutely nowhere, I go to leave my house and poof, there he is." I snapped my fingers. "Just like that. Like a fucking genie. And then he asked me to watch his daughter."

Faith's jaw dropped. "Wait. You watched Alice?"

"Yup," I said, popping my 'p.' "The man said he had an emergency and just left his daughter with a complete stranger!"

She held up a finger. "*Wait*, you're the stranger in this scenario?"

"Yes! I'm an unfit guardian. And she doesn't even *know* me. And the worst part of it—she likes *pineapple on her pizza!*"

Faith gasped in mock indignation. "Not pineapple on pizza! Sacrilege!"

I playfully pushed her arm. "Oh, shut up. You know it's questionable."

Faith rolled her eyes. "Let the innocent seven-year-old decide what she likes and doesn't like on her pizza."

I crossed my arms. "You're not seeing a problem with any of this?"

Faith shrugged. "Honestly, not really. So the guy you had a one-night stand with and never called you back moved in next door. NBD."

I hitched forward. "No. Big. Deal? Are you serious right now? Aren't you supposed to be my friend? You literally just said that Beck is the guy I can't stand."

Faith smiled coyly. "Don't you think all that built-up tension means something?"

I poured another glass of Pellegrino. "Please. It means we're likely to combust when we're together."

Faith narrowed her eyes. "You know, you never did tell me what happened between you two."

I crossed my legs. "That's because nobody needs to hear this story."

"You realize that only makes me want to hear it more, right?"

"I promise. It's not that exciting." Panty-melting sex was actually very exciting. What happened after? Not so much.

"Tell me. Tell me," Faith chanted.

I shoveled a giant forkful of noodles into my mouth.

"I'm pretty sure you're the one who encouraged me to climb Sebastian like a tree. Why clam up now?" Faith asked. "Besides, now might be the time to throw that sage advice back in your face."

The noodles tasted like soap on my tongue. I set the bowl down and used the napkin from my lap to dab the corner of my mouth. What happened between me and Beck was something I never spoke about. To anyone. It was too embarrassing and nothing embarrassed me.

Except the sharp pain of rejection that came from the hottest man to walk this planet.

I mentioned the multiple orgasms, right? I'm pretty sure I mentioned those once or twice.

How I'd canceled plans the day after we hooked up in anticipation of his call. How I watched the screen to see if he'd called, going so far as restarting the phone because something certainly had to be wrong with it if he said he was going to call but didn't. I'd checked the charge no fewer than half a dozen times that day.

And when he still hadn't bothered to call days later, the feeling of being let down crushed me. Reminded me of another man who was full of promises and no follow through.

But Beck...

I felt the loss of the *potential* of him. I didn't love him—I wasn't crazy enough to fall for someone that quickly—but there was something kindling between us.

Or so I foolishly thought.

Faith's teasing grin disappeared. "Now I'm worried he hurt you and I need to go kick his ass or something."

"He didn't physically hurt me, if that's what you're concerned about."

"Hurt isn't always physical." She set her glass down on the coffee table with a thunk. "I'm going to pull a you and kick his ass."

Faith went to stand, and I tugged her arm down. "Fiiiin-neee. You win. I'll tell you everything."

I pulled the pillow out from behind me and placed it in my lap, playing with the little poms that surrounded all four sides.

My mouth suddenly felt dry as the Sahara. I sipped my water and cleared my throat. Faith looked on as if she were biting her tongue, waiting for me to begin.

"It was eight years ago."

Faith squealed. Her eyes bulged. "I knew it!"

Her wine almost sloshed over and onto the couch.

"Careful!" I shouted.

Faith settled, swiping up a streak of wine from the outside of her wine glass looking properly chastised. "Sorry."

"Eight years ago. We were at a party hosted by one of my

college friends. I was on the prowl. Beck fit the bill. And voila, we hooked up." I made a grand gesture with my hands.

Faith's smile fell. "Worst. Storyteller. Ever. Don't quit your day job."

"I never said the story was going to be good."

"Stop lying to yourself. Obviously it left an impression. Everyone who is everyone knows there is some sort of combustible history between you two. The story has to be good if it's left this much of an impression."

She had me there.

Faith tucked a strand of hair behind her ear. "And I know you aren't used to all this girl talk, so I'll take it easy on you."

A laugh burst from my chest. "How kind of you."

"Let's start from the beginning," she said, ignoring me. "Tell me exactly how you felt the moment you first got a look at him. Please tell me he was wearing a leather jacket."

I laughed again, some of my unease ebbing. "He wasn't wearing it when I met him at the party, but he definitely had his leather jacket on when he took me home."

Faith clapped her hands together. "I fucking knew it."

So I shared with her everything that happened at the party.

"Who suggested taking the party elsewhere?" Faith asked.

My lips twitched. "Me."

"Yes!" she said. "Love an empowered woman who knows what she wants."

I pointed to myself. "And this woman wanted him. All of him."

"And you got him."

"I did." I patted myself on the back.

"Something tells me it's the *after* that was the problem."

"That's where it got messy. Or didn't because he didn't call."

She narrowed her eyes. "He asked for your number but didn't call you?"

"Mmhmm."

"And you're still mad about it?" she hypothesized. "It seems like something you would have brushed off."

I suddenly became very interested in my nails. Perhaps I should swap out the cherry-red polish for something even darker. A deep navy or maybe just go all black.

If I had to really examine it, I would venture that I was still mad about it because if he had called me, I might not have gotten into the situation that happened mere days *after* Beck and I hooked up.

"Luna—"

"Faith—"

She poked my arm. "You like him. That's why it hurts so much."

I swallowed. "I like him a lot."

"As in present tense?"

I shook my head. "No. No present tense. Dude didn't call me. If he was the man for me, he would have figured out a way to reach out."

Her brows knitted together. "When did you see him after that? When was the first encounter?"

"He came to my club with Sebastian once."

Faith gawked. "No, he didn't."

I nodded. "He did. Didn't know it was mine. He damn near tripped over his feet when he saw me. Luckily I'd worn my best bustier. The man practically had his tongue hanging out of his mouth."

"So what happened next?"

"Once the initial shock wore off, he had the audacity to be mad. At *me*."

"Why would he be mad at you if he's the one who didn't call?"

"Great question."

"And have you asked him that question?"

I sank back into the couch. *Had I asked him*?

If I was being honest, I probably hadn't. I couldn't think clearly through the red haze of anger that had overtaken me that night. Sebastian hadn't mentioned he'd be bringing a friend, and I don't think I had been kind to either of them. Sebastian had pulled me aside afterwards to ask what had happened, but when I didn't answer him, he didn't push it.

Smart man.

That was six months ago. I'd seen him several times in the past couple of months now that he was busy protecting Faith from aggressive paparazzi and public interest in the former socialite. Luckily, that interest died down, making it safer for Faith to go out on her own.

"Have you?" Faith prodded.

"Probably not…" I said, sheepishly. "I'll ask him next time I see him."

Faith tilted her head, as if to say *really*?

I nodded reassuringly. "I promise. Besides, I've cooled off. I'm totally fine now."

My friend arched a perfectly tweezed brow.

"Yep, totally fine."

CHAPTER 6

Beck

"YOU'VE ALREADY POTTIED three times. I think you're fine."

Alice held up a finger. "Just one more time, Daddy."

I scrubbed a hand down my face. "Fine," I said as she shuffled past me, out her bedroom door and into the connecting bathroom. "Last time and then you need to go to bed. For real this time. You have school in the morning. We can't be late."

Alice went through these phases of challenging me every time we went to bed. Her excuses ran the gamut. I was sure I'd look back at this stage and laugh, but at this moment, the only thing I wanted to do was put on some sweatpants and relax on the couch or grab a beer with a friend— anything to distract me from thinking about the woman next door.

I took my phone out of my pocket, shooting a quick text to Sebastian while Alice washed her hands.

BECK

Join me for a beer before you head back upstate.

Sebastian would probably come up with some excuse to

avoid hanging out with me. The man preferred to spend his time with Faith Waters. I'd never seen my friend smitten with a woman and I'll be damned, but my grumpy friend was completely enamored with Faith. They were basically attached at the hip.

I'd teased him about it endlessly once the job he hired me to do was completed.

Returning to the present, I could still hear the water from the faucet. "Alice, your hands are clean. In bed, now."

"But I haven't sung the ABCs!" she protested.

I motioned for her to hurry up. "You could have sung the ABCs multiple times by now. Come on, we don't want to waste water."

Alice huffed, shutting off the water and bumping into me as she passed by. She flung herself onto her bed, pouting some more as if my request for her to get some sleep was a major affront. It was already past nine.

I winced just thinking about waking her up in the morning. She'd be a grumpy bear, and I'd have to deal with it.

I'd rather deal with a bastion of ex-Marines on a warfront than deal with a sleepy Alice.

"Good night, sweetheart." I kissed the top of her head and adjusted the comforter. She was very particular about it covering up to her chin.

I headed downstairs and grabbed a beer from the fridge when my phone buzzed in my pocket.

SEBASTIAN

Sure.

I reread the text a couple of times.

BECK

Wait. Seriously?

SEBASTIAN

Is that a real question?

BECK

I was half assuming you'd say no. I figured you'd be too busy with Faith to get away.

SEBASTIAN

Are you trying to uninvite me now?

BECK

I would never.

SEBASTIAN

What time should I come over?

BECK

Now work?

SEBASTIAN

Yes. I'll be over soon.

Less than two minutes later, my phone alerted me that someone was at the door.

Maybe it's Luna. I picked up the pace, only to be sorely disappointed to find my best friend on my stoop.

Sebastian frowned. "You asked me to come over and you give me that sour puss look? What the fuck man?"

I shook my head. "Sorry. It's just that I thought it might be —" I shut my mouth. "Never mind. I just figured it was too fast for you to get here, so I thought it might have been someone else."

He assessed me in that shrewd way of his, like he was mentally cataloging people who might stop by as I opened the door the rest of the way to let him pass.

Finally, we shook hands like we always did.

"Beer?" I offered, lifting my glass.

"Just one," he said, clapping me on the back.

He followed me into the kitchen, and I pointed to a few

things along the way including the bathroom and my small home office since it was his first time here.

I headed to the fridge and grabbed a bottle of the IPA I was drinking. "Take a seat wherever. I'd give you a tour of the rest of the place, but Alice is asleep and I don't want to risk waking her up."

Sebastian waved me off. "I get it. The place is nice, not that I had any doubt. I just can't believe you're actually out of the city."

I palmed my glass. "Right? Took me long enough."

He smiled. "I'm sure Alice tells you that every day."

"So how the hell did you get here so quickly? If I didn't know any better, I'd assume you were in a car outside just waiting for me to extend an invite."

Sebastian chuckled. "The real reason is hardly that exciting. Faith's visiting Luna next door. I was getting some work done at a coffee shop across the street."

I nearly levitated out of my seat. "She's next door? With Luna?"

"Yes. I thought it was interesting when you texted me your new address the other day." The statement was heavy with the words left unsaid.

Besides, distracting myself from the woman next door was the whole reason for this impromptu hangout to begin with. Now that I knew for sure she was home, it would be even harder to concentrate on my friend.

"Tell me," he said.

I dragged my thumb across my bottom lip and suppressed a smile. "I moved in next door to Luna."

It wasn't the big bombshell I expected it to be, especially since Sebastian had already figured it out.

He shook his head as if I were the biggest idiot in the world. "In a city with this much housing, you decide it's important to buy the house directly next door to the one woman who bites your head off every time you're in the room with her?"

I shrugged. "It was a good deal."

"Bullshit."

Bullshit indeed. Still.

"I needed more space and happened to like the area when I stood watch over your girlfriend earlier this year."

Sebastian raised a brow, clearly skeptical. He was like an older brother to Luna, so despite his friendship with me, I didn't share everything with him.

Because the truth is, I knew exactly what I was doing when I found this place.

It was time to do what I had wanted to do since the woman reappeared in my life: make Luna Marks mine.

CHAPTER 7

Beck

AS SOON AS SEBASTIAN LEFT, I took a quick shower, pulled on my sweats, and slid under the covers of my Cal King.

I stared at the wall across from me. We'd officially been in the house a week. It had been twenty-four hours since I'd unceremoniously dropped Alice off with Luna.

The woman lived on the other side of that wall.

Technically, I didn't know where her bedroom was, but I suspected her upstairs layout mirrored my own.

Luna *fucking* Marks.

The woman who stirred something in me. Something I hadn't felt with anyone else.

That night we met had been the most memorable sexual experience of my life. But it wasn't just about the sex. No, it was *her*.

The way her red hair fell in a curtain around her face. The blunt bangs gave her an edge that I found intriguing. The quirk in her smile even more so.

Luna Marks was the kind of woman who knew what she wanted. Her success wasn't by accident. No, she worked hard in business, honing her image and she knew her mind.

And *that* night I thought our minds had been as in sync as our bodies.

I thought she was the fucking one for me.

The giddy smile I wore the day after made my face ache, and I didn't even care.

Then I called her that night, after thinking about her all day. The line trilled, and I knew exactly what I wanted to say to her. I'd been practicing it in my head all day.

The line trilled and trilled some more.

"Paccino's Pizza. May I take your order?" a man answered.

My smile faltered.

I glanced down at my phone, my brows furrowed. "Sorry, wrong number."

I ended the call and then glanced at the contact information I'd input. I read the digits one by one, comparing them to the Sharpie on my arm where I'd written the number as Luna relayed it to me post orgasm.

"We have to do this again. Listen up, buttercup," she had said to me. Then Luna proceeded to rattle off her digits, but my phone was buried under my clothes somewhere in the entryway of my apartment where I had shed them earlier.

Too far. They'd been too far, so I used the nearest tool at my disposal. I grabbed the Sharpie from my nightstand and wrote it on my arm and transferred it to my phone later.

After calling the number again and getting the same result, I realized what happened.

She gave me a fake number.

What a slap in the face.

I nursed beer after beer that night…

An incessant knock on the front door pulled me out of the past, thrusting me back into the present.

Took her long enough.

I threw my covers off, padding down the hallway and the stairs.

ness empire. You can watch my seven-year-old for two hours while I handle an emergency."

Had he been keeping tabs on me? Sure, we had a few recent run-ins no thanks to our respective best friends Faith Waters and Sebastian Steele, but that didn't mean he had a window into my life. When that happened, I immediately made Faith promise not to share anything about me to Beck Bennet.

"You can order a pizza," Alice suggested. "I like Hawaiian."

Then she swept past me into my brownstone, plopping down on the cute armchair I had in front of my TV. The little girl picked up the remote and navigated her way seamlessly to a show she must have deemed suitable, all the while I stood in the doorway, mouth on the floor watching the whole thing go down.

By the time I turned around, Beck was gone. "Son of a…"

But I caught myself because there was a tiny human in my presence.

I stared blankly at her. She was solely focused on the TV in front of her.

My phone beeped.

BECK

> Her name is Alice. I'm texting you this because you're undoubtedly in a stupor and not sure what to do next. You'll do fine. I'll be back in two hours. Three tops.

How the hell does he have my phone number now? Where was this eight years ago?

BECK

> I got your number from Sebastian when you were housing Faith. Don't read into it.

I rolled my eyes. So he's a mind reader now? Beck had

The Steele Cyber Security app on my phone confirmed my suspicions.

I opened the door wide. "Hello, Marks."

She glared. "Bennet."

We stood there, staring at each other. She was as beautiful as ever, even though her makeup had been wiped clean from her face. Her hair pulled back in a messy high bun on top of her head.

What the fuck was she wearing? I couldn't help myself as my eyes traveled down her tight and toned body. She'd encased it in black leggings, which served as a second skin. Her breasts strained against the black crop top she'd paired with the tight leggings.

Christ, I could see her nipples through the fabric.

I stopped myself from scrubbing a hand down my face. "You're late."

Her glare faltered. "Late for what?"

"My scolding." I reached forward, closing the front door behind her. "Come."

I headed for the kitchen. It was set in the back of the first story of the house, farther away from the stairs, which meant Alice was less likely to wake up.

It was a good thing Luna hadn't woken her too, because I'd applied the *you break it you buy it rules* when it comes to Alice and her bedtime routine. If you wake up my sleeping kid, you're officially responsible for putting her back to bed.

"Can I get you something to drink?" I asked, back turned to her as I opened the fridge and pulled out another beer.

"I'll have tea."

"Okay." Not what I was expecting, but then again, I never knew what to expect when it came to Luna Marks. That's half her charm.

I opened cabinet after cabinet.

"Something wrong?" Luna asked, arms crossed as if ready to jump back into our verbal volleys.

I scrubbed a hand across my scruff. "I don't actually have tea."

A hint of amusement crossed her face, disappearing so quickly, I'd almost thought I imagined it.

She dropped her hands to her sides. "What do you have? Decaf coffee? Sparkling water..?"

"Juice box?" I held one up. The green box with the little plastic straw fastened to the back.

This time the corner of her lips twitched. There was no doubt about it.

I ignored the seed of satisfaction that bloomed in my chest.

I went to put the juice box back in the fridge.

"Fine. If that's the best thing you have to offer, I'll take it." Luna lunged forward, swiping it from my hand. Well, she tried to. She was fast. I was faster.

I lifted the box in an iron grip above my head.

Luna tried to reach for it, her chest brushing against mine before realizing it was futile. I had almost a foot on her. Especially since she'd left her heels at home.

Just when I thought she'd given up, she jumped again, her body coming flush against mine.

Fuck her nipples were hard.

I let go and the box fell to the floor. She didn't catch it in time.

The box burst on impact, splashing juice everywhere.

We both froze as if a bomb had detonated. Then, breath held, we looked up as if waiting for the pitter patter of tiny feet.

"Daddy?" Alice called from upstairs.

"Shit," Luna swore.

I dragged a hand across the top of my head, not ready to be done with Luna. To hash things out. To find some footing...

"Daddy, are you there?" Alice sounded scared this time.

Right now my baby girl came first.

"I'll clean that up later," I said to Luna, pointing to the mess on the wood floor, before turning toward the stairs. "Everything is fine, Alice. Just a little spill. Nothing to worry about."

Alice was my first priority. And to think if things had gone right with Luna in the first place, I might not have Alice.

"I'm coming," I told Alice again. "Rain check on this conversation?" I asked Luna.

Luna nodded her soft gaze hardening when it returned to meet mine.

"An eight-year rain check?" she muttered, striding towards the door.

I got there first, her comments razing my hackles. "At least I know I have the right phone number this time."

CHAPTER 8

Luna

"AT LEAST I know I have the right number this time."

What the hell did he mean by that?

I was so dazed I almost didn't realize he'd closed the door in my face.

Rude.

I went down his stoop, taking the stairs slowly. They were narrower than mine, the wheelchair accessible ramp taking up the other half.

My security system beeped after I successfully plugged in my code.

That was a total bust. Adrenaline still coursed through my veins. It needed an outlet since I'd been denied a verbal sparring.

I threw on my running clothes and hit the streets, eager to burn off the extra energy, hoping a tired body would quiet my mind.

Afterwards, I showered and slid into bed wearing my favorite silk two-piece set. A delicate camisole and matching shorts.

As I fell asleep, I replayed Beck's words over and over again. "At least I have your correct number this time."

———

A few days later, I found myself back at the construction site for The Chateau.

Things were turning around. Walls were up, and materials delivered.

No migraine in the forecast today.

I breathed a sigh of relief. This project was my baby. It felt like everything I'd been working towards culminating together.

My career started in the service industry. I'd worked my ass off slinging drinks and learning the ins and outs of bar and club life.

That's where I met my mentor, Gigi. She nurtured my interest and let me take risks. It was one of the best things about her. Then, when she was diagnosed with stage-four lung cancer, she let me take over managing her businesses.

She left me the bar when she passed away six months later.

That had been years ago. I was only twenty-five at the time.

My businesses have exploded ever since. Because I worked like a dog chasing a bone. Determined to make something. A legacy.

And that left no time for romantic relationships or close friendships. I funneled all my energy into my work at the expense of my personal life.

That one night with Beck made it seem like I could have space for both... and what happened a few days *later* confirmed to me that I couldn't.

"Have you read the reports I sent you last night?" Parvati asked.

I cleared my throat. "Yes, I saw them. Keep this up and you're officially hired for all my future projects."

Not only had Parvati kept things on track, but she was

also able to work some of her connections to help speed up the delivery of the materials we needed. The woman was like a patron saint of construction.

"I gladly accept," Parvati said with a rare smile. The woman was formidable, making me look as sweet as a bunny rabbit. "I do want to make sure we get those security cameras set up soon though. With the increase in tools and supplies, the potential for loss grows. We know how tempting it can be for folks to steal from worksites."

This hadn't been much of a problem during previous renovations I'd overseen. With my hands on my hips, I surveyed the site. She was right. The fence that ran the perimeter would only deter people so much. Cameras were necessary.

Luckily I had a guy. "I'll call my friend and get them set up ASAP."

Parvati tapped her pen against her clipboard. "Very good."

We continued our walkthrough until we'd covered all the updates, then I hopped in my car and Darnell took me over to Club Deux.

It became a habit to walk the floor every night. Stopping to greet the city's elite as they drank and partied in my place of business. I arranged VIP lounges for them, personally greeting billionaires, politicians, actors, musicians, and everyone in between.

This was part of the gig. I loved it—loved saying hi and mingling. Except it usually depleted me of my remaining energy.

It was usually why I had to binge watch period pieces when I got home in the middle of the night. I longed for the slower pace, the clenching of hands, and solitude for those living in privilege during the time of Austen.

As I entered my office, shucking off my heels, I mentally planned a rewatch of the original BBC version of *Pride and*

Prejudice for later in the evening. That would be the perfect way to unwind.

Then, with a few clicks, my laptop woke up, and I video called Sebastian.

"It's late," Sebastian grumbled.

"Oh, poor baby," I crooned.

"It better be an emergency," Faith yelled, sounding far away.

"It totally is," I shouted right back.

"What is it, Luna? Are you okay?" Sebastian asked, sounding more awake this time.

I propped my legs up on my desk, leaning back in my chair. "I need you to install your fancy security system at my construction site in Atlantic City."

Sebastian sighed. "That's not an emergency, Luna."

"It will be if someone goes and steals a bunch of tiles, *Sebastian*. I ordered top of the line tiles. That means they are *very* expensive."

"Jesus."

I suppressed a smirk. I loved giving him shit.

"I'll call you in the morning for details, Luna. Until then, fuck off."

I overheard my friend gasping at Sebastian's audacity before the line went dead. I didn't take it personally. By the sound of it, I'd probably interrupted them mid-session and nobody likes a cock block.

I was just about to return to my actual work when Monroe knocked on the open office door. "Hey, there's someone here to see you."

"Who is it?" I'd reviewed the VIP list and made the rounds already. As far as I knew, nobody else was on the roster.

A frown tugged the corner of her mouth, and I watched as she tried to rearrange it back into her usual smile. "Carter."

The blood drained from my face. Carter was the most

recent in my attempts at having a normal personal life. We'd dated for a few months and yet we hadn't gone further than kissing and a little heavy petting.

The man never pressured me and was basically the nicest human being I'd ever met.

But despite his gorgeous face, Clark Kent glasses, and overall goodness, there wasn't a spark to be found between us.

Well, on my end anyway.

It was rather unfortunate actually.

He liked me. *A lot*.

Breaking up with him felt akin to kicking a puppy.

Yet when he suggested we make things more serious between us, I knew I couldn't do it. Couldn't keep stringing him along like that.

Not when I wished he would swap his clean-cut demeanor and tailored suits for scruff, tattoos, and leather. Because dammit if Beck hadn't actually ruined me for all men. Well, him and the *other* man.

The breakup with Carter was months ago. Plenty of time for him to get over me and move on, and yet he'd continued to reach out, to maintain that connection between us.

Monroe lifted her brow. "So, are you going to go see him or do I need to come up with an excuse?"

I bit my tongue, tempted to have her do just that. But that wouldn't be a very nice thing to do and dammit if this man wasn't the nicest man on the planet.

"He said he's been trying to reach you, but he can't seem to get through…" She phrased it as a statement, but I heard the question in it.

"I blocked him. So sue me." And now I'm a defensive asshole. *Shit*. "Sorry, I didn't mean it to come out that way."

Monroe smirked. "You're free to block all the men. And if you *don't* want to go out there, boss, that's fine, I'll handle it.

If you *do* want to see him, then I can go with you. Be the backup you need."

I nodded. "Let's do that."

"And you say the safe word and I'll get you out of there."

I cackled. "Deal."

The safe word was something Monroe and I had come up with when she started working for me.

Foliage.

If it was good enough for Michael Scott in *The Office*, it's good enough for me.

I fished through the bottom of my designer bag for my Badass Bombshell Red lipstick, using the small vanity in the corner of my office to check I hadn't smudged it anywhere. It gave me that extra boost of confidence to make sure Carter knew where things stood between us.

I threw my shoulders back. "Let's do this."

We wove through the back hallway until we emerged at the main floor of the club. The room pulsed around me as the DJ played their set from the booth. We took the long way, Monroe leading me around the floor to give me some extra time before arriving in our lounge area. Not quite VIP status, but an elevated experience for people looking to be in the mix without being smack dab in the middle of it.

I sighed at the sight of him. Carter Huntington. Handsome as ever in a fitted Armani suit, hair perfectly coiffed, and glasses sliding down his classic Roman nose.

The antithesis of Beck Bennet in every way. I picked him for that specifically.

We'd met at the Sexual Assault Survivors Network Gala last year.

Gigi had always encouraged me to network and because of my past, I found myself naturally drawn to the Network's mission. I'd been supporting them ever since, starting small with my donations and growing my financial support when I could, offering my time when I couldn't. After some gentle prodding, I'd been roped into helping the gala planning committee last year.

The director of the Network had placed me at a table with Carter and a bunch of local politicians decades older than us. His sweet smile endeared me to him right away. We ended up chatting most of the night, just the two of us.

Carter was clean cut, nice, and earnest.

He came from money, but he loved academia. He served as an adjunct professor at NYU but occasionally helped out his parents by attending these events. It didn't hurt that he sometimes convinced others to patronize the university's research.

Frankly, I didn't even realize he was hitting on me until he asked for my number at the end of the night.

I only said yes to him because he was the exact opposite of the man I was still—after all these years—trying to get out of my head.

We went our separate ways six months ago, after I finally summoned the courage to break things off after we'd witnessed a couple at the table next to us getting engaged and Carter turned to me, full of earnestness, and told me he wanted marriage some day while his thumb traced my ring finger.

It took all the power inside of me not to fake an emergency and get the fuck out of there, roadrunner style.

I'd never thought much about marriage, yet I knew if I did want it, it wouldn't be with Carter. There had only ever been one person I had even considered marrying, regardless of how fleeting that feeling had been.

So, I cut things off with Carter via text.

It wasn't my proudest moment.

He wanted an explanation; I wanted out.

So why on Earth would he be dropping by?

Carter's sudden reappearance brought back all the guilt that I'd shoved far beneath the surface.

I plastered a smile on my face. "Hi, Carter."

He stood and kissed my cheek. He smelled like mint and honey. "It's good to see you."

"You too," I said, lying through my teeth.

We stood there, and I waited for him to tell me why he was here—instead, we stared at each other in anticipation.

My brow lifted expectantly.

He shook his head. "Right. The next Sexual Assault Survivors Network Gala is just a few weeks away."

"I know. I'll be there." I'd been attending the gala despite not sitting on the planning committee this year. I had to take a step back with everything going on with The Chateau.

Carter clutched the back of his neck. "Right, of course you will be. It's just that, I wanted to let you know that I'm bringing a date."

Date. He said it as if it might hit me like a bullet. Except the pang in my chest never came. In fact, it was quite the opposite. Here Carter was trying to tell me he was bringing someone to the same gala we had met at, and I felt nothing.

Zero.

Zilch.

Nada.

Yet, clearly he felt he had to warn me. Couldn't this have been an email?

Oh wait—I blocked him. *Damn.*

"In fact, I want you to meet her," he said, his hand motioning for someone to come over.

Wait, what the actual fuck?

Sure enough, a petite blonde woman with a hell of a side swept bang emerged from behind him, her hand outstretched. "Hi, I'm Delaney."

I didn't know what was happening, but I knew that I wanted no part of it. I was too busy for whatever little show this was. Not only did I have to manage the club, but I had to get The Chateau up and running and begin tracking down items for the gala auction. I might not be able to be a full planning committee member, but I could still do my part to raise money for a great organization. To top it all off, I had the one-night stand of my dreams move in next door playing out the sexy single dad trope.

Life was busy. Too busy for whatever *this* was.

Still, I was a lady and shrewd. I couldn't very well ignore someone especially when they were in my place of business, so I shook her outstretched hand, and exchanged pleasantries with her.

"She loves Club Deux and wanted to come here. I didn't want it to be weird," Carter said sheepishly. Of course he would be a gentleman and make sure I knew he was here, especially with another woman. He wouldn't want it to be weird but that was impossible given the circumstances.

I prayed for a sinkhole to swallow me whole.

"Well, you clearly have great taste," I said to Delaney. "And I'll get a bottle of Dom sent over ASAP. On the house."

"Oh you don't have to—" Carter started.

"I insist." Anything to get me the hell out of here.

Then a text appeared on my screen.

I clicked it immediately looking for a distraction.

BECK:

Stop running in the middle of the goddamn night. It isn't safe.

My brain took a few seconds to comprehend the message.

Excuse me?

That bastard.

"Excuse me, I have to take this." I gestured to my phone because damn if that little text from Beck didn't send a jolt of dopamine straight through my body. "Have a good rest of your night."

I ignored the look of confusion that swept over Carter's face and started heading to my office as I reread the text.

BECK:

> Stop running in the middle of the goddamn night. It isn't safe.

How does he know I run at night?

BECK

> You set off my motion detector at 1 am last night and at 3 am the night before.

I frowned, fingers itching to respond.

LUNA

> I'm not sure that's any of your business.

BECK

> You're interrupting my sleep, which makes it my business.

I gasped at his audacity.

LUNA

> YOUR business? I'm sorry, but my running habits are exempt from your business.

BECK

> You're my neighbor, which means you're my business.

I scoffed, head shaking as my fingers flew across the screen.

LUNA

> Mr. Rogers never mentioned spying as one of the ways to be a good neighbor.

BECK

> I bet Nationwide is on my side.

LUNA

You need to work on your dad jokes. I'm embarrassed on Alice's behalf.

BECK

Stop running at night and you won't have to deal with my terrible dad jokes.

LUNA

I was too pissed to come up with anything cleverer. In a few steps, I entered my office and slammed my phone face down on the desk. "That's enough of you, Beck Bennet."

CHAPTER 9
Beck

IT TOOK LESS than five minutes for me to find the footage.

Luna *fucking* Marks stretching on her stoop at two in the fucking morning. My Steele Security app caught her in the act. It even captured her looking directly into my camera. *Smirking*.

Now she was just playing dirty.

I shucked off my sheets and scribbled a quick note for the nanny. Mrs. Corbett was healthy again and officially living in the downstairs guest room. She'd moved in two days ago and I heaved a sigh of relief at having another adult on the premises capable of watching Alice. I wouldn't be missed.

I anticipated this might happen, so I slept in my workout gear. It only took a few seconds to tie my shoelaces and then I was off into the night to follow Luna.

Unlike the woman I was trailing, I wore a high-visibility outfit. It didn't do much to attract the opposite sex, but it would do a lot to attract the attention of drivers who might otherwise miss me.

Luna should be wearing something equally protective. Although with her and that body, she'd attract creeps like a moth to a flame. That wasn't her fault. Just a fact.

It only took a couple steps to catch up with her. The woman wore a fucking sports bra and shorts. Sure, it was a balmy eighty degrees with humidity, but seriously? Could she have picked something else?

Headlights flared as a car barreled down the street.

Fuck. My instincts took over. I grabbed Luna's elbow, tugging her back from the street. Before I knew what was happening, she punched my throat.

"Back off, fucker!" she screamed, lifting her leg to kick me —probably in the groin.

My reflexes returned. I thwarted her next move, but just barely.

"It's me," I growled, my register higher than normal. I rubbed my neck once I was certain she wouldn't try to attack again.

"Beck? What the hell?" She drove her hands through her hair, her ponytail coming loose. Then she planted her hands on her hips, eyes flaring as she put two and two together. "Wait a minute. You followed me? You *actually* followed me? And attacked me, no less. How *dare* you," she seethed.

Of course she'd spin it like that. This woman could infuriate me like no other. "If you hadn't noticed, there was a car coming. I just saved your life."

"Please, I was stopping. This isn't my first time running in the city. This isn't even my first time running in the city *this week.*"

I scrubbed a hand down my face. "Don't I fucking know it."

Suddenly, Luna took off, resuming her run, as if we weren't just in the middle of a conversation.

I launched into motion, following behind her and shouted, "I'm not done talking."

She flipped me off. "Sucks for you, because I am."

"You need to at least take those earbuds out. You can't hear the oncoming traffic."

She tilted her head while maintaining her steady pace. "And yet I can hear you perfectly."

The woman stopped at the next light, bouncing on the balls of her feet to keep her body warm. When the light turned, she glanced left and right then proceeded to cross. I kept pace next to her.

She threw me a nasty look. "Go *home*."

I glanced at Luna. Her shoulders were tense, and she had a look in her eye I didn't like. "What's wrong?"

She didn't bother to look at me. "I already told you. Go home."

That response didn't sit well with me. Sure, I knew she wanted me to scram, but the way her body tensed reminded me of fight-or-flight mode. My senses were screaming at me, something about her reaction felt overblown. Sure, I may have scared her, but that would normally have been a temporary reaction, something easily shaken off. Either something else was bothering her now or something happened in the past.

I knew that mode and I knew it well. Seen it dozens of times with the people I'd served with. I saw it with clients my people and I were assigned to protect.

Because of this experience, I knew how to approach people in that mode. As frustrating as it could be, it wasn't about approaching it directly. You had to let the person come to you in their own time.

And I could be patient.

I kept pace beside her. "I might as well accompany you for the rest of the jog. I'm a completionist."

"Don't I know it," she said with a wink and a smile that didn't quite reach her eyes, even if her tone had oozed sex and implication.

Danger, Will Robinson.

I shifted, grateful my pants had extra room. The last thing I needed was to sport a boner while jogging next to a woman in the middle of the night. I refused to become the kind of creep I was out here to protect her from.

Luna sped up until we made it to the base of the Brooklyn Bridge. "Are we really crossing the bridge right now? It's the middle of the night."

We'd already logged a mile and a half, and I anticipated we'd turn around any minute now and make the return trip.

"I'm just getting started."

CHAPTER 10
Luna

"I'M JUST GETTING STARTED."

If that was how he wanted to play it, then game on.

I hadn't meant to go this far. Honestly, I thought I'd jog a mile or two, just a little loop and then go back home and stretch while watching the newest BBC version of *Emma*.

But then he scared the absolute shit out of me. My heart was still racing, and it wasn't from the exercise. My body needed the run at this point, and I had to keep going until the adrenaline fled my body. It reminded me too much of the *other* night that I couldn't stop thinking about—the night just a few days after I slept with Beck.

That night had haunted me and probably had more to do with my inability to be intimate than Beck's prowess ruining me for all other men.

Now, in this moment, despite the futility of it, I tried to escape Beck. I sped up as fast as my legs could carry me, but Beck kept pace with me. It was too much to hope that he couldn't keep up. The man did serve overseas and ran an elite bodyguard business. Being in shape was basically a job requirement.

That didn't make it okay for him to hijack my thinking time.

The fact that he thought he could just grab me off the street and make me go home was outrageous. Nearly as outrageous as my current quest to span the Brooklyn Bridge before circling back toward my brownstone.

I groaned inwardly at my own stubbornness. I didn't usually run this far, and the bridge felt like a fun-house mirror, forever elongating.

Maybe this was a bad idea...

But it was too late to turn around now. Once I committed to something, I committed all the way.

It would help if Beck was a little bit winded. Unfortunately, the man looked unbothered by the exertion, whereas I was on the verge of wheezing and making an absolute fool of myself.

Reluctantly, I slowed my pace and came to a stop in the middle of the bridge under the guise of wanting to stretch.

Beck came to a stop as well, stretching his calf next to me. "Nice place for a mid-run stretch."

I rolled my eyes and sank into a squat. "Just taking in the view. You know, a *stop and smell the roses* kind of moment."

He pretended to look around. "No roses around here, Marks."

"Metaphorical roses, *Bennet.*"

He kicked my foot with his. "You're favoring this leg. If you don't take it easy, you'll injure it for real."

"Am not." I hadn't noticed anything wrong with my gait.

He shot me a devilish grin. "Are too."

"And you know everything, is that it?" I raised a brow, while bouncing on my heels to keep my body from stiffening up.

"I know how to prevent knee injuries." He glanced down at my feet again. "How old are those shoes, anyway? If you plan to keep running, you need better shoes."

I waved my hands wildly in the air. "According to you, I'm doing this whole running thing wrong."

He slid his hands in his pockets. Unlike *my* jogging wear, *his* had pockets. "You said it, not me."

I narrowed my eyes. My feet started pounding pavement again.

"Are you coming?" I taunted him.

This asshole. If he was going to try to tell me how to live my life, I would make his a living hell and keep on pretending this jog was hurting him just as much as it was hurting me.

"Why are you doing this, Marks?" He kept pace beside me, his breath even. "You know if you tell me, it will make life easier for both of us."

Talk to Beck about my ex? Hard pass.

Although it was the whole reason I was out here in the first place. Well, that and the mountain of other obligations and to-dos that made my mind reel and my body require physical exertion to help me sleep.

Maybe it would be a good thing to tell him…see how he reacted. At the very least, maybe it would stop him in his tracks and give me a little breather.

Fuck it.

"My ex stopped by the club tonight."

Beck's eyes grew curious, glinting under the harsh lights. "Did he do something to hurt you?"

The idea made me smile. "No. He didn't hurt me."

"Do you still want him?" Beck's voice was low, harsh even.

That elicited a tiny laugh. "Absolutely not."

We finally made it to the end of the bridge, then we turned around and headed back toward our respective brownstones. My lungs were on fire and my body would hate me for the hell I'd put it through, but at least my mind would be clearer. The physical strain took away the mental one.

"Let me get this straight. Your ex stopped by your work today, and you're *fine* with it."

I gulped some air. "Yep."

Confusion swept across his face. "Then why the fuck aren't we in bed sleeping?"

I nearly stumbled.

He didn't mean it how it sounded.

Because he absolutely didn't mean it to sound like we should be sleeping together.

"What's your excuse for last night and the night before? I'm going to ask you again, is he bothering you?" he continued.

A red light. Thank God. I bounced in place, enjoying the bit of respite. "Slow your roll. He's not bothering me. He's a *nice* guy." I let that little implication hover in the air between us.

Beck wasn't convinced. "If he's such a nice guy, then why are you so bothered?"

"He stopped by tonight and I needed to process it." I pressed a hand to the stitch in my side.

He grunted. "What did you need to process last night?"

"That's none of your business."

The light turned green, so we picked up the pace, much to my body's dismay. "Fine. Then let's talk about what you're processing tonight."

"Pretty sure we established eight years ago that you're not a doctor, and you're definitely not a therapist, so you'll excuse me if I don't want to have you do a pseudo psych analysis."

Beck brushed against me, and I tried to pull away but a group of twenty something's were taking up the majority of the sidewalk as they drunkenly stumbled home from the bars, not a car in the world.

"Sometimes we just need a friend to listen," he said softly.

My heart pounded loudly in my ears, and I wasn't

convinced it was all from the exercise. "Are you saying we're friends, Beck Bennet?"

"No but if something's bothering you, I'm here to listen. Preferably not in the middle of the night. Or if it is the middle of night, at least have it be in the comfort of our own homes."

"I do my best thinking in the middle of the night. So if you can't handle that, then you can leave."

"Since we're going in the same direction, I think I'll stay."

Fucking cheeky bastard.

"It didn't bother me that he showed up." The words slipped from my lips.

"What do you mean?"

I shrugged, slowing my pace. "I felt nothing. Shouldn't I feel jealous or regretful? Shouldn't I feel *something?*"

We jogged in silence for a few beats as I waited for a response.

I shook my head once. "Never mind. I'll just talk to Faith, she's good at this."

"Don't count me out just yet, I'm trying to understand what you've shared. It just takes me a minute," he said in his defense. "You regret not feeling regret? That sum it up?"

I shrugged. "In a nutshell."

He tsked. "You can't spend your energy on that."

Such a man answer.

"Great idea. What didn't I think of that? Maybe if I just snapped my fingers, all that pesky guilt about not feeling guilty will just vanish into thin air. Woosh." I snapped my fingers and dramatically waved my hands around.

Beck's lip twitched. "Are you finished now?"

I lifted a finger. "Maybe I need to do some sort of incantation. That might help."

His lips thinned. "What exactly did he say to you?"

"He told me about his new girlfriend," I murmured.

Beck belted out a laugh. "What a twat. I thought you said he was a nice guy."

I slowed my pace and put my hands on my hips to catch my breath. "He *is* a nice guy. He wanted to let me know since she's a fan of the club and he didn't want it to be weird."

Beck hummed. "So he made it weird by trying not to make it weird."

"You could say that. We're also going to be seeing each other in a few weeks for this annual gala that we attend."

He lifted a brow. "Sounds fancy."

"Yep."

"Let me guess. He's bringing the new woman to that too?"

"Bingo." I winked.

Beck shook his head. "Still think he's a bit of a twat."

"He doesn't want it to be weird."

He probed. "Will it be? If he's there with someone else?"

Hair started falling out of my ponytail, so I pushed it back. "Not for me."

"It wouldn't hurt if you had a date too."

It wasn't a bad idea. "Maybe I will."

"I could be your date," he said so confidently that I stumbled. *Again.*

My body fell forward, and Beck was there, arms outstretched, bringing me toward him as we both barreled forward.

In some move straight out of *The Matrix*, he twisted, taking the brunt of the fall. He landed with a thud, a hiss of air escaping his chest.

I had also twisted as we fell, and now my hands were planted on his muscular pecs, my legs straddling either side of him, our pelvises aligned. The pesky jolt returned, my body immediately reacting to his.

"Get a room," someone shouted.

A laugh burst from my chest. A giggling, full-body laugh that had me falling forward until my forehead collided with his. For just a moment I was transported back to that night— our night. "New York, amiright?"

Beck smiled so wide his dimples popped under the harsh light of the bridge lamps. "Fucking New Yorkers."

My gaze dipped to his lips. His grip on me tightened.

Then *poof*. Without warning, the man lifted me off him.

"Can we please head back now?" he asked, his voice sounding like it had been over hot coals.

I fixed my ponytail, needing something to do with my hands, trying to shake off the feel of his hard chest. "Are you *actually* asking me nicely?"

Annnnd with another shot fired, the battle resumed.

This was us… where I was most comfortable, with the barbs back and forth.

He grinned, as if he knew exactly what I was doing and let me do it anyway, and I wanted to wipe that cocky smile off his face.

So I broke into a run, shoving his offer to the back of my mind.

———

I limped into work the following day, Monroe hot on my heels.

"What happened to you?" she asked, clipboard in hand.

"Beck Bennet happened to me," I grumbled.

Monroe blushed. If I didn't know any better, I'd think she had a crush on him. He had that effect on people.

"I think I need a massage." I flopped into the chair at my office, my knee practically screaming at me. "And maybe physical therapy."

Monroe sank into the seat across from me. "Well, you're on your own for those things, but I could help with doing the rounds tonight."

"That would be great. I appreciate it. Will you make sure that Harrison Barnes gets the VIP treatment tonight? Sebastian texted me asking us to make it nice for his new client."

"You got it, boss." Monroe saluted me and left the office just as my phone began to ring.

What is it now?

Parvati.

I picked it up immediately. "Hi. I plan to swing by the site tomorrow."

"I have bad news. Someone broke into the storage unit."

My stomach dropped. This was the exact thing we'd been trying to avoid.

Sebastian hadn't managed to get to the Chateau yet, but he promised he'd be there tomorrow, come hell or highwater, to personally set up the security system for me.

"Fuck," I swore softly.

Parvati huffed from her side of the line. "Yes. I'm pissed that the fence and lock didn't deter them. We need those cameras set up ASAP. I've already called the insurance company. They are understanding this time…"

"But they won't be as forgiving next time. Got it." I really should have thought about security earlier. I'd been foolish not to consider it until now. "Sebastian and I will be there in the morning."

Parvati hummed. "In the meantime, I recommend we have someone stay onsite tonight. I'm sure I could offer a couple hundred bucks to one of the workers to just walk the premises."

A couple hundred bucks to protect thousands of dollars' worth of materials sounded like a deal to me. "You have my permission to do that. Invoice me and I'll handle it.

"Will do."

The call ended, and I sighed as the sharp pain between my eyes returned.

CHAPTER 11

Beck

SOMEONE POUNDED ON THE DOOR. But it wasn't my front door. No, it was the neighbor's.

Luna's door.

I had dropped Alice off at school since the nanny had a doctor's appointment and stopped back home to get something from my office when I heard the knocking.

I opened the front door to find Sebastian on Luna's stoop.

"What the hell are you doing here?" I asked my friend.

Sebastian turned. "I'm supposed to go to the job site with Luna this morning to set up her security, but I haven't heard from her."

I frowned. Luna Marks might have pulled a disappearing act on me nearly a decade ago, but the woman lived for her work. There was no way she'd be intentionally late or miss a meeting.

Something's wrong.

"I assume you called her?" I asked while jogging down my steps and then up hers.

Sebastian gave me a look to let me know exactly what he thought of that dumbass suggestion.

I held my hands up. "Got it. You know her passcode, right? Use it. It could be an emergency."

He glared at me.

"Now," I growled.

The man rolled his eyes, something I'd bet money he picked up from Faith, turned his back to me, and punched in the combo.

"Finally," I muttered, pushing past him, a swell of panic rising inside me. "Marks, you here?"

I jogged into the kitchen and living area, finding them both empty.

A groan sounded from upstairs, and my gaze went skyward. I took the stairs two at a time, launching myself toward her bedroom, slowing down when I found it slightly ajar.

I ignored the sounds of protest behind me from Sebastian and pushed open the door. There was a mound of sheets on the bed, but no Luna from what I could tell.

Another moan.

My feet swallowed the distance between me and the bathroom.

For a second my heart stopped.

There she was, in a black silk two piece that hardly covered anything, her red hair slicked back against her face, falling out of a loose bun, and her head resting on top of the toilet as if she had fallen asleep there.

Christ. I'd bet my company she'd fallen asleep there. Her heavy eyelids flickered as I knelt next to her.

I rested a hand on the nape of her neck. "It's me. The bane of your existence."

"Ugh," she groaned. "Go away."

"You scared us," Sebastian said from somewhere behind me. "I'll get you some water."

He left, and I took in every detail of the woman in front of me.

She winked an eye open and somehow managed to glare with her good eye.

"Go," she croaked.

I tsked. "Is that how you say thank you to the man that saved your life?"

She narrowed that solitary eye even further.

I nodded to the toilet. "You done here?"

She leaned her cheek against the porcelain.

"I'll take that as a yes." I scooped her lithe body into my arms, easily carrying her back to her bed. My heart thudded in my chest, and I prayed that she was too out of it to hear it. The woman gave me a fucking scare.

With her safe in my arms, I finally managed to refill my lungs with oxygen. I hadn't done that since the front door unlocked.

"Go home, Beck," she said, exhaustion coating her tongue.

I drew the covers over her body, averting my gaze as I hid her smooth, exposed skin.

Luna curled up into a ball, brow pinching. "Fuuuuuck."

Just then Sebastian reappeared, glass of water in hand. "Drink this."

Luna stirred. "Sebastian is here? Why?" Then she must have remembered because she groaned out, "Missed our meeting."

I sat on the edge of her bed as Sebastian rounded the other side to hand her the glass.

"Don't worry about the meeting," he said.

Luna sat up with a hiss.

Seeing her in so much pain made me feel panicked in a way I usually managed to avoid. Being in the military had made me cool under pressure.

All that training was tossed out the window at the sight of Luna Marks in bed looking more helpless than I'd ever seen her.

"What can we do to help? Do I need to call an ambulance?" My voice was gruff. What would have happened if she didn't have a meeting with Sebastian? If I hadn't gone home to get some work done before going to the office?

We would have missed this.

I would have missed this. How long would she have laid here suffering? When I was little, I saw my dad suffer from the odd migraine, so I'd recognized this for what it was. She needed care. More than we could give her.

Luna tried to sit up but pinched her eyes and started back down. "Take care of my project site, Sebastian. I need those cameras."

"Work can wait," I scolded.

"I can take care of it," Sebastian told her, ignoring me.

Luna lifted her head enough to give me the evil eye before clutching her brow again.

"That's it. You're coming with me." I headed towards the dresser and picked out the first set of clothes I could find. There was no way in hell I was bringing her to the ER dressed as she was. I pointed at Sebastian. "You go work on her site, and I'll take her to the hospital."

Luna chimed in, voice strained. "No hospital."

I gently lifted her up, careful not to jostle her as I slipped on an oversized NYU sweatshirt over her head. I tried to be as nonchalant as possible, completely ignoring the fact that she still smelled like citrus and sunshine. Her hands slowly raised in the air for me to drag the fabric down, swallowing her toned body.

"Pants next," I said, trying to keep my tone light, not giving away how much it pained me to be this close to her body. The last time we'd been this close…

Not the time to think about it.

Luna mumbled but despite her protests, she was oddly compliant, stretching her legs off the edge of the bed, sending her shorts higher around her thighs.

I caught Sebastian's worried gaze. "Turn around."

Sebastian's brow knit in confusion glancing between us before turning to face the door. "You're taking Luna to the ER?"

"Yes," I said. Leaving no room for discussion. "You take care of whatever you were supposed to be doing for Luna. That way she can focus on getting better."

"Sure. And why should you be the one to take her to the ER?"

So much for taking me at my word and leaving.

Luna lifted a brow as if also wanting an answer to Sebastian's question while I wrestled the sweatpants on her. "Why the hell are these so tight?"

"Leggings," Luna and Sebastian said in stereo.

I continued to battle with the stretchy material. "They are the fucking worst, is what they are."

"You obviously haven't seen how good my ass looks in them."

I pinched her ass, and the woman yelped, a tinge of rouge touching her cheeks.

This formidable woman blushing? She must be sick.

By some miracle, I managed to get the leggings secured around her waist. Luna placed a hand on my chest to steady herself, her pupils dilating as if trying to focus on me.

A strand of auburn hair fell across her flushed face. My fingers brushed it aside, and a zing coursed through me at the touch.

Luna swallowed hard.

I held my breath as her eyes locked on mine. Then she shoved me. Not hard enough to rock me backwards but hard enough to break the spell.

She glanced over her shoulder at Sebastian. "Protect my job site. I don't want anything else to get stolen."

When she turned back to face me her eyes bulged, and her face turned green.

Uh-oh.

Luna scrambled off the bed and back into the bathroom, back to the spot we'd found her in.

CHAPTER 12

Luna

A MONITOR BEEPED from somewhere in the room.

My eyelids fluttered open and there, across from me, slept Beck Bennet. His figure slumped in a chair that was painfully small for his big frame.

My tongue slid across the front of my teeth, which were feeling fuzzy from lack of brushing.

Gross.

The memories of earlier returned in full force: puking up every last ounce of bile in my body. Beck finding me crouched in front of the porcelain goddess of a toilet I splurged on because I needed a fancy Japanese machine to help keep my lady bits clean while on my period.

I vividly remembered telling myself *not* to puke on the buttery leather seats as Darnell maneuvered expertly through Brooklyn's mid-morning traffic to the nearest hospital.

The drive nearly made me lose consciousness, my head splintering apart in pain despite Beck's attempts to shield me from light and sound.

In my haze, I overheard Beck whispering sternly, relaying messages to whoever was on the other end of the line.

When we arrived at the hospital, Beck didn't bother

waiting for anyone to greet us at the emergency room door. No, the man swept me up in his arms, cradling me next to his firm chest as he whispered sweet affirmations to me, promising to take care of me.

The beeps grew louder, my pulse quickening at the memory. That was the last thing I *could* remember.

Beck stirred, an eye popping open to scan the scene. Seeing me staring at him, he immediately roused. He was on his feet in a blink, swallowing the distance between us. "You're awake."

I blinked. "Obviously."

His gaze swept down my body in a way that didn't feel like he was checking me out. No, it felt entirely like he was making sure no new injury or ailment had befallen me.

I waved him off. "I'm better now."

Beck's jaw clenched. "Let me get a doctor or nurse."

Without another word, he left the room, leaving me there to assess my body. I sat up, careful not to disturb the IV. Mentally, I was foggy. Physically, my body ached, and yet I still considered that a victory in and of itself. Being able to assess my body without my stomach clenching, bile rising, and my head splitting felt like a tremendous success.

I tucked the sheet around my body tighter just as Beck returned, a crew of hospital staff in tow.

I raised a brow at him, mentally communicating that this was overkill. In return, he shot me a glance that said, you haven't even begun to see overkill yet.

If I was like Faith, I'd roll my eyes at him. Instead I flipped him off as the medical staff checked my vitals, my pupils, and rattled off a series of questions. I felt victorious seeing him suppress a smirk.

"On a scale from one to ten, ten being the worst pain you've ever been in, what's your pain at right now?" *A five.*

"To the best of your recollection, when did the migraine start?" *Around 2 a.m.*

"When was the first date of your last menstrual cycle?" I smiled broadly, staring directly at Beck. *Five days ago*.

This continued for a while. The doctor nodded attentively as I answered question after question.

The doctor typed away on the computer in the room, likely adding notes to my chart, then sat back. "I want to get some water and food into your body and see how you handle it. You've taken in two bags of fluids; you were severely dehydrated. I imagine your body is going to take a few days to recover."

"Is it going to happen again?" I ask, knowing that it undoubtedly would.

The doctor clicked on a few things and then turned the screen to face me. On it listed my previous hospitalizations. She did her best impression of a Vanna White wave. "If this is any indication to go on, then yes, you will continue to have migraines."

Beck swept around the other side of my bed, sidling up next to me, his hand white-knuckling my bed rail.

The doctor sent him a look of appreciation before turning her focus back to me. "It looks like you're out of refills on your migraine meds, so I'm going to place an order with your pharmacy. But your type of migraine is brought on, primarily, by stress." She pushed the screen out of the way, her body fully facing mine. "I recommend working out."

"I do that," I jumped in.

"Managing your stress."

My top teeth sunk into my bottom lip and Beck chortled at my side.

I glared at him, and the doctor's brow lifted. "I'm guessing you're *not* doing that."

I didn't bother answering.

"Maintaining a regular schedule helps too."

This time *I* chortled. "Well, we can toss that suggestion out the window."

This old song and dance again. Was there anything more annoying than being told that you need to lower your stress levels? It's like when someone tells you to calm down in the middle of a heated convo or to just relax. That things will figure themselves out.

No, actually, they won't. There's no magical fairy godmother waving around a glittery wand coming in to fix things.

Things got done because I *got them done*. Just as I always have my entire life.

The doctor pursed her lips. "How about alcohol? Can you cut that?"

Finally, one thing I *was* doing right. "I haven't had alcohol in eight years."

Beck jolted, as if shocked by this revelation.

Little did he know the last time I took a sip of the stuff was just a few nights after *our* night together.

I ignored his pointed look, focusing instead on the surprised look on the face of the physician. Yes, yes, a sober club owner who made her living off of selling a substance she didn't partake in might seem strange to some. In my mind, it made perfect sense. The late nights already took a hard toll on my body. Alcohol wouldn't help.

Besides, I liked being in control. And drinking made me the opposite of that.

"That's a good thing. If you could limit caffeine too—that might help. Drink lots of water. Eat lots of nutritious foods. Every bit matters. Unfortunately, there isn't just one thing you can do to prevent migraines."

This was nothing I hadn't heard before.

"All of this information will be on your discharge papers. As soon as this IV finishes up, we'll get you out of here." She pressed a few buttons, and a lock screen appeared. "I assume you have someone who can take you home."

"I can take a cab," I said sweetly, while throwing Beck a saucy grin.

Beck scoffed. "Cab my ass. I'm taking you home."

The doctor's eyes volleyed between us. "Right…I'll let you two figure that out." Then she focused on me. "Take care of yourself, Luna. And at least consider trying some of the strategies we talked about."

"I will," I said solemnly, although I'm pretty sure the doc was astute enough to see through it.

I couldn't exactly change my schedule when I had The Chateau to get off the ground. All my money, everything I'd been working towards, was building up to this.

The nurse came in and removed the IV, the bag now empty where it hung down off the metal stand. She made a few notes on the computer and handed me my clear plastic bag of belongings.

Beck outreached a hand. "Come on, Marks. Let's get you home."

CHAPTER 13

Beck

"DADDY, why is the neighbor lady sleeping on our couch?"

I barely had time to drop Luna off at home before it was time to pick Alice up from school.

While I intended to drop Luna off at her house, she'd promptly fallen asleep the second the car departed the hospital.

Despite my attempts to rouse her, I failed. I carried her inside my house and gently laid her on the couch, making sure to cover her in the fuzziest blanket we had available, before heading right back out to get Alice.

Did I forget to mention our house guest to my daughter?

Yes.

But not because I'm a bad dad.

It was because I had a rather loquacious kiddo who proceeded to talk my ear off the whole journey home, regaling me about the hottest gossip in the second grade. How Avery liked Luke, but Luke didn't like Avery, and how that essentially...

Actually, never mind.

Now, she sat stunned into silence, unsure what to do about the woman sprawled on our couch.

"Daddy?" Alice asked again. Then, on her tippy toes, she walked closer to investigate. You'd have thought my daughter had just stumbled upon a giant cake in the forest the way she was looking at Luna with awe and wonder.

Then Alice poked Luna.

Luna's hand rose and swiped through the air, as if swatting an invisible fly, missing Alice's nose by a hair.

Alice giggled, approaching again, this time lifting up the corner of the blanket and swiping it across Luna's face.

"What the—" Luna startled some more. Her eyes flew open, and her hand lifted as if to swat again. I swooped in, picking up my daughter before she—rightfully—got bonked for disturbing someone's sleep.

"Snack time," I told my daughter, carrying her to the kitchen. The open floor plan allowed me to keep a good eye on Luna.

I opened the fridge and removed a brick of cheese before heading to the pantry to get some pita chips and peanut butter. Alice loved the disgusting combination and who was I to stand in the way of her getting some good nutrients into her body?

While I was at it, I sliced some more cheese, making a plate for Luna.

I wonder if I have saltines…

When I looked up, Alice's chair was empty, and she was back in the living room staring curiously at disoriented Luna with questions.

"Alice, come here and leave her alone," I whisper-shouted.

Luna had given me a hell of a scare and her body needed rest. Given her track record, it wouldn't surprise me if the woman popped off the couch and decided to take off for another midnight run.

She wouldn't dare do that under my watchful eye…

Would she?

Luna shuffled into the kitchen, the blanket a protective shield around her. Her bedhead did nothing to diminish her natural beauty. With her face clear of any trace of makeup, she looked young and innocent with a hidden naughty streak.

Those plump lips of hers twisted as if she knew exactly how dirty my thoughts were.

Alice tailed behind Luna peppering her with questions.

Why were you sleeping on our couch?

You're pretty. Did you know you're pretty?

Can we do another pineapple pizza party? I'll even try watching that boring movie you like so much.

Using her whole body, Alice pushed the high-top chair away from the counter, making room for her to climb up onto the seat before diving into her snack.

Luna laughed lightly. "Hungry, Alice?"

"Starrrrrving," my daughter said dramatically, clutching her belly.

I walked around the counter to support Luna as she got on the chair next to Alice. She wobbled a bit, but I caught her unsteady form. "*Careful.*"

My hand gripped her tight, and I ignored the pang in my chest that she elicited with just her mere presence. Instead, I focused on the external clues to assess how she was doing. The color that returned to her cheeks, the purple under her eyes that wasn't as pronounced as before. The time at the hospital combined with the impromptu nap had done wonders.

After a fleeting look of what appeared to be appreciation, Luna resumed her normal glare. "You can let go now. And I'll take an orange juice for the road."

Reluctantly, I released her, my senses returning more with each step back I took.

I slid the plate in front of her and pointed. "You finish that without hurling and I'll walk you home with a to-go cup."

Just then the nanny arrived. After a quick round of introductions, Mrs. Corbett took over Alice's care for me with a silent warm handoff. I gave her an appreciative nod as she ushered Alice out of the room, firmly letting her know that it was time for homework.

"Wow. The nanny *does* exist," Luna quipped once Mrs. Corbett and Alice were firmly out of earshot. "For a while, I thought you'd made up the fictional nanny story just to mess with me."

I blinked. "You thought I was lying about my nanny having an emergency? That I would just drop my daughter at your doorstep to mess with you?"

Luna began to trace the lines in the marble countertop, her gaze not meeting mine. "When you say it out loud like that…"

I leaned forward, my hand cupping her chin so that I could peer into her eyes. "It sounds ridiculous?"

She scoffed. "Ridiculous is a strong word."

"In this case it's the right word."

She narrowed her gaze. "You calling me ridiculous, Bennet?"

I grinned. "Never."

Her top teeth sunk into that plump bottom lip, and I suppressed a groan. "I should take you back now. Make sure you get home safely."

Luna sighed. "If you insist."

CHAPTER 14

Luna

"HAVE you had enough water today? Let me get you more water." Monroe exited my office before I could stop her.

It had been two full days since my body went rogue in the most unhelpful way. I shook my head, still in disbelief that Beck of all people took me to the hospital and then took care of me afterwards...

In the corners of my memory, I recalled the feel of his arms around my body as he whisked me to the hospital, the little statements of reassurance he whispered in my ears when he thought I couldn't hear him.

All the little things that panged my heart and made me wonder, what if...

"Ah, shit," Monroe cursed as she walked through the door, water sloshing over the glass she brought me.

I lifted my giant ass water container from behind the desk, displaying it prominently.

"You already have water," she said, deflated.

I made a gimme motion. "I'm sure yours is better. I'll start with your glass and move onto this monstrosity. Sound good?"

A deep seed of pride found purchase in my chest for

doing something on the doctor's to-do list. I wasn't *that* terrible of a patient.

"Take a seat and catch me up on what I missed." I had spent yesterday on site at the Chateau, figuring that needed my attention. By the time I finished walking through and getting briefed by both Parvati and Sebastian, I was wiped out and went home to rest.

That meant I hadn't been at the club for days. I'd never gone this long without checking in with my staff and the club. My emails were piled high and though I triaged as many as I could at home, there were people I wanted to chat with in person on a few outstanding issues.

Once I was fully briefed, I did my rounds, and schmoozed with the VIP clients, before checking in with my barkeep. They managed the inventory and the prices from our distributor were going up, which meant we needed to think closely about what we kept in stock. So after picking the barkeep's brain, I walked back to my office to call my bookkeeper so we could review invoices and price out various combinations of hard alcohol and the different brands. The last thing I wanted to do was raise drink prices, so I sought a solution—any solution or combination of solutions—to prevent that from happening.

Our ambiance and fair prices were what kept us successful during economic booms and busts. I'd like to keep it that way.

My phone pinged as I poured over inventory spreadsheets.

FAITH

You haven't responded to any of my calls or texts. Please tell me you're okay before I make Sebastian drive us to the city before our designated day. You know how he feels about impromptu trips…

FAITH

Best friends do this thing called texting. Or calling. At this point, I'm not too picky.

FAITH

Okay, now you're making me mad. Sebastian said Beck took you to the hospital. BECK!? Seriously. I need all the details.

FAITH

And why it took my live-in lover days to tell me this is something I will deal with him directly about. In the meantime, I need YOU to tell me what happened.

FAITH

Packing my bags...

SEBASTIAN

Please text Faith back to let her know you're alright. She's packing her bags and Willow is getting upset.

SEBASTIAN

Seriously, my dog is pacing the room because she's worried about Faith and because Faith is worried about you. You're the only one that can stop her.

FAITH

What's the name of the driver that picked me up in the middle of the night when Sebastian was being an idiot? Do you think he's on standby?

I rolled my eyes and waited for the little dancing dots next to Faith's name to do their thing.

FAITH

> Or...

A knot formed tight in my stomach.

FAITH

> Or I could just call Beck and get the details from him.

FAITH

> Yep, I think that's what I'm going to do. Good night!

My fingers couldn't type fast enough.

LUNA

> I'm fine. Promise.

Then I double tapped the button on the side of my phone, enabling the camera. I snapped a quick selfie and sent it over.

LUNA

> See. All good. No need to pester Beck.

FAITH

> Since when do you protect Beck...

Well, she's got me there.

I tapped the phone a few times. I'd just call her to talk for a few minutes and clear things up.

"*Now* you call me?" Faith berated me as she answered the call.

I tilted my camera toward the computer screen in front of me. "I have work to catch up on. Just needed to make sure you didn't send the cavalry. It would interrupt my flow and I'm knee deep in catch-up mode."

I'd basically given up on getting to sleep at a decent hour.

Faith narrowed her eyes. "Is that what the doctor would want?"

But before I could answer, Sebastian walked into frame. "So are we good, or are we going to have to trek to the city in the middle of the night?"

I pointed back at the screen. "That's up to your girlfriend, but I promise I've got it covered. I even meditated this morning!"

Faith beamed. "You did? I'm so proud of you."

Technically, I sat down and closed my eyes for a few seconds with the *intention* of meditating. My legs were crossed and everything before my phone chimed, and I had to triage something with Parvati.

Details, details.

As if she could now see the truth on my face, Faith's smile faltered.

She was quick. I was quicker.

I blew a kiss. "Love you both. I promise to check in tomorrow. Bye-eee."

Then I hung up the call and slammed the phone on the desk, hoping they'd just accept my responses and be done with it.

But a little seed of doubt was planted, and I knew it wouldn't be the last time I had this conversation.

CHAPTER 15

Beck

"I CAN DEPLOY two of my guys. Just tell me when and where. Let me add my assistant to the call so we can get the details jotted down correctly." I seamlessly added my assistant Miles to the call so he could make sure I didn't fuck up any of the numbers.

That happened from time to time but now we had strict protocols in place to make sure contact information was collected correctly so that I didn't send my security team out to the wrong address. The dyslexia friendly font helped, but it wasn't fool proof.

I'd just set down my phone when a text came through.

SEBASTIAN

We're in the city and Faith wants us to grab dinner tonight. You free?

I glanced at the oversized clock above the door of my office. "Shit."

It was almost time to pick up Alice. Mrs. Corbett picks her up most days, but I always picked her up on Fridays. It was our evening to watch movies and spend time together. That hadn't really happened yet in the new house since we were still unpacking. Well, Alice's room was all set up, it was the rest of the house that required my attention.

BECK

I can't. It's pizza and movie night with Alice.

SEBASTIAN

Faith says she loves pizza. Why don't we come over and join you?

Alice loved Sebastian. She found his grumpiness hysterical. Yet we hadn't spent a lot of time together, just the two of us. With all of these changes she'd been a little grumpier than normal. Just this morning she'd decided to give maximum-level sass before school, refusing to get dressed, eat, or brush her teeth. Everything was a battle, and it was on my to-do list to ask why.

Perhaps I should explore getting her back into therapy, just to help smooth out these transition periods. I decided I'd call them immediately to reestablish visits and tomorrow would be a daddy daughter day.

That still left the matter of pizza tonight.

BECK

Let me check with Alice first. Make sure she's okay with it.

FAITH

Oh, please, I want to meet Alice. I haven't had a chance to meet her yet. Pretty pretty please.

FAITH

I promise I'll be good. I'll bring the pizza and get some local ice cream too. It's on me. You don't have to do a thing.

SEBASTIAN

I think we're coming over, whether you want us to or not.

I sighed but was secretly happy that my friend and his partner wanted to come over. Usually it was me dragging Sebastian out to get some adult time.

BECK

I figured it was a losing battle as soon as Faith got involved.

SEBASTIAN

You're a wise man. Sometimes.

BECK

Don't be a dick.

I darted out to pick Alice up from school. When I told her the plan, she squealed at the idea of visitors. My extroverted kid wasn't bummed at all that we weren't going to have the evening to ourselves. I tried not to let that bother me.

"And I get to meet Uncle Sebastian's girlfriend?" she asked.

I nodded. "You do."

She damn near skipped all the way home.

I had just finished cleaning up the kitchen an hour later when I heard a knock on the door.

"They're here!" Alice screamed, in her high-pitched voice. It sounded like a stampede tramping through my hallways as she vaulted toward the door. Alice flung it open to let my friends in without bothering to look through the peephole, not that she could reach it. I quickly followed behind her, grabbing the door before it slammed into the drywall.

Faith beamed and even Sebastian looked amused to find my daughter greeting him.

Alice tugged Faith's hand, trying to tow her in an acrobatic move that would impress a Cirque du Soleil performer, Faith passed the boxes of pizza to Sebastian without spilling a slice.

Then Willow burst through the door following Faith and my daughter. The lovable lab enjoyed bouncing between the city and the country house.

Thankfully, I was a dog guy.

Sebastian's normally grumpy demeanor cracked. And, for a second, I thought I saw a sense of longing in his gaze as he watched Faith and Alice walking away together.

Had he and Faith talked about children yet?

I'll be damned. Sebastian Steele had found the woman for him and that brick facade was crumbling bit by bit.

My gaze slid to the wall between my house and Luna's. For a brief second I considered what it might be like if she were here, greeting *our* friends *together*.

Then I chuckled. *Maybe in an alternative universe.*

I clapped my friend on the back and headed to the kitchen where Alice was rattling off her favorite pizza combinations to Faith. The women stared at my daughter, completely enamored. Alice had that effect on people.

There was mischief in Faith's eyes as I poured the adults glasses of sparkling water and milk for Alice.

"How's my bestie doing?" she asked.

I winked. "I'm doing great. Thanks for asking."

She narrowed her eyes like she knew exactly what I was doing. "Love that you think you're my bestie, we should talk about that. I was referring to..." She pointed at the wall separating my place from Luna's.

Alice's head whipped toward the wall and then back at me as if trying to puzzle things together. "You know Luna?"

Faith's mouth twisted like the damn Cheshire Cat. "I do."

Alice lit up. "So do I. She's so nice. Do you know she

babysat me? Although she didn't think Hawaiian pizza is a good pizza. She's wrong about that. Otherwise, she's cool."

Faith nodded sagely. "She is very cool. She's one of my best friends." Then she turned to me. "So how is my best friend doing?"

I busied myself with the pizza, making Alice's plate first. "And why would I know what your friend is up to?"

Sebastian cut me a glare.

Faith stood straight, reaching her full height. "You seem to have no problem keeping tabs on her midnight running sessions."

"She hasn't done that in six nights."

Faith looked like the cat who caught the canary. "Oh, really? Six *whole* nights? And you know that because..."

I pretended to remove a piece of non-existent lint from my shoulder. "I own a billion-dollar bodyguard business. It's my duty to know these things."

"Sure, you just happen to keep tabs on a woman who you aren't contractually obligated to protect." She nodded. "That makes a whole lot of sense." Sarcasm dripped from her lips like honey from a honeycomb.

"Can I eat?" Alice piped in.

Faith startled as if remembering there were little ears in the room. Her face softened as she turned to my daughter and asked her about school, making sure to throw me one final glance that promised we weren't done with this conversation.

I made plates for everyone. Sebastian and I ate standing up since we only had two barstools, and we'd offered them to our girls.

"How's it going with Harrison Barnes?" I asked. Sebastian finally got the white whale of clients. Something he'd been working towards since he started Steele Cyber Security a dozen years ago.

Sometimes our work overlapped, which meant we often passed clients back and forth. Unlike my friend, I didn't care about the cache that comes with some of the wealthiest people in the world. No, I preferred to protect people who deserved protecting. To be fair, most people fall under this category. Luckily, I've made a great name for myself, which means I can cherry pick my clients.

"It's fine. I have to fly back to London a couple of times and I'm trying to convince Faith to go with me. I think she's onboard for one trip and then needs to be here for a few gallery meetings. Apparently they are going to set up another show with her and a couple of other artists and she wants to hold the meetings in person. It's more professional that way."

"She wants to be taken seriously given her last name. That makes sense." Being a former socialite meant that a lot of people judged Faith based on her name alone.

Sebastian ran a hand through his scruff. "I was hoping you'd have someone watch over her while I'm gone. Just a few days." He rattled off the dates. The first trip was just a few days away.

I nodded, already combing through my mental Rolodex to consider who I might be able to dispatch. "You sure as shit didn't learn your lesson from last time?"

He shrugged. "I knew you'd figure something out."

"My team has a full roster right now." And Sebastian couldn't be bothered to give me more of a heads up.

He grinned like he knew exactly what I was thinking. "You could always do it."

I frowned. "Yes, I watched her before, but that was an unusual circumstance, and you know it. I come in, get the client comfortable, and do the soft handoff with my team. That's how it works."

Sebastian folded his arms across his wide chest. "We can just pretend anytime that Faith is involved is a special circumstance."

A laugh burst from my chest. "You would ask for that."

My friend's face turned hard as steel. "For that woman, I'd ask anything."

I loosed a sigh. "I'll see what I can do, I promise. It gets complicated with Alice. I don't like spending more than a night or two away from her."

Sebastian shrugged. "Simple. Bring her with you."

"That's not how this works."

He shrugged again. "Think of it as house-sitting."

I had a few choice words for my friend. None of which I'd vocalize in earshot of Alice.

"I'll consider it." Knowing full damn well I'd say yes in the end.

CHAPTER 16

Luna

"THE PERMIT DIDN'T GO THROUGH."

Parvati didn't even wait until I fully exited my town car to tell me. Nope. She held the door open and casually dropped the latest in a series of setbacks.

"Fuck," I swore, adjusting my dress to make sure I didn't show the goodies to the men wandering around the active worksite.

Parvati performed her typical Sorkin-inspired walk 'n talk, taking us from the street to the main entrance of the job site. By the looks of it, there were a handful of folks erecting the steel beams that would keep the place upright. Things were busier than ever, and yet there managed to be setback after setback.

"I swear it's like the city doesn't even want us to build with the way they are putting up one bureaucratic barrier after another. It's bullshit, is what it is. This happened to me once before on a job site in Southern California. Let me tell you, I started attending every damn city council meeting to make sure they saw me and knew exactly what they were doing by stalling our project. It was for a non-profit that got unhoused folks back to work! And they tried to stop me."

She huffed, as if the challenge was nothing but a battle to win.

Despite my increased heart rate and the sour taste in the bottom of my esophagus, I knew for certain that Parvati would do everything she could to remedy the situation. That was the kind of leadership and badassery I wanted around me at all times.

I looked at her pointedly. "You tell me when the next meeting is, and I'll show up with red lipstick and my eyes lined so sharp they could kill a man."

Parvati smiled smugly. "You up to some vigilante shit?"

"Something like that."

She nodded approvingly. "And in the meantime, I'll pay the city a little visit. I've dotted my tees and crossed my 'I's. I know the paperwork is perfect and their excuses are total bullshit. If I have my way, you won't have to step foot in a city council chamber."

Parvati waved me forward to the trailer that served as her headquarters. Thanks to Sebastian's surveillance equipment and the new "Business" tab on my Steele Cyber Security app, I was able to check in on the project whenever I could.

I wonder if this is how parents feel who have nanny cams throughout their house. It had felt a little like spying when I first got access, but honestly, it's my site and I found it soothing to watch the feed in the wee hours of the night while I laid restless in bed.

We each took a seat at the small round table inside the trailer. "We also need to talk about the designs for the break-fast buffet. Drew sent them to both of us. Have you had a chance to take a look?" Parvati asked.

I groaned as I considered the interior designer I'd hired for this project. "I did. My list of changes is probably going to drive Drew away, but I can't have a breakfast buffet in a luxury, boutique casino and hotel that looks anything less than perfect. We already have cheesy-kitchy covered by the other casinos. I'll be damned if I let mine get steered in that direction. People are going to spend almost a hundred dollars for breakfast. It can't look like they are stepping into a bottle of Pepto Bismol."

Parvati released an unhinged giggle. It clashed with what I knew about the woman who—in my mind—embodied the term "put together." "I've been trying to figure out what it reminded me of. That's exactly it."

"Oof, I knew it the second my peepers laid eyes on that god-awful design."

As Parvati continued to talk through the items on her agenda, I already started mentally planning to visit my bestie and get her input.

———

"I'm gassing up the PJ and coming for a visit."

Faith blinked. "Excuse me?"

I pulled my suitcase out of the hallway closet with one hand and held the phone in my other hand, granting Faith a shaky view of me and my brownstone.

"I need your design expertise, and I need to escape the city for at least twenty-four hours."

Faith laughed. "You're always welcome here."

Sebastian groaned in the background. "Who is that?"

Faith set down her paint brush. As usual, my friend was creating masterpieces in the atrium of the gorgeous house she shared with Sebastian. "It's Luna. She's coming for a visit," she shouted over her shoulder before turning back to me. "You aren't really taking a private jet here are you?"

"Nah, there's no good place to land. Besides, all my money is going into this casino, so I have to be smart with it. Town car it is. I should be there in three hours. Make sure you brew a pot of coffee; we're going to need it."

I watched Faith leave her easel and sit down on a nearby couch. "Ohh, what are we doing this time?"

I threw a swimsuit in my bag and a couple of bras and undies. Clothes. I still needed clothes. "I need to provide feedback on the buffet and, oof, it's a doozy. That brilliant brain of yours better be ready to brainstorm. This designer is getting feedback like they've never seen before. Frankly, I might have to switch interior design firms. It's that bad."

I pinched the spot between my brows, a headache forming.

My friend's brows knit together, her voice soft. "Have you taken your medicine?"

I shook my head. "Not yet. I'll take it now." Heaven knows if I didn't do that I'd be up a shit creek. And then how would I get back to Drew in time.

Fuck.

My meds were in the downstairs bathroom, so I trekked there to grab a pill. "I should probably keep my migraine meds on me like an EpiPen."

I said it flippantly, but a frown tugged at the corner of Faith's lips. "That might not be a bad idea."

"Aha!" I found the bottle and tossed the pill in my mouth. After setting down the phone, I turned on the facet and got some water to wash it down.

The room spun.

Fuck, I felt like I was going to fall over. I pinched my eyes shut and took a few deep inhales—in through my nose and out through my mouth.

"Luna? Luna, can you hear me?"

My friend's voice broke through the whine that pierced my skull.

"Going to go lay down and the second I feel better I'm heading upstate."

I ended the call before Faith could protest and laid down

on the plush rug, grateful for past Luna who splurged on bathroom decor for the tiny half bath just off the kitchen.

It was there I clutched my head and willed the pain to go away.

———

A knock startled me awake.

Disoriented, I rose on my forearms and swiped away the drool dripping down my chin. The cursed piercing abated. Not fully; it still felt like pain was knocking on the door of my frontal lobe but at least it wasn't barging through with a pickaxe.

I savored the little win for what it was.

The pounding resumed, and for a second I wasn't sure if it was the door or my head.

"Definitely the door," I mumbled, getting to my feet. It took me a good few seconds to feel sturdy enough to move forward.

By then the pounding stopped. I'd just turned the corner in my kitchen when my security system beeped, and the door swept open revealing a frantic Beck. His normally well-kept hair was swept every which way as if he'd been tugging on it.

"What's wrong? You need me to watch Alice again? Because it's really not a great time." I grabbed the base of my neck, trying to massage away the stiffness there.

Beck didn't stop barreling toward me, pulling me into his strong arms. I collapsed into him, too tired to protest, especially when he smelled so good. So safe. So *him*.

I think I even released a little sigh.

Beck lifted me into his arms and whispered, "You can't keep doing this, Luna. You scared the shit out of me."

I played with his hair. "You love taking care of me and you know it. You weirdo."

He practically growled in my ear. The warmth of his

breath sent a shudder along my spine. "We're going to my place."

I made a pathetic attempt to swat at him. It resulted in more of a feather-light graze at best. Ugh. This was twice now he'd come to my rescue, like some damn damsel in distress.

I loathed the feeling. The feeling of helplessness. I'd been on my own for so long now that the idea of any man—*this* man—stepping in to help felt completely foreign. More foreign was how much I liked it.

When we reached his house, Beck didn't drop me off at the couch like he had last time. Instead, he traversed the stairs. I hadn't been up here yet, so I peeked my eyes open to find photos of Alice on the wall. He must have made that one of his first priorities since moving in.

The hallway itself was painted a lovely neutral gray. We passed a room that had to be Alice's with a pink ruffled bed skirt that was similar to the one I'd wished for as a little girl. Beck's long strides made it impossible to catch a glimpse of anything else.

I wonder if we're going to his bedroom…

And despite the dull headache that remained, a pool of heat formed low in my belly. The idea of being alone with Beck in his bedroom excited me. In all those years since our night together, I hadn't longed for a man the way I had him.

In fact, quite the opposite. A few days after our romp together, I'd adopted a sober lifestyle and licked my wounds, not just the emotional ones left behind by Beck's disappearance but by the man that came *after*. The one who I didn't want and yet he took something from me without asking.

That loss of control was something I could never forget and never forgive. It was why all of my bars had a code for women and anyone else that felt uncomfortable or uneasy. To make sure what happened to me didn't happen to the happy people who patronized Club Deux. It was also why I made sure to offer free self-defense lessons for staff and had strip tests readily available for people to test their drinks for date rape drugs.

All these safety measures made Club Deux the most popular place to party for women and LGBTQIA clientele. Creating that safe space was essential and part of my mission as a business owner in hospitality.

I may never feel able to have fun and experiment in a way I once did, but I wanted to reduce as much risk as I could for others.

Beck carried me into a bedroom. Probably not his since the floral decor screamed guest bedroom. Without losing his grip on me, he lifted the corner of the comforter and slid me into the luscious satiny sheets.

"Stay here. I'll get you some water and call your doctor."

The man slipped out of the room, and I immediately felt the loss of his presence. My eyelids grew heavy, and I fell fast asleep.

CHAPTER 17

Beck

THE SECOND I saw Faith's name flash across my phone screen, I knew something was wrong. While she occasionally texted in a group chat with Sebastian, Faith had never used my phone number despite having given it to her numerous times, including when I was hired to protect her from the overzealous paparazzi.

I excused myself when the call came through, passing off the team meeting to my second-in-command to finish facilitating our strategy for the next big gig: protecting celebrity clients at an upcoming festival in the California desert.

"What's wrong?" I answered.

"It's Luna. We were on the phone, and she was complaining about her head hurting when just seconds earlier she said that she was coming to visit me. I don't think she feels okay and I'm too far away to check. Are you home? Can you stop by?"

My steps quickly swallowed the distance between the conference room and the exit. "Already on my way. ETA is..." I glanced down at my watch. "Twelve minutes." At this time of day, I'd have to fight through some congestion on the sidewalks, but I'd lived in the city a long time. I knew how to navigate the town regardless of the time of day. It wasn't worth trying to flag down a taxi; I'd just waste time sitting in the car.

For the second time in the span of a week I'd barged into Luna's house. This was a pattern I wasn't fucking enjoying.

And when I brought her upstairs I damn near set her on my own bed, remembering only at the last second how inappropriate that would be.

She zonked out the second her head hit the guest pillow. I'd had Luna's doctor on speed dial since the day she entered the hospital. Adrenaline surged in my body as I waited for someone to answer my call. Luna wasn't in any imminent danger and yet my body reacted viscerally as if waiting for the next shoe to drop.

"Thank you for calling the office of Doctor..." fucking voicemail.

I left a message and called Faith to let her know that I was with her friend. In usual Faith form, she demanded regular updates. "Don't make me come out there."

Faith did confirm that Luna had taken the migraine medicine. She seemed much more together than the last time I found her passed out over the toilet. That likely meant she'd caught it in time.

Still, it unnerved me to think of what might have happened if Faith hadn't been on the phone with Luna.

I pinched my brow. "Fuck."

My phone started blowing up with text messages. Some from the office asking where I'd rushed off to. Some from Sebastian.

I took a closer look at the one from Sebastian.

SEBASTIAN:

Harrison Barnes wants me in London
TOMORROW.

SEBASTIAN

> Fuck, I thought I had more time. I know this is extreme, but can you come and look after Faith while I'm gone? The insane press has died down, but I still don't fully trust them not to track her down.

SEBASTIAN

> Bring Alice. It's the weekend, so she won't have school.

SEBASTIAN

> Faith says that Luna is not feeling well. Call me when you can.

Alice would be out of school in an hour. I could swing by, get her, and call Sebastian en route, a kernel of a plan forming in my mind. Luna wouldn't love it but at this point I couldn't care less.

I was about to become Luna's personal bodyguard whether she liked it or not. If she wouldn't protect her body, then it left me little choice but to do it myself.

———

"This is kidnapping."

Luna stirred awake the next morning. Yes, the damn woman slept on and off all night. I slept with the door open to my room, getting up to check on her occasionally as if she were some newborn I had to check to make sure she was breathing.

Sebastian requested my help, and Luna was getting it whether she wanted it or not. I made the executive decision to bring her with me upstate where I planned to spend the weekend watching Faith or at least just being nearby so my friend could focus on his business deal, and I could pull

Charlie or someone else Faith knew to take over babysitting duty.

Besides, it sounded like Luna planned to visit Faith anyway. I'd found a half packed to-go bag, so I grabbed that and figured I'd just go out and buy whatever I missed.

Alice had her headphones on singing Taylor Swift's latest bop as Luna finally came to.

"Where are we going? Are you taking me into the woods to murder me because this is really sketchy? And frankly this outfit is not the vibe." She sniffed her shirt and winced.

Then our eyes met in the rearview mirror. I'd placed her in the backseat to give her more room while making sure I could watch over her.

"We're spending the weekend at Sebastian's house upstate. He left this morning for London and doesn't want Faith all by herself."

Luna rubbed her temples. "Faith's a grown woman. She can look after herself. But as it so happens, I do need her help. So this works out just fine. Except for the kidnapping bit. That's not cool."

She reached over and smacked my head from behind.

"Hey, I'm driving here."

"Oh, please, I barely hit you. Suck it up, buttercup. You don't get to pull a kidnapper move and then complain when I get pissy about it," I grumbled, still waking up.

"Daddy, what's a kidnapper?"

My eyes darted to Alice who now had her headphones in her lap. *When did that happen?*

"My bad," Luna whispered before turning to my daughter. "So let's talk about consent. Consent means someone says yes to something. For instance, I didn't say yes to this excursion because I was unconscious. It's impossible to give consent when you're sleeping off a migraine. Does that make sense?"

Jesus Christ. The woman wasn't wrong, and I was all for

age-appropriate discussions about bodily autonomy. This wasn't the place and time…

I had to step in. "Technically, Luna is right, honey. I should have waited for her to wake up and make sure she was okay with the plan before putting her in the car and whisking her away to her best friend so that she can get some much-needed girl time and fresh air so that she can let her body rest because her body is battling her right now."

Alice frowned. "Is your body okay, Luna? Do we need to go to the hospital?"

Annnnd I made it worse.

I opened my mouth to respond but Luna beat me to it. "I'm okay now. Don't you worry about me. Now tell me, have you been to Faith's house because let me tell you, I love it. We can explore the woods, play with Willow, and enjoy the fresh air. It's delightful."

"I love Willow! She'll be there?" Alice asked.

Luna smiled. "She'll be there. Last time Willow cuddled me all night. It was the best feeling ever."

My daughter's eyes were as big as saucers. "Can she sleep in my bed tonight?"

Luna hummed. "I'm sure she'd love that. We just have to check with Faith first."

Alice put her hands in prayer. "Daddy, can we get a dog? Please. Pretty please."

"My bad," Luna said again, this time a little louder.

I knew this was coming. Hell, it was one of the reasons for the new house. Maybe this weekend could be a trial. "Let's take good care of Willow this weekend and then we'll see about getting a dog."

Luna tapped her painted nail on her plump lips. "You know, Sebastian does help out at the local animal shelter. Maybe you could check it out…"

My eyes collided with Luna's.

"Riiiiight." She made a zipping motion with her hand before throwing me a wink.

The damn minx knew exactly what she was doing.

"I'm going to take very good care of Willow, Daddy," Alice said firmly.

My face softened. "I know you will, sweetheart."

CHAPTER 18

Luna

"THANK GOD FOR LADY TIME. I swear, that man drives me nutty."

I enveloped Faith in a hug the second she opened the door to the sprawling country manor house owned by Sebastian Steele. I could practically feel Beck rolling his eyes behind me.

And while I usually said that statement with venom dripping from my red-stained lips, this time it felt a little less weighty. Like it wasn't quite true anymore and even my body could detect the lie for what it was.

But I seriously needed girl time. I loved the badass ladies who worked for me, but they worked *for* me, which meant that inherently we had a wonky power dynamic that I didn't want to fuck with.

Faith however didn't work for me and even though I'd only known her a few short months, it felt like we'd known each other all our lives. With her wealth, she could have been stuck up and conceited and a real asshole and nobody would blink. But she was the opposite of that. And she'd managed to break down those brick walls around my friend Sebastian's heart, which meant she was a keeper.

The second the hug was over, I beelined for the guest

room I'd stayed in before, hopping immediately into the shower.

I tried to forget that Beck had once again seen me at my worst, and probably smelling my worse if I was being completely honest.

I scrubbed away the grime and felt like a new woman. Then I took my time lining my eyes and my lips, carefully painting them both until I felt more like myself.

Fortunately for me, I'd left a few pieces of clothing in the closet the last time I crashed here. I selected a black bodysuit and chic red leather skirt with a peekaboo slit that skimmed the top of my thigh.

Eat your heart out, Beck Bennet.

With that complete, I padded down the hallway to my favorite room in the house. I found most of the crew: Alice and Faith were there.

Beck wasn't.

Curious.

And a smart move. The man should keep a wide berth after the shit he'd pulled this morning.

Willow was in the kitchen too. The sweet dog peppered me with kisses, and although I usually identified as a cat person, you couldn't help but fall in love with Willow.

After giving her a final pat on the head, I sank into a chair in the cozy kitchen with its wooden cross beams and European chic vibes as Faith set out plates of veggie and tofu stir-fry. It was a little early for lunch, but my stomach grumbled all the same.

"Where's your dad?" I asked Alice as she picked up a fork and poked at a mushroom.

Faith rolled her eyes, chiming in for Alice. "He's doing a perimeter check."

I laid a napkin in my lap. "I'm guessing that's more for Sebastian than for you."

Faith nodded. "Absolutely. You know Seb is going to

require proof-of-life photos. I'm sure Beck is documenting everything he's doing to ensure my safety."

"Is your house dangerous?" Alice asked with her mouth full.

"I'm perfectly safe," Faith said with a reassuring smile. "Sebastian has a state-of-the-art security system and this house would be safe even if we didn't have that in place."

The little girl's brow furrowed. "So why is Daddy doing a perimeter check then?"

Faith leaned in close, like she was going to reveal a big secret. "Because Sebastian is a bossy billionaire."

Alice nodded sagely, as if that explained everything. "My daddy is a billionaire too."

I spat out the swig of ice water I'd just taken a sip of. "Say what now?"

Faith smirked. "Didn't you know? Beck is a billionaire. Some family money plus a booming business."

"And he's bossy too," Alice added. "Maybe that's why he's such good friends with Uncle Sebastian." Alice's forehead crinkled, deep in thought.

The back door squeaked as it opened, the hinges in dire need of some WD-40. In walked Beck, hair slicked back with sweat, his shirt clinging to his chest.

Lust shot down my spine. "Look what the cat dragged in."

Beck flashed me a smile like he knew my words didn't match up with my inner thoughts.

I moved my hand to flip him off when I remembered Alice was in the room. The man was a menace, but he was a good dad—anyone could see that—and I would never say anything disparaging in front of the man's child.

Tease him? *Of course.*

Put him in his place? *Absolutely.*

But say something negative? *Hard pass.*

Kids had enough drama to navigate without new lady friends messing up their heads.

Besides, as far as I could tell, Alice's mom wasn't in the picture. My dad hadn't been in the picture either, so I knew the feeling of being raised by a single parent. They took on all roles.

Beck was a goddamn superhero with his hands on his hips, his broad chest tapering down...

Where was I going with this...

My stomach growled and suddenly everyone was looking at me.

Alice's fork clattered on the table. "All done. Daddy, can I go play with Willow now?"

Beck dragged his eyes from me, and they softened as they landed on his daughter. "Sure, just make sure you stay where I can see you."

Faith pushed back her chair. "I'll go with her. Show her some of the cool tricks Willow can do."

Before I could protest, my best friend and Alice rushed outside, an excited Willow in tow until Beck and I were alone in the room. He still towered near the door and had the audacity to tug the bottom of his shirt up to wipe his brow. The movement revealed a chiseled set of abs that would make Adonis jealous.

Fucking hell.

I gulped, lurid images springing to mind. I scooted back and proceeded to escape the kitchen, bringing my veggie stir-fry with me.

Heavy footsteps sounded from behind. "You haven't finished your food."

"No shit, Sherlock."

"You don't need to leave the kitchen to eat."

I stopped myself from turning around. "Personal preference."

"Your personal preference is to haul your bowl around the downstairs of Sebastian's house?" Beck asked, and I could hear the smile in his voice. The taunt.

I headed to the atrium where Faith spent her days painting. The greenhouse-like glass roof provided gorgeous natural light and made for a happy place. You couldn't be annoyed in a happy place like this.

Although if anyone could make that statement untrue it was Beck.

I sunk down on the plush couch and Beck took the seat beside me, the couch buckling under his weight.

"Tell me about Alice's mom."

The words slipped out of me. By my calculations, Alice must have been born nine or ten months after *our* night.

Had he met someone so quickly? Were they in love? Was it a one-night stand?

Pain flashed in those hazel eyes of his, before being smothered like the extinguishing of a candle. The spark vanquished before it could fully ignite.

"Jasmine. Her name is Jasmine."

In moments like this I wish I still drank. It might take off some of the edge. But then I took some deep breaths as I nodded my head, urging him to continue.

Beck's Adam's apple bobbed, the charming, shit-eating smile he usually wore scrubbed from his face. "We slept together one night, and she got pregnant. She said she wasn't sure she was ready to be a parent and when she saw that I was, she decided to have Alice. She signed away parental rights immediately after birth. Alice is a hundred percent mine."

A million follow-up questions sat on the tip of my tongue. One rose above the rest. "How long?"

Beck tilted his head.

"How long after us did you sleep with Jasmine? Or was it before us?"

Beck leaned forward, forearms on his thick thighs. "It was four days after us."

I chuckled, but it held no mirth. "So you wrote my phone

number in Sharpie on your arm just for fun and then ignored it? Was my number still on your skin when you decided to sleep with someone else?"

Fury flashed in those hazel eyes. "You gave me a dud number."

I scoffed. "Oh, please."

"You gave me a fake fucking number, Luna. Trust me, I called multiple times. You wanted nothing to do with me, so I moved on." His tone was lethal.

"Rather quickly," I damn near shouted. "And what's this bullshit about a fake number? The number I told you was real. I watched you write it down on your arm."

He pointed to his chest. "I wrote it down verbatim."

"Then you wrote it down wrong," I nearly shouted.

Beck slid closer. "I wanted to see you again. I wanted more."

I swallowed. "Then you should have called."

He scrubbed a hand down his face. "Jesus Christ we aren't getting anywhere with this."

"I waited for you to call. You didn't call."

His jaw clenched. "I tried calling. Hell, I can still remember the number."

Beck proceeded to rattle off the numbers, and they were *almost* correct.

I frowned. "That's not my number."

He threw his hands in the air. "Exactly, you gave me the *wrong* number."

"My number ends in a nine not a six."

He narrowed his gaze at me, and I watched as the blood drained from the man's face. Beck sat there staring at me for a full minute before he whispered, "I fucked up the numbers."

I couldn't wait to hear what bullshit explanation he'd come up with next.

He dragged his hands through his short hair. "I fucked up the numbers."

It was almost a whisper, like he was talking to himself.

My stomach plummeted.

I scooted closer to him, pulling Beck's hands out of his locks. We didn't need him to do any permanent damage to those gorgeous strands.

"What do you mean you fucked up the numbers?" I held my breath awaiting his answer.

His eyes pierced mine. "I'm dyslexic."

I blinked once. Twice. The puzzle pieces falling together in some cosmic joke that wasn't the least bit funny. I inhaled through my nose and released my breath slowly through my mouth.

"You *wanted* to call me? You *wanted* to see me again?"

He flinched, as if affronted. "Of course I fucking did. Do you remember that night?" He tapped his forehead. "Because I have seared it into my brain. I can play it like a fucking DVD. And you know what? Most nights I do just that. I grip myself and replay that night together. Sliding the straps off that dress and struck dumb as it pooled round your feet. I loved every second I spent shamelessly exploring that bare skin of yours. Those little moans you made when I licked you while driving my fingers deep. Fuuuck. It's a sound I'll never forget."

My throat went dry as I silently urged him to keep going.

Beck shook his head as if to clear the haze of his memory. His attention returned fully on me, and he closed the space between us. He leaned in and the scent of pine tickled my senses, my nipples pebbling in excitement.

This man…

"I called you. I wanted to have so many more nights where we stayed up talking for hours and then get intimately acquainted with every inch of your body. And not just once. Over and over again. I figured you gave me the wrong number on purpose. That's why I didn't go after you. That's why I didn't put every resource at my disposal towards tracking down the woman who could have changed everything."

I felt dizzy. My body swayed forward, and Beck was there in an instant, catching my arms in his hands.

I gulped. I'd been fighting with this man every time I saw him because I thought he rejected me after that night. I was just another notch in his belt, a conquest to be won.

His grip remained firm, holding me steady.

This close I could see the sincerity written on the planes of his face. This wasn't his usually jovial volley of cute remarks that raised my hackles. Or the playful looks that hid deeper feelings.

This was real.

"You mean that? You called me? You wanted me to answer?" I held my breath.

The man looked damn near tormented. "Of course I fucking did. I called that number a dozen times and I should have fucking considered that I messed up the numbers. That my dyslexia came to play at the worst possible time."

Then Beck's eyes traced the outline of my face, his gaze softening as he tucked a stray hair behind my ear.

I leaned into the touch.

"Beck—" I sighed.

A door flung open, and footsteps bounded down the hall.

We flew apart until we were on opposite sides of the couch. Just in time for Alice to find us, Willow in tow, and Faith bringing up the rear, eyebrows raised in blatant accusation. "Well, well, what do we have here?"

CHAPTER 19

Beck

THE REST of the evening was pure torture. We didn't have any alone time. Not when Faith insisted on having us all cook dinner together and then called Sebastian so she could show him that she was just fine.

Alice kept giving me a strange look, probably because both me and Luna were unusually quiet.

Luckily, Faith used her socialite sparkle to smooth over any weirdness.

Still, I sat there dumbfounded as I took a bite of bruschetta. I'd fucked up the numbers. Luna had wanted me to call her. I'd been holding onto this ridiculous grudge for years wondering how things might have been different had we...

"We're going to have dessert after this, right?" Alice asked.

Alice.

I wouldn't have Alice if I had gotten the phone number right all those years ago. As much as I had envisioned a future with Luna after less than twenty-four hours of knowing her, if she had answered I wouldn't have my precious girl.

I wouldn't have been stupid enough to go out and drink, seeking solace in someone else. Not when I'd just met who I thought was *my* person. My end game.

Now I just had to sit here eating dinner like I hadn't just had the biggest revelation of my life. I couldn't even taste anything, my mind and body were too busy thinking and replaying the interaction from earlier.

I glanced at the clock across the room. Alice would go to bed in a few short hours and then I'd corner Luna and make her tell me her side of the story.

I'd been such an asshole to her. Egging her on because I thought she'd tossed me away like yesterday's trash.

When all this time she'd been thinking the exact same thing about me.

How had we fucked this up so bad?

Probably pride. At least on my end.

Then Jasmine got pregnant with Alice, and I had no time to pine over what could have been with a woman I thought didn't want me.

Hypotheticals and *what ifs* swirled around in my brain.

"What do you think, Daddy?"

Alice had asked me a question, and I had no idea what it was.

"Sorry, sweetheart. What was that?" I narrowed my focus on her, tuning out everything else around me. The exact opposite of the rigorous training from my time in the Marines and frankly the antithesis of what I should be doing as someone actively on guard watch despite there being little to no threats to Faith and her safety.

Alice had her hands on her thighs as she bounced in her chair, the food half eaten on her plate. "Can I have a slumber party with Faith and Sebastian's mom?"

Constance had joined us for dinner. Sebastian's mom lived in a cottage located southwest of the main house. I had an unobstructed view of the front door which was painted a bright barn red. Because it was on Sebastian's property, the house came fully equipped with the latest and greatest Steele Cyber Security had to offer.

I shook my head. "You want to do what?"

Constance wiped the corner of her mouth with a linen napkin. "I made a chocolate silk pie earlier today, and I thought the girls might like some. Then I figured we would turn it into a girls' night..."

Faith nodded along, picking up where Constance left off. "We want to set up in the living room, play some board games, maybe decorate cookies, and braid hair. You know, girly things."

"I'm all for a girl's night but I'd rather sleep in a real bed," Luna said.

"Oh, you're not invited," Faith said with a smile.

Luna reared her head back. "What do you mean I'm not invited?"

Faith held her ground. "You need your beauty rest, and you can't manage that if you're sleeping on an air mattress. Nope, I won't hear of it. You need to spend time in the main house where it's quiet and you can be near a bed."

Faith's eyes volleyed between Luna and myself.

What is she planning?

"Pie and cookies!" My daughter's eyes were as wide as saucers. Her hands immediately folded into prayer. "Please let me go to this sleepover. Faith promised to braid my hair like a princess, Daddy. A princess!"

Alice suffered enough of my fumbling with her hair after watching hours of YouTube videos to no avail. Having someone who could actually braid her hair had her buzzing with excitement.

I looked at Constance and Faith. I'd met Constance a dozen times over the years and while I didn't know her that well, I'd heard plenty from Sebastian. And Faith, for that matter.

I trusted them both implicitly. After I ran a thorough background check the first time I met each of them.

"We will take good care of her," Faith promised.

"I'll be good, Daddy." Her sweet face filled with excitement and anticipation. Then she climbed out of her chair and came over to mine, crawling into my lap. "Pleeease. I've never had a girl's night before."

What a gut punch. My baby girl didn't have a lot of strong women role models and now there were three in this very room. She wanted to spend time with two of them. To be silly and have sweets and stay up way past her bedtime.

I hugged her tightly. "Sure. Just make sure you listen. And if you need to find me at the main house, make sure someone walks you over okay?"

Faith waved her phone. "And we're just a phone call away."

Alice flung her arms around me. "Thank you, thank you, thank you."

Then she ran from the room, probably to get her bag.

Luna crossed her arms. "I'm really not invited to girl's night? That's fucked up."

"Language," Constance scolded despite the fact I've heard the woman swear like a sailor. The woman grabbed our plates.

"I can take care of the dishes." I stopped her, pushing back my chair and lifting the plates from her hands.

Constance patted me on the cheeks. "Thanks, sweetheart. I'm going to set up the house. I never had a daughter; this will be fun."

She left with a wave and there were only three of us left in the room.

"I should go pack too and then I'll take Alice over when we are both ready," Faith said with a little finger wave.

Finally, it was just the two of us.

Me and the woman who'd had me buzzing all afternoon.

I didn't even care that Faith had clearly cooked up this girl's night to give me and Luna privacy. I was damn well happy she had.

"This will give us plenty of time to catch up," I said, breaking the silence.

Luna lifted a brow. "You stuck in the past, Beck Bennet?"

"I'm stuck in the *what could have been* and making up for lost time."

Luna shot from her chair, and walked toward me, then leaned against the large marble countertop near where I stood at the farmhouse sink. "You found your solace in Alice's mom. You didn't waste much time."

I shut off the water so she could hear me clearly. "I will never regret that because it gave me Alice, but trust me when I say she didn't compare to you. No one could even come close to comparing to you and our night together."

I watched, mesmerized as she swallowed hard.

"Is that so?" she asked

Planting two hands on either side of her, I got up close, the smell of her citrus shampoo marrying with the scent of basil from the bruschetta. "It's the truth. Maybe if we stopped this stupid bickering long enough, we could actually tell more of the truth."

Luna pulled her shoulders back, her lips twitched. "What's the fun in that?"

I nipped at those wicked lips, relishing in the sharp inhale of her breath. "Don't test me, Luna. It's been way too long since I've been inside you."

Luna lifted herself onto the counter, nearly knocking me in the chin in the process. We were nearly the same height, although she still had to tilt her head up to get a good look at me.

Her legs widened, and I stepped in between them. "Don't tease me, woman. I don't have the patience for it. Not tonight. Not with you."

Somewhere in the house Faith told Alice they'd go out the front door.

Smart woman.

I held my breath, staring at Luna and feeling the heat of her core near my stomach as the security system beeped, letting me know we were now officially alone.

My patience snapped like a ripcord. My hands dove into her hair, tilting her face up so our lips could collide.

She responded immediately, her legs wrapping around my waist, squeezing me tight as her hips rocked closer. Our teeth thrashed together, both of us eager to be closer before I slowed it down, my tongue dragging across her bottom lip before meeting hers. The small mewl she emitted from the back of her throat had me instantly hard.

My cock pulsed with need, as I slowly began to kiss a trail down the slender column of her neck. My fingers found the barely there strap that kept her top in place, and I slid it off her shoulder with a mere flick of the wrist.

The exposed shoulder did little to quell my thirst for her. It felt like that first night all over again. Like I'd never have my fill of her.

My palm unthreaded from her hair to palm her full breast, her nipple pebbling beneath my touch. The silky grazes across the fabric were nothing compared to the feeling of shedding her from the top altogether. The hiss that left her mouth when I exposed her and put my mouth on the perfectly pink nip was heaven.

How many times had I imagined doing this again? Gently, I dragged my teeth across the bud and Luna's fingers dug into my shoulders.

"We can't forget about this one," I said, releasing her and dragging my attention to her other perfect breast.

Luna tossed her head back as she held me to her chest, the possessiveness in her grip damn near making me explode in my pants like a horny teenager. I hadn't even gotten a chance to venture below the belt and she already had me bucking against her, seeking as much friction as I could through the thick denim that separated us.

"More, Beck. I need more." The plea dripped from her lips.

She was *begging* for it.

And I had to stop.

I halted my ministrations, gently bringing her shirt up to cover her.

She whined. "What are you doing? Why are you stopping?"

"Hold on." I carried her down the hall toward the guest room she'd claimed earlier. The woman continued to gyrate against me and her mouth found that spot behind my ear that drove me wild. "Behave, Marks."

"What happens if I don't want to behave?" she whispered, voice heady.

"Then this is going to be quite embarrassing for me."

Her arms straightened so she could get a better look at me. "I didn't take you for a premature ejaculator."

"Jesus—"

"I don't think he's going to help with this," she quipped before grinding against me like we were at a middle-school dance.

"Woman—" I hissed, kicking open the door and dropping her on the bed. She sat up on her forearms, licking her lips. Pure possession in her glance. Her heavy, lust-filled eyelids narrowing as her gaze trailed down my body.

I wanted to stop. I should've stopped. It had only been a couple of hours since my world had been tipped on its axis.

And yet...

I didn't want it to stop. Not when I'd gone this long without her. It had been years between our first encounter and the next. When I saw her again my immediate reaction was defense mode leaving us bickering like a couple who had spent decades together.

You wouldn't know it now. With Luna licking her lips as I placed my hands on either side of her body.

When I hovered on top of her, our bodies aligned...

And she *flinched*.

CHAPTER 20

Luna

BECK IMMEDIATELY LIFTED off me and moved to the other side of the bed.

My hands were shaking as I pressed my palms to my eyes. "Fuck."

"You have nothing to apologize for," he assured me.

I took a jagged breath.

The man was worried. For me. He even scanned the room as if looking for some invisible threat and then came up short. "Talk to me, Marks. This isn't the time for that smart mouth of yours to go quiet."

Dropping my hands, I winked an eye open. "Dammit, I want to have sex with you."

He looked skeptical. "Maybe you wanted to, but the way your body is reacting, I'm thinking you changed your mind. In case you don't know, I'm going to tell you it's okay to change your mind."

What the fuck is going on with my body? "Fuck, I thought this would be easier."

Beck propped his head in his hand as he studied me. "What's going on in that head of yours? Do you need me to get my medical kit?"

My chuckle sounded forced. I didn't embarrass easily and yet I could feel my cheeks flushing.

Beck brushed my hair back, face sober. "Did someone hurt you?"

I blinked. "Don't be so dramatic."

The man was the opposite of amused. His jaw clenched, and I saw his fist do the same before he took a deep breath and relaxed it. "Who. Hurt. You?"

I shivered. Fuck I hadn't spoken about this since the night it happened. I somehow managed to make it to the police station to file a report and then again when I started therapy. Outside those spaces, I kept it locked up tight. Not even Faith knew about what happened.

Besides, sex sells. I know that and in my industry, I'd be an idiot not to think about it...all the time. Immediately after that horrific night I wanted to cover up, to dim my shine, until I decided to fuck that. Some asshole didn't get to take away my bodily autonomy. That was mine and mine alone. I'd wear whatever the fuck I wanted, whatever made me feel beautiful. My own little way of taking back control of my life.

Just like not drinking had been a way of taking back control.

"Let's get you under the covers." Beck went to help me and then must have thought better of it. The tilt of his head screamed, *Is it okay if I touch you*?

I swallowed and nodded, letting him. Once I got cozy, Beck pulled back, but I grabbed his hand. "Get in with me."

His face crinkled. "Are you sure?"

I needed his grounding presence. "Hold me."

He scrubbed a hand down his face. "Nothing is going to happen," he said. His voice was firm, authoritative.

I patted the spot next to me. "Come."

Beck slid under the covers and despite my brain telling me this was a bad idea, I placed an arm across his chest and nestled my head against his neck. I inhaled his calming scent as his heartbeat thudded under my hand. My body relaxed immediately, as if tuning itself to him.

He ran his fingers through my hair. "I fucking hated seeing you flinch like that."

"I won't apologize." Even now, even like this, with the brick walls crumbling around us, I still felt compelled to challenge him. To poke at him.

His hand paused his ministrations. "You have nothing to fucking apologize for. But I am going to need a name, sweetheart."

I sighed heavily, his arm possessively coiled around me. "He's not worth it."

Beck tightened his grip, before coming to his senses and loosening it. I could hear the man's heart ricocheting in his chest, damn near bursting out of it.

"I hate this," he grumbled.

"I can tell. Your heart's racing like you're being chased by a polar bear."

A chuckle rumbled from his chest. "As opposed to a brown bear."

I shook my head. "That would be a totally different cadence."

"And you're a bear expert now?"

"Yup. Bar and bear expert."

He blew air out through his teeth. "Quite the resume you have there."

I shifted my body, draping my leg over him.

Beck hissed. "Don't make me shove a pillow between us."

"You would if I asked you to."

He planted a kiss on the sensitive spot behind my ear. "I would."

"It happened one night at Paige's apartment."

His grip tightened, and I'd bet money he'd done it inadvertently. It was as if he were bracing himself.

"Paige was my best friend at the time. I was pissed you

hadn't called me, and she insisted we go out to take my mind off things."

I inhaled deeply. "We went to a club and then Paige invited some guys home. She'd insisted even though I asked if we could just walk home and grab a slice of pizza along the way. The confusion started before we even left the club. I'd been upset about—" Beck turned to me, eyes colliding with mine as he listened. "I'd been upset about how things had gone down between us and between that and the long days and nights of working, I figured I just needed sleep. But then the dizziness started, and I knew something was very wrong. I was passed out on Paige's couch when I came to. One of the guys was fondling me with one hand and his dick in the other hand. My limbs felt like lead and my head was fuzzy, but somehow I managed to shout. My voice probably was barely above a whisper but somehow Paige heard it. She stormed out of her room and kicked him out when she saw tears running down my face."

"I'm glad she was there to stop him," Beck said fiercely, jaw clenched.

Sometimes I was grateful for that too, but mostly I hated that she left me alone with him. How could she not have seen how fucked up I was? She'd trusted these strangers implicitly.

"Deep down, I know it wasn't her fault. Countless hours of therapy taught me that. By knowing something in my head and feeling it in my heart were two different things. I can't separate it out, no matter how hard I try. And trust me, I've tried."

He hummed in understanding.

"It's like all the fear and feelings from that night are tied up with her too." I turned so that I faced Beck without craning my neck.

"Are you still friends with Paige?"

I shook my head. "I stopped talking to her. I tried to

remain friends at first. But then I changed so much after that night. I stopped drinking, I stopped partying for fun. I cut off most of that friend group, opting to focus on my work and my business and making sure that what happened to me didn't happen to others."

Beck combed my hair with his fingers, the little gesture a soothing balm over the heavy conversation. "Do you miss it?"

The air whooshed from my lungs. Nobody has asked me that. Most of my current friends only knew me as a sober person. Everyone I hung out with in the *before times* were no longer part of my circle. I don't think I'd even asked myself the question. And I definitely didn't say anything to my mom. She would have somehow blamed me for getting myself into that situation. Probably would have asked what I was wearing and how much I drank, as if that made it okay for anyone to lay their hands on someone without consent.

But the partying—*did I miss it*? "I'm not sure."

Beck waited for me to continue, his grip even tighter than before. He proceeded with caution, the little groove between his brows deeper than I'd ever seen it. The expression on my face silently asked if how we were laying was okay.

"It's hard to miss it when I'm surrounded by it."

Beck frowned. "Does that not make the temptation greater?"

"For me, it doesn't. Once I'd made the decision not to drink, it just stuck. Like I no longer needed to even consider it because the possibility has been wiped from the table."

"Because you needed to feel in control."

I nodded. "Exactly."

"And you don't trust anyone to see you out of control."

I blinked back the tears that threatened to spill. Fuck, if I cried then I'd run the risk of another migraine and that was the last thing I needed.

"Beck?"

"Yes, Marks?"

"I'm tired," I said through a yawn. It went beyond that. I was exhausted.

He nodded solemnly, taking the cue to leave. Beck leaned forward and placed a kiss on my forehead. The movement was slow and controlled. Not asking or wanting for more.

Beck's firm grip loosened, and the sudden loss of him felt like a sharp dagger to the chest. He slipped out of the bed and placed another kiss on my head.

"Sweet dreams, gorgeous," he whispered. Leaving me all alone.

CHAPTER 21
Beck

I'D JUST TAKEN a sip from my first coffee of the day when Alice burst through the door. "Daddy!"

She ran into my arms looking like a little princess, her hair intricately braided like she came straight from singing on the streets of Arendelle.

I'd been up half the night replaying Luna's words in my head, feeling grateful that she'd shared her truth with me while simultaneously seething and wanting to track down this man and single-handedly ruin his life.

And I wasn't foolish enough to think that one conversation would fix what could have been between us. It meant we knew the truth—the full truth, but it didn't mean we were suddenly together. It didn't erase all those hurt feelings from the past eight years.

Now reality had set back in. Real life. Responsibilities.

"Daddy can I have a sleepover every night?" Alice asked wide-eyed, pulling me back to the here and now.

I squeezed her tight. "Sleepovers are great every once in a while, but not every night. They would lose what makes them special."

"But it's so much fun." Alice broke into a yawn mid-sentence.

"We also don't live here and maybe Constance and Faith don't want to have a sleepover every night."

My daughter nodded enthusiastically. "I'm sure they will say yes."

I grinned, loving Alice's precocious nature all the while feeling completely inept to navigate the situation, so I fiddled with one of her braids only to have her swat at me. "Not the braids, Daddy!"

My hands flew above my head in capitulation. "I'm standing down."

Alice threw me a look befitting a teenager.

Luna swept into the kitchen wearing an emerald silk pajama set she'd changed into last night that showed off her long, lean legs and complemented her auburn hair. "Love the braids, Alice."

My daughter blushed, hand reaching up to touch her hair. "Thanks, Luna."

"Morning, Beck," Luna said, shooting me a sly smile as she headed straight to the coffee maker.

My heart thudded in my chest. "Morning, Luna."

"Daddy, I'm hungry."

I stood. "How does French toast sound?"

"Delicious," Luna answered.

My lips twitched. "I was asking Alice, but it's good to know what you like."

Alice walked right up to Luna and tugged on her arm. Luna bent down as Alice cupped her hand and whispered in Luna's ear.

Luna broke into a wide smile, then cupped her hand and whispered back into Alice's ear.

They were fucking adorable conspiring together. The tableau had me absently rubbing the spot over my heart.

I'd wondered what it would be like to raise my daughter

with a partner. With someone who wanted both of us—the packaged deal.

They both straightened, mischief written all over their faces.

"We want donuts," Alice said firmly.

Luna raised a finger. "And a latte. Preferably vanilla."

I crossed my arms. "Is that so? And where do you expect us to get said donuts and vanilla latte?"

"In town," Alice said.

Luna nodded enthusiastically beside my daughter as she pointed at me. "You're driving."

Is that so?

They both nodded some more, the corner of Luna's lips upturned.

"What about Faith?" I was here to babysit, and I took that seriously. "Are we supposed to just leave her here?"

Alice gasped. "I'll get her!"

In a flash, she was out the door, her little legs carrying her across the back cobblestones toward Constance's cottage. I watched the whole thing through the glass pane covering the top half of the door.

Luna recaptured my attention. She leaned against the marble countertops, her forearms resting on the counter behind her.

"I should separate you two. You're a bad influence."

Luna placed a hand on her chest. "Little 'ole me? Never."

"I'll call bullshit on that." I swallowed the space between us, and her arms came up to rest on my chest, the movement effortless, like we'd done this song and dance a million times before. "The bed was cold without you."

When I finally emerged from my own bedroom this morning, I caught a glimpse of her on her phone talking to one of her associates.

The woman never rested. It was no wonder her body kept shutting down on her.

Luna extended a finger, dragging it down my chest, and I held my breath wondering what would come next.

When I stepped back, her brows furrowed.

"How are you feeling about last night?" I asked.

She blinked. Twice.

"Coffee," she croaked. "I need more coffee before we talk about last night."

I stepped to the side, blocking her path. "Talk first, coffee second."

She crossed her arms and sank into her hip. If I were to have Faith paint this image, I'd dub it *Unamused*.

"You shared a lot last night," I prodded gently. "I'm glad we cleared some things up, even if I will be kicking myself for the rest of my life for not getting your phone number right. And for how I've treated you these past few months."

Luna peered at her fingernails like they were the most fascinating thing in the world. "I wasn't exactly a peach, either."

My lips twitched. That was one way of putting it.

Still, I loved all the poking and jabbing and fighting.

I took another step toward her, closing the gap again, her hands once again finding their place on my chest, her eyes focused there.

Gently, I lifted her chin. "Thank you for sharing that with me. I fucking want to tear the world apart to find the asshole that hurt you." She shuddered underneath my palm. "And I'm so proud of you for everything you're doing to make sure something like that never happens at Club Deux. You're *incredible*."

She gulped, eyes shining. "Thank you for saying that."

I pulled her in tight, and at first wasn't sure what to do; she just kind of froze there. Then, eventually, her arms tightened around my waist as I enveloped her in a hug. Luna sighed and a wave of content flooded my veins.

Eventually, Luna tilted back, smirking. "I could really use that coffee now."

"You're released," I said, reluctantly dropping my hands.

She hummed and made her way to the coffee pot. "Monroe called. Sounds like I might have to fire one of our bartenders for being snippy at some customers."

I clicked my tongue. "The customer is always right. Don't they know that?"

Luna blew on her piping hot coffee, before saying, "That's a common misconception. The customer is often wrong, but it's not for us to judge that unless they're being an asshole. Then my staff have every right to call security and kick people out. I have a no assholes rule at Club Deux, and I stick by it religiously."

I stayed put, keeping the distance between us. "And was the customer an asshole?"

She shrugged, the movement shifting her top until it slid down her shoulder revealing her creamy pale skin. Luna quickly adjusted the material but not before she caught me staring. "It sounds like something activated the bartender and they responded inappropriately. I plan to give them a call once I'm caffeinated. I don't tolerate rudeness from them, but I want to hear them out. If they were having a bad day, maybe they just need some time off to cool down. If they aren't amicable…" She shook her head. "Then good riddance."

"You'd give them another chance?"

Luna cocked her head to the side. "We're human. We have bad days. I certainly wouldn't want to be judged by how I acted on my worst days."

"It's generous, is all."

"I wouldn't have a business if I didn't have great people around me. Do I make terrible hires? Sometimes. But most of the time I can tell if someone has the same principles as me."

That reminded me of something I saw the last time I'd visited Club Deux. "You have posters up in the bathrooms."

"You mean the warning signs about what behaviors to look out for that might indicate human trafficking?"

"It's related, isn't it?"

She blinked. "Yes. It's related."

Alice dashed back into the house, and our conversation ceased. "Faith's coming!"

Sure enough, I saw Faith yawning as she traversed the pathway to the main house.

Luna got up. "I guess I should go get dressed."

"We should too." I pointed between me and Alice.

Luna walked past me, my nerves all but crackling at her proximity and my mind reeling.

Where the hell do we go from here?

CHAPTER 22

Luna

"PLEASE TELL me you have good news," had basically become my mantra since the beginning of this damn casino project.

Turns out my dream was riddled with roadblocks.

Parvati and I fell in sync with each other as she walked me around the project site. "The good news is the city officially issued most of our permits. There is one outstanding one we need to resolve. I'm finding out more information about the specific official holding it up so we can have an informed meeting with them."

"Excellent." I waved at some workers nearby who were clearly taking a lunch break. "I assume that good news comes with a side of bad news I should brace for."

Parvati's face fell. "Unfortunately, it does, and not for lack of trying."

"I would never assume."

"Well, turns out there is a small hiccup."

"What's that? Rip off the Band-Aid," I said, bracing myself.

"Drew quit this morning. Said it was too big of a project

and that she bit off more than she can chew," explained Parvati.

Fuck. I'd gone out on a limb for Drew, and I liked her style. It just took some coaxing to get her style and my vision to match. I needed to handle it delicately. Hence the reason why I brought in Faith from time to time to help me articulate my feedback.

"She wants to quit mid-project? We've finished half the designs." I should have focused on this more. I kept getting distracted.

Parvati consulted her clipboard. "We still need to finalize the room designs and decor as well as the hallway style for the hotel room tower."

"It's essential to get that right. People are drawn in by the glitzy casino but want to stay there because of the chic rooms. That's always been the plan. Make them luxurious and lovely and different from what the rest of Atlantic City has to offer. It's the hook." And I couldn't afford to get it wrong.

"It could be a case of cold feet or imposter syndrome. I recommend you talk to her. She might respond better to hearing from you since you engaged her at the beginning of the build."

I nodded, knowing Parvati was right. Sometimes it took some coaxing. "I'll schedule a coffee. Something casual."

"Good. Report back. In the meanwhile, I'm getting recommendations for other designers that we could engage if we can't figure things out with Drew."

"Perfect. Send me their portfolios as you get them so I can review and vet them."

She jotted down some notes. "You got it. Next we have…" Parvati started, running through the usual list of things we had to account for. Luckily, nothing else big, just small problems that she easily handled or she needed my input on.

Before I left, I asked one more question. "With all the setbacks, are we still on schedule?"

Parvati tucked her clipboard under her arm. "Pending we finalize the designs for the room tower and can source the materials, then yes. If there are issues with that, it might delay us. I'm optimistic."

"Appreciate you," I said as I waved goodbye. "And send me the details on the final permit. I'll see what additional info Sebastian can dig up for me."

I slid into the black sedan that would take me back to the city. Rather than staring at my phone the entire drive, I forced myself to put my air pods in so I could listen to calming ocean sounds while I closed my eyes.

It lasted five minutes. *Better than last time.*

Maybe this meditation thing wasn't fully for me, but I'd keep trying anything that had the potential to give me relief.

After finding Sebastian's name, I pressed the call button.

"It better be a fucking emergency," he grumbled.

"Well, hello to you too."

Sebastian muttered unintelligibly on the other end of the line. "I'm still in London."

I glanced at my watch. "Oh, shit. I assumed you came home yesterday after we left your house."

"That was the plan. Then Harrison changed it."

I tsked. "Sounds like his motto. You just let Beck go back to the city?"

It was his turn to sound affronted. "I made him send backup."

That made me laugh. "Of course you did."

"Luna, I stepped out of a very important contract signing with Harrison because I thought this was an emergency. You have sixty seconds to convince me it wasn't a mistake to answer your call."

"No need to get testy with me. You know, just because you landed this big whale of a client doesn't mean you get to just toss aside us little plebs."

"Luna—"

"Okay, okay. Here's the thing. I only need one final permit for the Chateau and there is some sort of weird hold out. I don't know the full story yet. The part I do know is that I need your super sleuthing skills to figure out who I need to schmooze at city hall." I crossed my fingers.

Sebastian quietly counted to ten.

I frowned and took a look at my phone, totally confused by this dramatic display of his. "There a problem over there? Do I need to send an SOS to Faith? I know morse code." Well that wasn't quite the truth. "I watched one class on morse code, so I could probably make it work."

"Luna—"

"Sebastian."

He sighed heavily. "This could have been an email."

"But then you wouldn't have the honor of hearing my voice," I said sweetly.

"Send me what you have, and I will look into it as soon as I'm done in London."

The line went dead.

"What a dick," I said with a smile on my face. I dialed the next person who came to mind.

Faith answered on the first ring. "I was wondering when you would check in with me."

"Well, I wondered when you were going to check on me. How does it feel?"

Faith chuckled, and I heard her set down her paintbrush. "What's going on?"

"When were you going to tell me that Sebastian isn't home yet?"

"Not you too. Beck was basically a glorified babysitter."

"Not to defend Beck or anything—because you know how much I hate that—but he could probably kick someone's ass if he wanted to."

Faith hummed, and my antenna went up.

"What was that?" I asked.

"What was what?"

I pressed the Facetime button so that I could look at her while we spoke. I didn't trust the tone of her voice.

I nodded in her direction. "You did a little hum thing there."

She did it again, while looking at me like a goddamn Bambi.

"You said something nice about Beck. Willingly too. Don't think I didn't notice," she said, with a sly smirk.

I waved her off. "Beck's an ass but he kind of knows what he's doing."

Her eyes narrowed more, and I watched her take a seat on the leather couch in the little library in Sebastian's place upstate. It was where they fell in love, Faith had told me once. In that very room.

"Your boyfriend hung up on me," I said, throwing Sebastian under the bus to distract her.

"Sounds like something he'd do."

I paused, because surely there would be more of a reaction to this. When no more explanation came I couldn't bite my tongue. "And you're not remorseful on his behalf?"

She smirked as if she could see right through my attempt at diversion before saying, "I am not in the habit of apologizing for Sebastian. That's up to him."

"Well, I won't hold my breath," I pouted.

"What made him hang up on you?"

I gasped. "Wait, are you taking his side?"

"Absolutely not, I just figured you poked the bear, and he retaliated." Faith smiled back at me.

"Fine, apparently the bear doesn't like to be disturbed when he's inking million-dollar deals."

"Seems reasonable," said Faith before taking a sip of her water.

"Ugh, fine. Anyway, I need his skills to help me figure out a permitting issue."

"I'll make sure he does it as soon as he gets home. Well, he has a few things to take care of first." Faith winked.

"Ew, gross. I don't need to hear about your sexcapades."

Faith threw her head back and cackled. "Since when? You love hearing about them."

I glanced at my fingernails. "Bald-faced lie."

Faith guffawed. A full-on guffaw. "Don't think I won't forget you defending Beck. What happened to you guys when you were here anyway? I never managed to debrief with you. For some reason, you were never alone after that night when we left you two alone together in the big house."

My cuticles suddenly became interesting. "Nothing interesting happened."

She narrowed her eyes. "Then why be so coy? And why hide from me?"

"Who said I was hiding? I just wanted to spend some quality time with my new gal pal, Alice."

Faith's interrogation-face softened. "She does seem to like you."

I waved a hand down my body. "What's not to like?"

"I'm being serious, Luna. She was glued to you the morning after the sleepover."

I tilted my head back against the headrest. We were back in the city and closing in on Club Deux where I'd spend the second half of my day. "It's the red hair. It makes people think I'm cool."

Faith rolled her eyes at me. "You are cool and it's not just that. She feels safe with you. That's important, especially if you still have googly eyes for her dad."

"Now you're going to make me puke."

"Dramatic much?"

Then I remembered the other reason why I called Faith, and it wasn't just because I wanted to complain about her partner. This conversation had already taken more turns than my sensitive stomach could take. "I might need to employ you to help with the design of the rest of the Chateau."

Faith sputtered, sending water droplets over the camera lens. "Excuse me?"

"Turns out my designer is getting cold feet. I'm worried she can't handle the pressure of a project this size."

Faith finished drying her face with a tissue she'd found nearby. "I know she's struggled a bit with the designs, but I think it's completely normal to get client feedback and recalibrate. That's the name of the game when it comes to design projects, especially ones of this magnitude."

I nodded along. "I think so too, and we always end up with a great design, it just takes a few iterations to get there."

"Again, totally normal."

I sighed. "I'm going to get coffee with her and see if we can work things out. If not, consider yourself on notice."

Faith turned the camera to show me her easel. "And what about this?"

"You can do both. You're my supremely talented friend. You've already course-corrected so much on this project. I think I'll name something after you."

Faith perked up. "Naming rights?"

"Mmhmm."

She tapped her finger to her chin. "Well, this changes things."

"Think about it."

My phone rang with another incoming call. "I've got to go, Faith. I'll call you later to follow up."

CHAPTER 23

Beck

"YOU HAVE another meet and greet downtown. A prospective client who doesn't trust anyone. I think it's some boy bander from the early aughts." My assistant scanned his tablet to find the name. "Tyler James."

I pinched the bridge of my nose. He had just named the biggest male pop star of my teenage years.

"You don't know Tyler James?" I asked, just to be sure.

He lifted his head from where it was buried in his tablet. "No. Should I?"

"Jesus Christ," I muttered under my breath. My assistant just made me feel like an old man. "Make sure to run a thorough background on him and give me all the info his agent sent over. I need to play this right, or he'll never go with us. Where are we meeting?"

"They keep changing the location."

I knocked my knuckles on the desk. "Once they make a decision, make sure to get the driver to pick me up two hours early."

He gave me a quizzical look. "Two hours?"

"Yes, I'm going to get there ridiculously early to scope out the place. I want to make sure my best crew is there too." I rattled off three team members that would blend in with a former heartthrob. People that fit his age profile and could pass as friends. I threw in Margot Madison's name for good measure and she'd either love me or hate me for it. By the end of our conversation, a plan had formed, and I knew if anyone was going to get Tyler to agree to protection, it was going to be me.

Spending the weekend upstate meant I had a mountain of work to address. I made my biweekly calls to each person on my team to check on them, see how their active assignments were going, and gauge their mental health. In this job we oscillated between the mundane and the life threatening. It was exactly the thing that brought adrenaline junkies to me for work and was also the reason I needed to keep an eye on them. They had me, personal coaches, and a therapist to support them.

A handful of staff also worked for the VA and understood what other resources were available to my team. These connections made a powerful support system.

It was the very thing that set me apart. People trusted people. My people could be trusted because they had that support.

Now that I had a minute to myself, I couldn't help but wonder what I could find out about the fucker that dared to harm Luna by slipping a roofie into her drink. The no-good asshole who thought he deserved her body despite not getting permission.

Fuckers like that didn't deserve to live. While I wouldn't do anything drastic, it didn't mean I didn't want to slam my fist into the guy's face and cut off his hands and dick so he could never assault another person ever again.

People who prey on others were beyond my limit of compassion. I wrote down all I knew and sent it off to Sebastian for his expert-level sleuthing. If there was footage to be found, he'd dig it up.

———

"Daddy, whenarewegettingadog?" Alice asked the second she shoved some corn into her mouth.

"Finish chewing please."

After an obligatory eye roll, she exaggerated her chewing until she swallowed. But that wasn't enough, no, she proceeded to open her mouth to show me that she had in fact finished chewing.

I crossed my arms.

"I'm done chewing now," she said, opening her mouth again to prove it.

I gently closed her mouth. "I can see that."

She beamed. "I was asking, when are we getting a dog?"

I swiped at the smile on my face. Frankly, the fact that she'd waited this long was a miracle.

"How about we go upstate next weekend to see if we can find a dog at the shelter Sebastian volunteers at?"

"Yes, please."

"I'll call him and ask if he can give us the tour. He prob-ably knows all about the dogs available." Then I pointed to her half-eaten plate of food. "Make sure to finish eating. You had a busy day and need some good nutrients for your body."

Alice dove into her dinner and I did the same. We picked up BBQ on the way home from school. It sounded good considering the warm weather and with the days getting longer, I figured we'd finally eat in the backyard. Especially since I managed to assemble the patio set that had been in boxes since we moved, too busy prioritizing the other rooms to pay much attention to the outside.

I cracked open a beer as Alice sipped on her lemonade while relaying the details of who likes who in her class. She loved regaling me with all the nitty-gritty details and despite my attempts to follow all the threads, I only managed to understand and retain about a quarter of the info volleyed at me.

Then a sliding door sounded from over the hedge, the side of the hedge that Luna was on.

Flip-flops cracked on the pavement, then the sound of something falling. *Hard.*

"Shit. Fuck," said Luna, said quietly

"Luna." I was out of my seat and trying to figure out the best way to scale the fence.

"I'm fine," she murmured. It was muffled, probably by the concrete.

The wood planks between our properties were well made, sturdy enough to hold a trellis of Virginia Creeper. Still, I wasn't convinced it would hold my weight.

Luna groaned again.

"That does it." I scaled the trellis and dropped down on the other side of the fence.

"You okay, Daddy?" Alice asked hesitantly.

My knees felt the shock of the fall and I suddenly felt my age. "Fine, honey."

Then those same knees helped me swallow the distance between me and Luna. "Don't move."

She waved me off, face still planted on the ground. "I think I'll just take a nice little nap here."

I swept her hair out of her face, my fingers gently trailing her body checking for injuries. Seeing nothing obvious, I slid my hands underneath her. "This might hurt."

Luna groaned as I lifted her from the ground, my thighs doing the heavy lifting.

Luna pushed me away once she was upright then pressed the heels of her hands to her eyes and immediately flinched. She turned her hands over and sure enough they were skinned.

I encircled her wrist gently. "Come. I'm taking you to my place to get you cleaned up."

She pulled her hand from me, and I let her. "I'm perfectly capable of taking care of myself."

"Daddy?" Alice whined.

"Luna's okay," I assured her. "Just a little scraped up."

She breathed a sigh of relief. "You have to come over to our house, Luna. I have Bluey Band-Aids."

At my daughter's offer, Luna's face softened. "That girl's trouble. She could probably convince me to do anything."

I chuckled. "Trust me. I'm fully aware of her superpowers." And I was well aware of the power the two of them could amass if they joined forces. They'd be unstoppable. I tilted my head toward my side of the fence. "So?"

Her lips pressed into a thin line. "I don't suppose I have a choice, do I?"

"Nope!" chimed Alice.

Luna's lips twitched, then glanced at me and her frown returned. "Lead the way and preferably not over the fence, thank you."

I towed her through her house, out the front door, and up the stairs of my stoop where Alice waited for us. She'd rushed to get the first aid kit I'd stowed away in the downstairs bathroom.

"Oh look at your boo boos. Daddy is going to fix it up for you," she promised. "He does this all the time."

Luna lifted a brow, completely unimpressed. Still, I kept hold of her until she sat down on the leather couch. I bent at the knee to take a closer look at her, her face a hair's breadth away from mine. Her chest rising and falling rapidly.

"I'll get you a blanket!" Alice declared. It broke the spell Luna had cast over me. In a fluid motion, I stood and went to get some paper towels. The scrapes were an angry red.

"What happened?"

Luna flashed me a strange look. "I was trying to get some fresh air."

"Instead you decided to faceplant on your patio?"

"It wasn't exactly planned. I forgot about the stupid step down out of my house." She shook the hair out of her face as I wet a clean cloth from the kitchen and lathered some soap on it.

Luna was wearing a goddamn leather dress that molded perfectly to that tight body of hers.

"Something tells me you don't use that patio much," I said as I started cleaning up her wounds.

"And here I thought it was the reason why I bought the house. Turns out wanting to have coffee outside in the back-yard is something one aspires to do but never actually does."

Alice came back into the room, her special pink blanket and favorite childhood stuffy in her hands. "These always make me feel better."

CHAPTER 24

Luna

MY VOICE CAUGHT in my throat as Alice came over with a tattered pink blanket and a stuffed bunny who had seen better days. They were clearly both well-loved and cherished by the little girl. "Thank you, sweetheart."

Alice squealed and plopped down next to me. "Those will make you feel better."

And because my hands were violently red and scraped, Alice set the blanket in my lap and settled the stuffy right next to me, cuddling by my side.

Beck's top teeth dug into his full bottom lip, his face the epitome of concentration as he used the warm, soapy towel to pat my hands clean. "You still never told me why you were outside to begin with."

I swallowed hard. "If you have to know, I was calling a therapist."

Beck sank back on his heels, the man kneeling before me, his muscular arms covered in tattoos, a shock of hair sweeping across his brow, his eyes determined and steely as ever. Fuck, if having this man on his knees in front of me didn't leave me wanting to pick back up where we left things the other day.

I felt the full weight of his attention. "You called a therapist?"

I cleared my throat, tossing my gaze in Alice's direction.

Beck caught my drift. "Alice, can you please find Luna a pillow from upstairs? Maybe one of the extra throw pillows you have on your playroom couch."

"Good idea!" She ran out of the room, eager to complete her mission.

Beck waited patiently for me to explain.

"After the other night, I figured it wouldn't be a terrible idea to talk to someone."

He nodded. "That's brave of you."

I smirked. "Turns out, wanting to have sex with a DILF without flinching is a good motivator."

Beck coughed uncontrollably.

Little footsteps announced Alice's return, and she immediately went over and started patting her dad's back. "Are you okay, Daddy?"

I, on the other hand, tilted my head into my chest to smother my smile. Beck deserved to know that I wanted to bang him again and the way he'd treated me with kid gloves made it perfectly clear that he wouldn't come near me with a ten-foot pole unless I addressed some of these underlying issues.

Hence going out to make a phone call. Pacing my brownstone hadn't given me the mental fortitude to actually press the call button to the therapist Faith recommended. I'd briefly seen a therapist after the assault and didn't keep up with it.

I was ready to pick up where I left off.

Beck finally stopped his coughing, his gaze on me lingering and his eyes darting to his daughter. No doubt he was thinking of ways to get me alone so that we could talk more.

Alice frowned. "Daddy, are you going to finish cleaning up Luna's hands?"

Sure enough, my palms were still upturned. While the skin was clean and clear of any obvious dirt, he'd yet to do anything else.

A groove formed between his brows. "Right."

The man grabbed the black bottle of hydrogen peroxide. "This might sting." He proceeded to pour a small amount over the open wounds.

I sucked in a quick breath as he lightly blew on the aggravated skin. Not only was he kneeling in front of me now, but he was also taking such good care of me. His scent was heady.

And I wanted him *so* bad, but the timing wasn't right. Not *yet*.

I stood, the pink blanket sliding off my legs. "I can take it from here."

"I haven't even put the Bluey Band-Aids on yet." He stood, hands reaching out to grasp me before he thought better of it and slid them into his pockets instead.

I went around him. "My hands are clean. I'll bandage them at home with some gauze."

Alice frowned too, but trailed behind me, nonetheless. "Take the Band-Aid box, at least."

I reached out to take the small box between my fingertips, avoiding the concrete burn at all costs.

"Luna—"

"Beck."

The man opened the front door, when I could tell by the tense muscles in his arm that he wanted to keep me hostage at his house.

My gaze pierced his. "I'll call you, I promise."

"You better," he grumbled. "I know where you live."

Wasn't that the damn truth?

———

The next morning I awoke with a start to the sound of a chainsaw.

At least I thought that's what the buzzing noise was.

The high-pitched screech that could wake the dead roused me from my bed. "What the hell? Is that a chainsaw?"

I trotted downstairs, wrapping my silk robe around my waist, careful not to accidentally hurt my hands which were wrapped up. They hurt if I applied any pressure to them, so I tried not to.

The noise seemed to be coming from the back yard, so I unlocked my French doors and found the source of all the kerfuffle.

Beck Bennet.

"What the hell do you think you're doing?" I shouted, hand above my brow to keep the morning sun out of my eyes.

There stood a shirtless Beck with a chainsaw—totally called it—and some protective goggles which made him look ridiculously handsome. While that was a sight to see, it almost distracted me enough from the gaping hole in the fence.

Almost.

"WHAT DID YOU DO?"

Beck lifted the goggles, pushing back his hair which was starting to grow out. It was only noticeable because the man liked his military cut. "Isn't it obvious? I'm making a gate."

He slid the goggles back into place and turned the chainsaw back on.

I tightened my belt, and turned on my heel, charging back into the house like a bull.

I searched my drawers, looking for anything that might resemble a tool or something I could use to stop him.

Coming up short, I planted my hands on my hips, scanning the kitchen. A large pot hung in the rack above the stove and an idea struck. "Gotcha."

Once I filled it with water, I stormed back outside, startling Beck who was busy erecting some sort of frame around the exposed ends of the shared fence.

He lifted his hands and backed up, "Whoa, whoa, whoa. What the hell do you think you're doing?"

I tossed the pot of freezing cold water all over him, drenching his skintight, dark-washed jeans. Now they were even tighter around his thick thighs and my throat was suddenly parched as I took in a wet Beck.

Where was my vibrator? I'd need to give it a workout later.

"Jesus, woman," he swore, water dripping down the planes of his chest.

I wagged my finger at him, approaching slowly. "You do not get to put a gate between our houses without asking me, Beck Bennet."

My finger stabbed his chest, and the smell of his sweat had me closing my eyes for just a second. I had to collect myself. "Put the fence back up."

He tilted his head down. "No."

I gasped. "No?"

"No."

"I'm sure this is illegal." I gestured wildly.

Beck lifted my chin with his finger, his touch simultaneously gentle and searing. "This will allow me to help you if you fall again."

My eyes nearly bugged out of my head. "That was *one* time."

"One time too many," he countered, wiping his chest and once again drawing attention to the muscles there. The sunlight connected with the water droplets to highlight the definition even more. It was practically blinding.

"Put. It. Back." I stabbed him in staccato. "And put on a shirt."

He leaned in, his lips just a hair's breadth away from mine. "Make me."

I stomped around him, lifting the chunk of wood he'd

removed. He'd cleared out a whole section of the fence, which meant the pieces were still bound together by two cross beams and damn they were heavy. The thing is I could lift it, but I couldn't do anything more than that, and my hands were screaming at me to drop it.

"Fuck," I muttered, setting the piece down to examine my palms. Sure enough, that white gauze was now stained pink with blood.

"Are you bleeding?" Beck asked with the patience of a man with a small daughter who undoubtedly went against his wishes on a regular basis.

I rolled my eyes. "Yes."

Beck slicked back his hair with his forearm. "Do you need me to fix you up again?"

I shoved my fisted hands to my sides. "I can fix myself, Beck Bennet. And I'm calling the cops." I pushed past him and back toward my side of the fence.

He smirked. "No, you won't."

He had me there.

"Well, I'm calling Sebastian," I called over my shoulder just before I slammed the back door shut.

———

I rushed into work, late, again, all thanks to Beck fucking Bennet.

The audacity.

I tripped and fell, and sure, I was a little stunned at first, but that didn't give him the right to jump over my fence like I'm some damsel in distress nor does it give him the permission to make a literal door between our backyards.

Easy access.

Okay, my lady bits were all riled up at the idea of him slinking over into my house in the middle of the night for evening acrobatics.

If only my head could also get on board.

Luckily, I did manage to make the appointment with a therapist.

Still, he had absolutely no right to do that. I'd have to get him back somehow.

Setting my revenge-plotting aside, I sat down to answer emails in my favorite booth at Club Deux.

There was nothing I loved more than spending time at the dance club during the day. With the house lights up, it felt like a different place entirely. Almost like the club had a secret identity.

After a call with Parvati to check in on the Chateau, a notification popped up in the bottom right-hand corner of my screen.

I double clicked the incoming email to find the invitation to the Sexual Assault Survivors Network Gala—the same event that I met Carter at.

Then another email popped up, a forwarded message from… "Speak of the devil."

I opened this new email to find a message from my ex:

I hope to see you there. - Carter

"I've been going to this event for years, but yes, you pretend like this is your event and I'm just invited." I shut my laptop and stood in search of a coffee or sparkling water, not wanting to examine why the simple, innocuous email elicited such a strong reaction.

"We aren't open yet," Chloe, one of my bartenders, called out.

I looked up to find a man walking into my space.

Beck.

Beck was here and Carter dissolved from my thoughts. "What are you doing here?"

He showed off a distinctive pink cardboard box. "Alice wanted me to drop off some donuts. She said it would make you happy with me."

"Wait—" I thought back to the little scene from this morning. "Was Alice at the house?"

"Yup. Witnessed everything from the bay window in her room. Luckily she wasn't privy to all the pretty expletives you used, but she is old enough to understand body language."

"Oh, shit," I mumbled as I sank back into my seat. Some things were meant to not be witnessed—or overheard—by children. I'd have to be more mindful of little ears.

A bemused Beck slid into the booth next to me, and I took a second to admire the view.

He'd showered and changed. And smelled like heaven.

My breath hitched, and I spoke to cover it up. "Couldn't you pay a delivery driver to drop this off?"

He shrugged, slinging his arm over the bench behind me. If I leaned back, we'd be touching.

"You said you were getting a therapist, and you called me a DILF and then proceeded to walk out of my house. Of course I came to find you."

My head whipped around the room, trying to make sure nobody would overhear us. I could be vocal about my wants and needs without having them broadcasted to my entire team.

Then I twisted in my seat to face him, face softening. This man tracked me down because he cared. That felt big. "I had fun the other night until I didn't. I want to do it again some time, preferably with a more satisfying ending."

Beck hissed. "Fuck, hearing you say it aloud makes it real."

I swallowed, and with the willpower of a saint, I scooted back, Beck's outstretched hand sweeping the back of my neck.

Beck frowned, but didn't stop me. Then, he said, "I want to take you on a date."

I blinked. "And here I thought you just wanted to fuck me."

"Don't get me wrong, I absolutely want to fuck you but

that's not going to happen. Not for a while if the other night was any indication, and I'm fine with that. Let me be clear about something, I don't *just* want to fuck you."

Something like hope blossomed in my chest.

He leaned in. "I want to get to know you. All of you."

I crossed my arms, figuring I'd make him work for it. "Where, pray tell, do you plan to take me on this hypothetical date?"

He lifted a finger. "One, this isn't hypothetical. I *will* be taking you on a date."

"So presumptuous." I kind of loved it.

"Two," he said, ignoring my quip, "you leave the planning up to me. I'll pick you up tomorrow at six. Dress casually."

"Tomorrow is Friday. I have work."

"Take it off."

My eyebrow rose.

"Not like *that*," he huffed.

"I need to work that night; we have a couple of VIPs that will need schmoozing. I am, however, available for a lunch date." I wanted the date, but I wouldn't compromise my work for it. Not a whim at least.

Beck pulled out his phone. I glanced at the screen, watching him scroll through his calendar. Then he called someone and asked them to move around some meetings. I sat there, watching the whole thing take place in a matter of minutes. "Done. Lunch it is. I'll pick you up from your place at noon."

My heart beat faster, and I hefted a shoulder. "I'll be there."

Then Beck leaned in. The smell of his aftershave had me squeezing my thighs together.

"See you tomorrow." He kissed the sensitive column of my neck before departing, leaving me alone in the middle of my club feeling hot and bothered.

CHAPTER 25

Beck

"I NEED A FAVOR."

"No, I won't do another background search on Luna," Sebastian answered.

"That's not what I was going to ask about."

The typing stalled. "Now I'm intrigued. So why are you calling then? You know I'm back in town and have Faith covered."

I laughed. "I'm sure you do."

"That's my future wife you're talking about," he said, immediately going on the defensive.

"Holy shit." He was actually admitting that this woman was his end game. I mean, I knew that already. Practically everyone who knew him understood this wasn't some fling. Faith was Sebastian's person.

Sebastian grumbled, dragging a hand through his hair. "Shit, I shouldn't have said that to you."

"Why not?"

"I should be telling *her* that, not you."

I shook my head. "No, man. That means you care for her and are excited about it. That's something you share with your friends."

"I officially asked her to move in."

"Asked? That's a surprise. I figured you'd just move her stuff and tell her she moved in."

He grunted.

"Holy shit, that's exactly what you did, isn't it?" I erupted into laughter and scrubbed a hand down my face. "How did she take that?"

"She told me she'd need a bigger closet."

I could see that happening. "That's it? Just wanted more space for her clothes?"

He clicked his tongue. "She also wanted to make sure that we kept a place in the city."

Made sense to me. "I assume you want yours because it's all tricked out."

"How did you—"

I laughed. "You're predictable, man."

"I'm going to say no to this favor request if you keep being a dick."

I bet I could change his mind. "It's for Alice."

A sigh was his only response. "Tell me."

I knew it.

"Alice wants a dog, and I figured I'd bring her to your shelter for a personal tour."

"Absolutely," Sebastian agreed without skipping a beat. "Actually, there is this great dog, Pepper, and I think she'd be great for Alice." He rattled off a list of information about the dog and I had to admit, a smaller dog who was a few years old would be better for the city than a dog like Willow who required more space to run around and get her energy out. "And Pepper is a sweetheart. When I walk her she loves getting pets from kids who are brave enough to touch her."

That caught my attention. "Why wouldn't they want to pet her?"

Sebastian took his time to consider this. "She isn't a cute puppy in the traditional sense."

I wanted to hear Sebastian utter the words "cute puppy" a few more times, maybe record it for later, but my curiosity got the better of me. "What makes you say that?"

Sebastian hesitated. "She's a little wiry and fluffy at the same time. I'm tempted to pay for one of those dog DNA tests because I want to know what breeds she's made of because it's a unique combination. It's the talk of the shelter."

So she's not cute. I could work with that. "But she's safe to be around, right? She wouldn't hurt Alice."

Sebastian belted out a rare laugh. "She wouldn't hurt a fly. Pepper would be the perfect family dog."

"Excellent. I want to meet her. You free this Saturday?"

"You know I'll be here." The man rarely left his home upstate except for the occasional trips to the city for work or to take Faith to the library where she volunteered teaching teenagers to paint.

"Great, I'll text you when we're on our—"

Then the line went dead. Either the call dropped, or he hung up on me. "Fucker."

———

With the plan to get a dog in place, I could focus my attention on planning my date with Luna.

The woman deserved to be seduced, and not all seduction meant getting naked. I'd have to get her to let her guard down completely, to feel absolutely comfortable with me before intimacy was even an option.

If this happened to her all those years ago, and she'd been living like this, I couldn't fucking imagine.

I'd slept with women occasionally over the years, nothing serious since my focus was on Alice and my business. It did help to quell the urges I felt. She hadn't had a chance to do that. In fact, the last sexual experience had been horrific.

I'll be damned if I let that ruin her forever. I was desperate to replace the terrible memories with good ones.

But first, I'd woo her.

Luna deserved an unforgettable night, but an unforgettable lunch would be a good start. With a few calls, I'd booked something that would surprise her and hopefully sweep her off her feet.

CHAPTER 26

Luna

I SHOOK my foot so hard, the table shifted, sloshing coffee over the rim. Today was the big day that Beck Bennet would take me on a date. Why on Earth did the thought of us being alone together—on purpose—make my heart feel like it was going to burst right out of my chest?

"Shit," I swore, using a linen napkin to tidy up the mess.

"Luna, are you there?" a little voice sounded from the other side of the fence.

I smiled. "Morning, Alice. Yes, I'm here. Want to come over?"

"Yes, please!"

A minute later, Alice knocked on the new wooden door that separated our backyards. I tugged on the string to open it, letting in the little girl. "Does your Daddy know you're here?"

She nodded. "I told him."

"Okay, good. Your dad may be okay with kidnapping, but I'm not." I said it loudly just in case Beck was within earshot.

Alice giggled. "That was only once, and didn't you have fun with us?"

I tugged playfully on her ponytail. "Well, that's true."

She puffed her chest out and started exploring my back patio, her smile drooping into a frown. "There's nothing out here."

I glanced around the small outdoor space and tried to see it from her perspective. There were pavers with moss in between them to give the patio a lived-in, old-world vibe. There were fences on either side and a building behind. Other than that, and the small cafe table I'd schlepped outside when I first moved in, the space was bare. The only greenery was the ivy that trailed over from Beck's side of the fence.

Huh, maybe she had a point. "Do you think I need to jazz up the place?"

"Uh, yeah," she said with the attitude of someone twice her age.

Ohh, Beck Bennet. You're in for it, that's for sure.

The idea made me smile and calm down for the first time today. I'd been practically buzzing since before my alarm went off. The anticipation akin to preparing for an early morning flight.

Except this was Beck. I gulped.

"Luna? We need a fairy garden," Alice said authoritatively.

I pointed to my chest. "You want to build a fairy garden in my yard. With me?"

Alice nodded earnestly. "We need to get you some decorations. It's boring out here."

I tapped my nail to my lips. "That's a great idea. What if we put it by the tree?" I pointed to the little corner that housed the only tree and square of dirt. "We could make a little fairy door here and maybe plant some cute little trinkets."

"Yes. Could we get a little fence?" Alice asked.

"Why not?" I shrugged.

Alice began listing a dozen other things we could buy or

build for our fairy garden. Then she slumped down in the cafe chair and smacked her lips.

I smothered a chuckle. "Can I get you some water? Almond milk?" I really didn't stock kids drinks in my fridge but maybe I should start.

"Water would be great."

"Coming right up."

I returned and set down a glass in front of her. Turns out, I didn't have any kids cups, so hopefully she'd be fine with the glass in front of her.

Alice took a few big gulps, carefully lifting the water with both hands while I sipped on my coffee, closing my eyes a bit to soak up the sun. There was a to-do list the length of a CVS receipt in my mind and I was mentally shifting and prioritizing as we sat there.

Then, out of nowhere, Alice said, "I heard you're going out with Daddy today."

The scalding hot coffee ran down my chin. I dabbed my face gently with the napkins and laid it back down on my lap, smoothing out the edges. "He told you that?"

She nodded enthusiastically.

I leaned forward, elbows planted on the small cafe table, trying to relax my face so I didn't look too eager to get information out of her. Consider my curiosity piqued. "Does your dad usually tell you about the people he goes out with?"

Her face twisted. "What other people?"

Hmm. Interesting. "Do you happen to know what your dad has planned for me today?"

She practically bounced in her chair. I reached over to hold the water glass in place. "He did…"

"What is it?"

A frown tugged at the corner of her lips. "Daddy said it was a surprise."

Fuck.

She shot me a smile that would make the Cheshire Cat proud. "But if you guess it…"

Aha. "Great idea, Alice."

I clutched my coffee cup like the lifeline it was. "You want to give me some hints or should I just start spit balling?"

She scratched her nose. "What's spit balling?"

"That's where I just list a bunch of things, and you say yes or no."

"Let's do that."

I nodded solemnly. "Is your dad taking me to a fancy restaurant?"

She shook her head. "Nope."

"To a sports game?" I crossed my fingers, desperately hoping that wasn't the case. I know Faith's brother met his girlfriend at a basketball game and honestly that sounds like a terrible meet-cute.

"Bowling?"

Alice giggled. "No."

I rattled off a dozen more date ideas, all better—or worse —than the next. At least it ruled out most of what I would consider a truly horrible date.

I narrowed my eyes at Alice as if that would give me some sort of telepathic connection.

Spoiler alert: it didn't.

"Mini golf? A movie?"

A screen door opened. "Alice, are you still out here?"

"Shit." I ran out of time and was no closer to having the answer I wanted.

Alice pointed at me. "You said a bad word."

Damn. "Sorry, about that honey. Do you want to just whisper where your dad is going to take me today? Help a girl out? I have no idea how to dress." While I usually dressed for myself and myself alone, I felt a certain pressure to get this right. I hadn't been on a date I cared about since, well, never.

Alice sat up and Beck's head popped over the top of the door that separated our backyards.

Wait a minute. "You can see into my backyard? Just like that?"

Beck pulled on the string that laid on *my side of the fence*, opening the door. "There you are."

Alice jumped up, and I followed. "Wait—"

Beck grinned at me as I moved toward him and his daughter who was now holding his hand. "Morning, Luna."

I shifted into my hip, the silky fabric of my robe moving as I sank lower. Beck's gaze dragged the length of my body, his face hardening. I glanced down to see the robe had come loose, my silk nightgown now on full display. If Alice weren't there, I'd leave it, but since she was there, I quickly tied the belt firmly around my waist.

"I'll see you later?" Beck asked, his voice all low and growly.

I nodded. "Yes, want to tell me exactly what we'll be doing so I can dress appropriately?"

"Come as you're dressed now."

Alice chuckled. "That's silly, she's in her PJs, Daddy."

Beck shook his head, as if the little innocent voice had pulled him out from his dangerous thoughts. Thoughts I wanted to explore.

"It's a surprise. Let yourself be surprised." The man held the door open for Alice to slip through. She ducked under his arm and mouthed the word "boat" and then made a motion with her hands indicating waves.

Aha.

"A surprise sounds great." I waved my goodbye, turning my heel to get back inside and get some work done before our date. Luckily, I knew exactly what to wear.

———

"A boat on the marina? How amazing." I'd tried infusing surprise into my voice, and it fell flat, even to my ears.

Beck crossed his arms over his chest, causing the fabric in his suit jacket to pull taut. I rarely saw him out of his usual uniform of a black t-shirt, dark-wash jeans, and black leather jacket, so this little ensemble had been the surprise of the day.

While I normally loathed surprises, I didn't mind this one. Beck was handsome as ever, the sun shining on his face and the city lights behind him. Without second guessing I wove my hands over his shoulders.

He peered at me, taking in my outfit. The striped, boat neck shirt and wide legged jeans were a far cry from my usual wears.

"How did you know?" he asked.

"I don't know what you're talking about," I deadpanned.

He tugged me closer to him, then assessed me closely, again making sure he had permission to touch me. I knew if I so much as gave one indication that touching wasn't okay, that he'd back the fuck off.

I sidled even closer, so close I could feel his cock hardening against my stomach. He captured my mouth with his, and the heat of his lips on mine sent energy skittering through my body.

My body melted into his, and then suddenly Beck pulled back and adjusted his sleeves. "We should probably board. The chef is scheduled to bring our plates out at one. You turn into a pumpkin at four, so we should get going."

We walked the long plank that connected the shore to the fancy yacht, Beck's hand on my lower back the entire way. I relished in the warmth of it, and the safety I felt from the simple act.

The captain and crew welcomed us with flair. The crew waved and the chief steward carefully balanced a tray of cocktails.

"Oh, I don't—" I said, trying to decline the outstretched

drink when Beck leaned down and whispered. "They're virgin daiquiris."

Something close to contentment bloomed in my chest.

I nodded and took a sip of the drink. Sure enough, I couldn't taste any alcohol, but the burst of coconut and pineapple was a refreshing treat. "Thanks."

He pointed to the front of the boat where there was a comfortable lounge area set up.

Before I let him lead me over, I skimmed my fingers along his jawline. "Thank you."

He tilted his head. "For what?"

"Today. This." I did my Vanna White wave, and we took in the waves around us. There was a handful of other vessels in the water, including some brave kayakers.

"You're thanking me for taking you out?"

He was going to make a big deal of this wasn't he? "Accept the thank you."

Beck tugged me even closer, his hands skimming the flair of my hips. The movement stole the oxygen from my lungs.

I backed up until my legs hit the double wide lounge area. I sank back on to the plush cushions, careful not to spill my drink.

Beck placed his glass on the small ledge on either side of the lounge area and began shucking off his jacket. A crew member swept in to grab it from him and stow it away somewhere safe. But he didn't stop there. No, Beck began unbuttoning his shirt.

"What do you think you're doing?"

His hands continued their path down the center of his shirt. I lowered my sunglasses, watching as he reached the bottom of his destination and began peeling the shirt away from his torso, but he didn't bother to remove it all the way, not that he needed to. I could see the planes of his tanned chest, covered in tattoos. They'd changed in the years since our night together.

Yet it was the sleeve of tats on his arms that really made me damp between my legs. Screw a six-pack, corded forearms could get me off. Especially since I knew those forearms were connected to very talented fingers that could ministrate their way to the ultimate pleasure.

"You like what you see?" he asked, voice like gravel.

"Ppff." I blew him off, lowering my glasses back into place and trying to keep my eyes from retreating back to the dessert of a man in front of me. Beck finally settled onto the cushions, sliding in next to me so that our thighs touched.

Any other man would have looked ridiculous in just a pair of suit pants. Beck, however, was not just any man.

My phone buzzed. I ignored it at first until Beck lifted the drink from my hands and insisted I take it.

CARTER

> Just a reminder, I'm bringing my new girlfriend to the Sexual Assault Survivors Network Gala next week.

Beck not so subtly read the message over my shoulder. "He's still in love with you."

I turned my phone over, suddenly regretting that I had unblocked Carter. "He's not." But then again, why did Carter feel compelled to let me know? *Again.*

Beck clicked his tongue. "He is."

I turned towards him, head cradled in my palm and let my elbow do the heavy lifting. "And why do you think that, Mr. Know It All?"

"You said it, not me, but I appreciate you acknowledging my wisdom." His eyes dropped to my chest before gliding back up to meet mine. My breathing hitched and yet I felt like I'd won some sort of standoff in my head.

"You have no idea what you're talking about." I picked up my phone and tapped away.

LUNA

Okay.

I was about to hit send when Beck grabbed the phone from my hands. "You're not sending that."

What the hell?

I lunged forward, and with some seriously expert ex-Marine skills, the man leaped off the lounge chair. His fingers were tapping away on my screen as I awkwardly scooted off the cushion, careful not to trip over my linen dress as I stood and went in to grab him. Just as I reached him, he handed back my phone.

I scrambled to unlock my screen, and I groaned when it didn't immediately do so. After blowing some rogue hair out of my face, my messaging app appeared on my screen. "Finally."

CHAPTER 27

Beck

LUNA GAPED at the screen before slowly lifting her blazing gaze to meet mine. "You didn't."

I nodded at the phone, because clearly *I did.*

"You told him I was bringing a date," she squeaked. "I had it handled, Beck. You didn't need to step in like the world's worst bodyguard."

Well that hit like a bullet to the chest. "World's *worst* bodyguard?"

"You told Carter I was taking you to the gala? Why on Earth would you do that unless you were trying to be some sort of unnecessary savior?"

"It seemed like you might need a date since he had one. Make him sweat a little. Let him know you've moved on." I'd offered before. This shouldn't be that big of a surprise.

She stormed off, and I immediately followed suit.

I'd have Sebastian do a background search on this Carter kid and then make sure I had the ammunition needed to make sure this guy knew she wasn't pining over him. That she was with me, even if she didn't want to admit it yet.

I continued to trail behind Luna as she stomped her way around the yacht.

"Is it such a hardship to take me to the gala with you?" I pressed her.

The withering look she threw over her shoulder would stop a lesser man in his tracks. We backtracked a few times until Luna found what she was looking for: the captain.

"Take me back to the harbor. Something's come up and I need to get off the boat immediately," she demanded.

"We just got out here—" I protested.

Luna lifted her hand in the air as if to silence me, not bothering to glance behind her as she addressed the captain. "You'll turn this boat around or I'll call the port authority."

I chuckled because this was escalating quickly and frankly laughing was the only thing I could think to do.

The captain, a distinguished-looking man, complete with gray hair and graying beard appeared downright terrified.

Luna lifted her phone, a silent threat that she'd do exactly as she promised.

The captain raised his hands. "Yes, ma'am, I'll head back to the harbor right away."

"Thank you, sir," Luna said before trudging back to the front of the boat, asking a nearby crew member for a drink top off and a bite to eat. "Might as well get some fuel before we head back."

Luna stationed herself at the outdoor dining area, phone in hand.

I sat down across from her, giving her as wide a berth as I could given the size of the table. "You're really going to jump ship?"

Her eyes flitted to mine, before dropping back down to her screen. Answering emails from the looks of it.

"Ignoring me? That's how you're going to play this?"

Jaw clenched, she didn't deign to give me a response.

"I only wanted to help," I continued to press her.

That got her attention because her head snapped up. "How many times have I told you I don't need your help?"

The sharpness in her voice was one I recognized from when I saw her again for the first time since *our* night.

I shrugged, not sure where she was going with this, but willing to listen because this was clearly about something more. "I'm helpful."

"Sometimes your help is *unwanted*."

I flinched. "How so?"

"You're pushing. I want to agree to the help, not have it thrust on me. I've been taking care of myself for much longer than I've known you, Beck. Just because I'm interested in exploring this thing between us doesn't mean I've cosigned on your deciding things for me."

Fuck.

This was about so much more than just offering to be her date. This was about me pushing myself onto her without consent. Not in a physical way, because I'd never fucking do that. No, the mental, emotional, that was just as bad.

I should have fucking known better.

I leaned forward, and both of us shifted as the boat turned. Luna had to stabilize herself and the movement finally broke the stalemate.

"May I?" I asked, nodding at her hands. I clasped them in mine. "I'm sorry. If you don't want me to go, I won't. I just didn't want you to have to face it alone."

Luna squeezed my hands reflexively. Clearly, she was still mad. That line between her brows was still deeper than usual. But I must have done something right because she was marginally less mad. I'd take that win for now until I could fully make up for it.

She searched my face. "I'll think about it."

"That's all I'm asking."

Someone cleared their throat.

One of the crew members had brown bags for us. "The chef packed a lunch for you to enjoy at your leisure."

Sure enough, we were docking. The rest of the crew were

moving like they were in a ballet, all synchronized and in their whites.

I circled the table and reached my hand out. Luna hesitated, but only for a moment before taking it. We walked hand in hand back to my car, and I drove her home, a comfortable silence between us. Something that felt a hell of a lot like respect and understanding.

CHAPTER 28

Luna

I SET my large-ass purse on the counter of the county office. "I'm here to see Delaney Taylor."

Turned out, I knew someone who worked for the county, and I damn well planned to leverage every connection I had to get this final permit.

Who knew meeting Carter's new girlfriend would have such immediate benefit?

"Your name," asked the woman behind the counter. She rocked a stylish silver bob and matching silver earrings. "And an ID, please."

"Luna Marks." I fished my ID out of my bag and handed it over.

After she jotted down my information, I signed the sheet on the clipboard in front of me and was asked to take a seat. "She'll be right with you."

I tapped away on my phone, slinging messages to Parvati and a few others. Parvati prepared me for the meeting this morning so I had all the latest info and paperwork to tackle this meeting.

Suddenly, the woman I was here to see strutted down the hall like a willowy model. For a second I wondered what made Carter go from me to her. We were as opposite as they come. With my silk cami and leather knee-length skirt, I balanced professional and edgy. She was the epitome of an ethereal runway goddess with her blonde waves contrasting with my red A-line.

Shoulders squared, I stood and shook her hand. "Nice to see you again, and in broad daylight too."

Delaney chuckled, her hand squeezing mine a little tighter than I would have expected given her delicate aesthetic. "I was surprised when my assistant said you wanted to meet."

She led me down a corridor straight out of an eighties procedural drama before waving me into an office that had her name on it. "Come sit down and tell me what's going on."

The woman had a legal pad and a pen and was ready to take notes.

I wasted no time launching into my spiel. At this point, I could talk about the Chateau in my sleep. "It's going to be the first woman-owned casino in Atlantic City. It's for women, by women. I want it to be the place for bachelorette parties and for women to feel like they can have fun and let loose all while being safe in my casino. I'm here to turn this city around and offer a menu of fun opportunities for people even if they don't drink or gamble, although there will definitely be plenty of that, of course."

She glanced down at her notes, then back at me. "Tell me what permit it is that you're having difficulty acquiring. That will help figure out next steps."

There was something in her tone that caught me off guard, but only for a second. I immediately dismissed it given the caffeine deficit I was working with.

I relayed the info from Parvati, sliding over a few documents that demonstrated what we applied for and how we completed the forms.

She read through them carefully, dragging a nude fingernail across the forms, reviewing the paperwork with a fine-toothed comb.

I glanced down at my nails, then scanned the room, basically trying everything to keep from squirming in my chair.

A frown tugged at the corner of her mouth. "Hmm."

That little hum set my Spidey senses tingling. "Hmm?"

She clicked her tongue and set down her ballpoint pen. The woman across from me no longer resembled the sweet-as-pie person I'd met at my club. Not with the groove between her brows and her lips set firmly in a straight line.

"Unfortunately, this form is incomplete."

I counted to ten in my head before speaking. My internal bullshit detector rang like a siren for a five-alarm fire.

"I had my legal team and my chief contractor complete this form and then I, personally, reviewed it just to make sure the 'I's were dotted and the 'T's were crossed."

She hummed again. "And yet it's still wrong. We can't permit this until another inspection has taken place, and the county has signed off on the build."

My heart damn near stopped. "Explain that to me again."

She folded her hands. "It's a step-by-step process and needs to go in order. You couldn't have filled this out correctly…" She proceeded to explain in lots of jargon why things hadn't gone through. I followed about half of what she was saying and frankly I wanted to question the authenticity of her words but without the backup of Parvati or my legal team, I didn't want to push too hard. Not yet at least.

Still, I pushed a little. "Can you or someone from your team help us fix it?"

"Sure," she said through a smile that didn't quite reach her eyes.

"Great. Let me relay this back to my team and I'll reach out again."

She nodded, then stood.

Class dismissed.

———

"Damn. I knew I should have gone with you." Those were the first words out of Parvati's mouth when I dialed her the second I left the county offices with my giant laptop-size purse on my shoulder.

Darnell awaited me around the corner with an iced coffee in hand.

I thanked him. "You're the best."

He saluted before closing the door behind me once I was safely stowed in the backseat, holding my phone to my ear like a pleb because I hated those little wireless earbuds.

I relayed as much as I could, grateful I'd pulled out my phone to take notes during the brief conversation. "I'm sending my scribbles to you right now."

"Perfect. Once me and the team review them, I'll circle back with you." I heard Parvati typing away on her side of the line. "Talk soon."

The efficient woman hung up the phone, and I tilted my head back and closed my eyes as I replayed the interaction in my head. What I had done wrong, what I would do differently in the future.

Part of me even was tempted to follow up with Carter.

Then I thought better of it. I didn't need him fighting my battles for me. Besides, I doubted it would earn me the good-will I needed to get this permit in place.

Rather than make my next call, I tested some of the meditation practices I'd seen on TikTok. I tried a few different breathing techniques and then imagined the sun was shining on me. That was harder to do given the threat of rain outside.

I lasted longer than other previous attempts and took the win.

Then my phone rang, and I jumped at the distraction, especially since I recognized the ringtone.

"Hey, bestie," I answered.

Faith chuckled. "Hello, back atcha. I'm shocked you answered the phone."

"I always answer the phone for you."

"But during working hours?" Faith countered.

Like that made a difference. "All hours are working hours."

"Is that what your doctor would want?"

I groaned. "Not you too. I'm getting this daily from Beck."

"We're just worried about you."

"Ugh," I said with an extra oomph of exaggeration, ignoring how her words actually made me feel cared for. How nice it was to have someone who cared about my well-being. It felt strangely foreign and yet exactly what I needed and one of the reasons why Faith was my best friend.

"Are you driving somewhere?" she asked.

I glanced out the window to see exactly where we were. "Yes, heading back into the city. I met with Carter's current girlfriend, the woman who apparently knows the correct paperwork I need to complete to get the permit for my multi-level parking garage. According to her, my team didn't fill out the paperwork correctly."

Faith scoffed. "I've met members of your team and there is no way they messed this up."

"Right? Especially Parvati—that woman is a powerhouse."

"Takes one to know one," Faith affirmed.

"Aw thanks. See, this is why you're my bestie. Love this confidence boost."

"You do the same for me."

"So, to what do I owe this impromptu phone call? You know those scare me."

Faith laughed. "Please, nothing scares you. Well, except Beck Bennet. That man frightens the fuck out of you."

"Pff." I waved off the comment, not that she could see me.

"He does and you know it."

"Ignoring that comment, I don't like unsolicited phone calls. I don't know a millennial that does."

Faith clicked her tongue. "Fair."

"Now remind me of the purpose of this call again..."

"Okay, boss. A certain handsome bodyguard type is trekking upstate to get a dog this weekend, and I thought you should know," she gloated as she relayed her intel.

That warmed my heart. Little Alice was obsessed with Willow when we were all there at Sebastian's house together. It was obvious to anyone with eyes that this kid wanted a dog. Hell, she said as much during our last visit. I changed the call from audio to video.

"How does this affect me?" I asked.

Faith blinked, her expression basically screaming *isn't it obvious*? "Well, you live next door to said bodyguard."

"Mmhmm. Still not seeing how this is my problem."

"Who said it was a problem? This is an *opportunity*."

Now she had me confused. "What do you mean?"

"You might be spending a lot of time with this dog, so I was thinking it could be good for you to come with."

I pursed my lips. "Faith Waters, now that's a little much. Don't you think?"

"Oh, please." She waved me off. "I'm just planning ahead. Something you should be doing."

My lips twitched. "This is going to be Alice and Beck's dog. Just because I want to—" I lowered my voice, realizing I was still in the back of the town car driving to Club Deux and didn't want to give Darnell a heart attack. "Bang Beck doesn't mean I get a say in the family dog decision."

Darnell, the picture of a professional, kept his eyes forward, never leaving the road.

"If I thought for even a second that all you wanted from Beck Bennet was to bang it out, I wouldn't have even called."

Observant little...

"Besides, if it makes you more comfortable, you can travel with them under the guise of coming up to visit your bestie."

"Sounds like quite the hardship," I deadpanned. "Especially since my bestie is being really annoying."

That made her laugh. "Oh, please. If anything, I've learned from the best."

I examined my nails. "Obviously."

"So what do you say?"

My heart picked up speed at the thought of spending time with both Beck and Alice. Damn it if that little girl hadn't left an impression on me. If I were being honest, I kind of want to be there too. Not because I felt like I had any right to be with them. This was for their family, and I was distinctly not part of it. But because I wanted to see the joy on Alice's face when she found her forever friend. I wanted to see Beck's face when he realized his daughter picked a dog that he didn't want but would eventually come to love because he couldn't help himself.

It was as if I could picture the whole scenario in my head.

"You're thinking a lot over there. I can practically hear it from here in the woods," Faith said.

I rolled my eyes as my mind reeled, every instinct telling me to go.

Faith lifted a brow. "What do you say?"

"I'll think about it."

———

FAITH

I guess you thought about it.

LUNA

Don't you start.

FAITH

I'm basically a matchmaking genius.

I scoffed and lifted my gaze to find Beck's attention on me in the rearview mirror. After my call with my former best friend yesterday I went to work at Club Deux. Things were running smoothly there—thank goodness—and luckily there were no surprises. No drop ins from an ex or missed shipments.

It was very late at night when I'd gotten home and decided to go back out on the patio. It had become a habit of sorts to spend time out there. One of my bartenders sent me home with a mason jar of mojito mocktail to test out so I poured myself a glass, added the sprig of mint for garnish as I was instructed to do, and quietly sat out in the dark, admiring the stars when I suddenly heard my neighbor's back door creak open.

I startled in my chair. It was well past two in the morning, way past most people's bedtime. Not for my neighbor who had gotten very comfortable traipsing back and forth between his back yard and my own.

I wondered how he'd react if I put a lock on the door...

"Luna, you out here?" Beck whispered, making his voice sound raspier than ever.

Then his head peaked over the shared fence of ours because of course the door was slightly lower than the rest of the fence, probably for this exact purpose. His eyes twinkled like the damn stars above us and my heart beat unevenly as I watched him tug on the string that lifted the gate latch.

His gaze lingered on my body, and I tugged the sleeves of my silk nighty to make sure there was no sign of goose-bumps. That would just get to Beck's head, and we couldn't have that.

"I'm glad you made it home safely," he said, voice like it was combed over hot coals.

I raised a solitary brow and teased him. "Were you waiting up for me?"

"Yes."

No hesitation.

I gulped, then crossed my legs, looking for something to do. "You don't need to do that."

"I'm your bodyguard next door. Of course, I'm going to wait up for you." Beck sat down across from me.

Tears pricked the back of my eyes, so I blinked a few times and willed them away.

"Well, if you want to waste your time, that's on you," I attempted to joke because I wasn't quite sure how to handle the kindness.

Beck rubbed a thumb over his lower lip, drawing my attention there. "Faith told me she invited you upstate."

I crossed my legs, ignoring the ache between them. "She did."

"And do you plan to come?" He glanced at this watch. "We plan to leave at nine."

"Not giving me much notice, Bennet."

"You can sleep the whole drive, Marks."

I shifted again. "You'll let me play sleeping beauty while you shuttle us to the country?"

He shrugged. "It's not a hardship to want to take care of you, Marks."

Without thinking, I scooted my chair back. Beck watched as I rounded the table. He was far enough away from the table that I could slide onto his lap. He welcomed me there, his hands resting hesitantly on my hips, applying just enough pressure to hold me in place without crossing into inappropriate territory.

"Tighter, Bennet."

He swallowed, and I bent down to kiss the column of his neck, his Adam's apple bobbing.

The man hissed, straightening his arms to put a modicum of distance between us. "Luna. Damn it, woman, you're torturing me here."

A chuckle rumbled from my lips. "Good."

CHAPTER 29

Beck

"GOOD."

It was like I had a steel pipe in my pants. The woman was pure sin. A goddess in her signature silk robe. Her hair was unbound and wild. Not the perfectly coiffed hairdo she usually wore.

I released a hand from its hold on her hips and drove it through her strands. She practically purred as she leaned into the touch.

"You're distracting me."

Luna leaned in and nipped at my ear. "No idea what you're talking about."

"Liar."

The smile that touched her lips was a ray of sunshine on a cloudy day. The exhaustion from a long day of new, demanding clients and shifting of staff to accommodate the chaotic schedules of the people we protected. She extinguished that all with one twitch of her lips, one broad smile. Suddenly everything was a little bit better.

I'd do everything in my power to hold onto that feeling. To hold onto her.

"Come with us tomorrow." I barely managed the words as

she proceeded to cup the back of my neck and drive her fingers through the bottom of my shortly cropped hair, her fingernails sending a shiver down my spine and straight to my hard dick.

There was no world in which she couldn't feel it harden beneath her. Suddenly, she pulled back, a hint of mischief in her eyes as she rocked back and slid her hands down the front of my shirt. I wore my signature black tee, having shucked the leather jacket the second I arrived home earlier in the evening. Now I wish I still wore it to put an extra layer between us. Well, my brain wanted that, my lower half wanted other things.

Luna rocked one more time against my dick, this time harder, the rocking, not the dick, before slipping off me.

I breathed a sigh of relief, but it was short-lived. The woman dropped to her knees in front of me.

"Luna—"

She ran her hands along my thighs and the sight of her down there, showered in moonlight, her wide eyes on me made me crave things, dirty things.

I made to stand, and Luna stopped me, her hands holding my thighs firmly in place. If I wanted to, I could break the connection. There was a war between my head, my heart, and my dick and I wasn't sure which one would win. "Are you sure?"

Her fingers toyed with the button that held my dark-wash jeans together. The button came undone with a pop, and her gaze never left mine as she drew down the zipper. I gently wrapped my hands around her wrists. "You don't have to do this."

She lifted a solitary brow. "I know."

Then, after a little coaxing, I lifted my hips so she could easily get me free. The second she had my dick out her eyes doubled in size. "Jesus, Bennet. You're packing. How could I have forgotten?"

My dick twitched. "Take what you can."

"Challenge accepted," she said breathless as her hands clasped around the base of my erection, her grip firm. I immediately tilted my head back, swearing up at the stars above. This was the single greatest sensation I'd felt in my life, and she hadn't even done anything yet.

Luna licked her lips as her hands began their work, twisting and tugging. Then she lifted one hand and dragged her tongue along the palm to wet it. The little gesture had me panting for her.

"Please," I begged, no longer interested in games. I wanted those pouty lips around my dick, and I wanted them now.

Luna bent down even lower, and I could feel her warm breath on me.

"Breathe, Bennet."

"Not likely," I hissed.

She chuckled, opened her mouth, and dragged her tongue slowly from base to tip, taking her goddamn time.

I white-knuckled the armrests, keeping my hands firmly in their place.

Then, the teasing stopped, and Luna took me deep into her throat, taking me as far as she could go. The moment she gagged, I tried pulling out, but Luna's fingers dug into my thighs so hard they'd leave a mark.

I almost forgot to breathe as she added her hands back to the base, gently twisting and tugging in an easy rhythm with her mouth. It was as if we'd done this dance a thousand times before.

In just a few strokes, the sensations threatened to consume me and there was no way in fuck I was going to blow after ten seconds like some sort of virgin.

Through hooded eyes, I stared at the woman who would surely be my undoing and tried to distract myself with unsexy thoughts.

Then she dragged a fingertip underneath my balls, and I was done for. "Fuck, woman. If you don't stop that, I'm going to come down the back of that pretty throat of yours."

A look of pure victory crossed her face. She doubled down.

In a few seconds, I started panting, the wood of the chair cracking beneath my palms.

"Luna," I growled in warning.

A warning she didn't heed.

Well, fuck. That very decision on her part sent me over the edge. Before I knew it, my cum was spilling down the back of her throat. Her hand milked me, and she took it all.

And my hand fell away, the wood shattering under my grip.

With my cum still in her mouth, she glared at me. "You had to go and break my chair."

Her glare wiped away in an instant, and the ridiculousness of it all came crashing down on us as I zipped my pants.

Luna shifted as she tried to get to her feet. I reached out to help her when she started swearing.

"Shit, my knee."

I swept her up and sure enough there was wood embedded in her knee. "You have a splinter. At least one. There must have been something already on the ground."

"If I knew giving you blow jobs was this dangerous, I might have chosen to go inside the second I heard your back door open."

I tilted her chin up. "Would you have changed what we did just now? Do you regret it?"

Her face softened, and she must have known exactly where my head was . This time, she slid her hands into mine. "I wouldn't change a thing." Then she snapped out of the softness. "But if you don't get this splinter out of my knee, I might reconsider going down on you in the future."

"We can't have that. It would ruin the whole orgasm thing."

Her lips twitched. "I think you should carry me."

I couldn't agree more. Bending at the knee, I lifted her up, her legs handing over my arm and her head cradled near my shoulder.

The sigh she released sounded like heaven.

"By the way, I'm invoicing you for that chair. I can't have you going all hulk on my furniture."

I chuckled. "These muscles aren't just for show, you know."

"Awfully cocky there, aren't you?"

"Confident, Marks. I'm confident. Let's not get it twisted." I knocked the door between our backyards closed with my foot before bringing her into my house, being extra careful not to bump her feet on the door. I would never hear the end of it.

"Can you confidently get this tiny piece of wood out of my knee before morning because it really feels like you're stalling and I need my beauty sleep," she said on a yawn. "Don't think I didn't notice that you're bringing me back to your house and not mine."

"I know where my medicine cabinet is, Marks. Besides, this is starting to feel like our schtick."

"You wish."

I kissed her temple. "I do."

Luna lifted her head from its place in my nook. "Are you trying to kidnap me again?"

"What will you do if I say yes?"

She cocked her head, then shook it as if shaking off whatever thought had popped into her head. I wanted to tease out that thought, whatever it had been.

I clutched her closer to my chest, before setting her down on the closed toilet seat in the downstairs bathroom. The loss of her warmth made me stumble back a step before I got back to the task at hand. Luna gestured toward the drawers in the vanity, amusement flashing in her hooded eyes.

The woman was clearly exhausted and needed sleep, so I got to work and when her knee was clean and splinter free—with only minor bouts of cursing from my patient—I put a Bluey bandage on her knee for good measure, certain that Alice would berate me if I didn't.

Rather than taking her back to her place, I lifted her again, bringing her back to my guest room, Luna nearly asleep in my arms.

Just before setting her on the bed, she shook her head vehemently and tightened her grip around my neck. "Not this bed."

My heart stopped, and I hovered over the plush floral comforter. "I'm not taking you home. It's late, and I'd feel better if you were here with me."

"Your room," she said, her voice a little louder, and a lot firmer than before. "I want to sleep in your bed."

"Luna—"

"I'll make sure to wake up before Alice does."

"This isn't about Alice." Although I appreciated that she considered what it might be like for my daughter to find a woman in my bed. Alice loved Luna. If anything, she'd probably be thrilled to have Luna in our house in the morning. I'd never brought a woman around my daughter before. I'd been very careful about that.

"This is about me not taking advantage of you," he confided.

Luna cupped my cheek. "I'm pretty sure I just took advantage of *you*."

"This body is yours. You can take advantage of me whenever and however you want."

I watched the long lines of her neck as she swallowed hard. Then I remembered her swallowing something else just a few minutes ago and remembered once again that having her share a bed with me was a terrible idea.

Luna tapped my shoulder. "Is that an invitation for round two?

I could feel myself getting hard again. This woman had my body reacting like a teenage boy.

"Take me to your room, Beck. Hurry before all the blood rushes to my head."

That's when I realized she was still hovered over the bed. Come to think of it, my arms were starting to feel the strain of the awkward angle. "Fine."

I walked down the hall and placed her in my bed, carefully bringing the sheets and comforter up to her neck. The woman would be well covered if I had anything to say about it.

Then I snagged a few extra pillows from the linen closet in my oversized bathroom and lined them down the center of the bed. Luna turned over, one hand under the pillow as she examined me. "What do you think you're doing?"

I shoved one final pillow between the head pillows. "Fixing the bed."

She lifted a brow, her face steeped in skepticism. "Is that so?"

Hands on my hips, I scanned the room to see if there was anything else I should add. Happy with the results, I headed to the bathroom where I grabbed a clean pair of athletic shorts and brushed my teeth. The day had been long and the last thing I wanted while also being the only thing I wanted to do was crawl into bed. I took my time washing my face, reapplying deodorant and making sure I flossed so thoroughly my dentist would be forced to give me a gold star.

I was stalling.

The sheets rustled. "Do you plan on joining me at all? Perhaps sometime before the sun rises?"

"Go to sleep," I said from the confines of my bathroom,

making sure to use mouthwash. You could never be too careful when it comes to dental hygiene.

Luna muttered something unintelligible. I could only imagine it carried a few expletives.

Finally, I'd run out of tactics and swayed on my feet, the long day catching up to me. "Fuck it."

I exited the bathroom to find a mound of pillows on the ground, my hard work undone. "Luna—"

"Beck—" she countered easily. "You're a grown up. You can handle it." There was nothing quite like having your own words thrown back in your face.

I scrubbed a hand down my face then slid into the California King.

Luna chuckled sleepily and patted the bed. "There's plenty of room."

I'd kept my body firmly along the edge of the bed, trying to take up as little space as my massive body could manage.

"I gave you a blow job. You can lay next to me like a normal human."

I bristled at that. "And nothing else is going to happen tonight."

Luna kept her eyes closed as she smiled. "Technically, it's morning."

I pulled the blankets over me, effectively tucking myself in and said, as pointedly as possible, "Good night, Marks."

"Good night, Bennet. By the way, get your suit ready, you're taking me to the gala."

CHAPTER 30

Luna

A WAVE of déjà vu washed over me as we exited the city in Beck's Subaru.

Yes, *a Subaru*. Apparently, it met Beck's rigorous safety standards for his daughter, and he wouldn't be caught dead on the motorcycles he told me all about that night we first met. I hadn't really clocked the make of the vehicle before because of the whole kidnapping thing, but now I found this little piece of the Bennet puzzle to be, well, puzzling.

Alice chatted the entire duration of the drive.

What's your favorite Disney movie?

Do you have a favorite color?

Do you like dogs?

Have you had a dog?

Do you think I should get a cat instead?

"No cats," Beck chimed in, putting a quick end to that line of questioning.

Alice pouted for exactly two seconds before she opened her mouth again, this time listing the number of things they'd need to buy to take care of a dog.

I turned in my seat to get a better view of Beck. He'd planted his arm on my headrest the second we exited the city and firmly kept it there. A small, possessive move that had me recalling how we'd woken up this morning, me the little spoon to Beck's big spoon, his raging erection digging into my ass.

We'd just passed the *Welcome* sign for the little upstate township that Sebastian Steele called home when I broke into another yawn. We'd only managed a few hours of sleep before Alice pounded on the door. I scrambled like a madwoman to hide under the bed but luckily Beck had the foresight to lock the door before going to bed.

When I yawned again, Beck glanced over at me and then used his turn signal. I sat up straighter as he turned the wrong way.

"I'm stopping to get you coffee," Beck explained.

I blinked as warmth spread through my chest. "Thank you."

He lifted a brow, clearly not used to this nice side of me. "You're welcome, Marks."

I sank back into my seat, tracing the lines of Beck's face as he navigated the few streets between us and the town center.

"Can I get a muffin?" Alice asked as we pulled into a parking spot.

Beck answered his daughter as a calendar item flashed across my screen.

Dr. Wozniac - 30 minutes

Shit. I'd forgotten about my therapy appointment. My doctor had a few highly coveted slots on Saturday mornings to accommodate her busier clients and I'd greedily taken one figuring it would be easier than a mid-week session where I was vollying back and forth between Club Deux and The Chateau.

"Everything, okay?" Beck asked, sliding his sunglasses into the top of his black t-shirt.

I lifted my phone. "I have a call in half an hour I need to take."

He nodded. "We'll make this quick and find you a quiet space at Sebastian's."

The words hit something low in my gut. On instinct, I leaned forward, placing my hands on his thick thigh and I savored the feel of him under my palms. If I inched up *just* a little further

"I'm starving," Alice grumbled from the back seat.

I pulled my hands back as if they'd been burned and reached for the door handle, my lungs desperate for air.

Beck chuckled and unbuckled himself, chatting away with Alice unfazed that I'd just had my hands on him. Yet, still, I could feel his attention on me. The curiosity in his glances as we walked into the homey coffee shop with its mismatched chairs and tables. The regulars in their seats, chatting with neighbors while sipping from unique mugs.

We stood in line, me beside Beck and Alice in front of Beck, leaning back on her dad.

He bumped shoulders with me and mouthed, "You okay?"

I nodded. The therapy session didn't scare me like it had when I'd first tried right after the incident. I'd only met with my new therapist once and we just clicked. Which felt weird, but also amazing, and left me actually looking forward to today's session. I saw it as a step toward *this*, this growing, palpable thing between Beck and me, and even Alice. They were a package deal, and I wouldn't have it any other way. The comfort of the car ride, the safety I feel in his arms—I wanted the possibility of that. *Forever.*

The idea alone made me dizzy.

But it wouldn't be possible until I'd worked out enough of my own stuff.

Still, therapy was helping. Talking about the past, putting it out there, understanding the trauma and my coping mechanisms and finding healthier coping mechanisms...it had a compounding effect, chipping away at the mental blocks that stopped me from being ready, being fully healthy—or healthy enough—to give this thing a real go.

When the person in front of us finished ordering, we scooted up and Beck began rattling off our order, starting with a cappuccino for me, an Americano for him, and a hot chocolate for the little miss.

"And a raspberry white chocolate scone, please," Alice chimed in. Beck added a few more pastries to the order, enough for us and our friends.

The barista read back the order, and Beck paid while Alice and I combed through the books in the little free library in the corner. I flicked through the romance novels and found an illustrated cover with a hunky hockey player kissing a redhead and immediately tucked it under my arm. Not that I had time to read, but maybe I'd make an exception.

We took our food and drinks to go, and I kept checking the time on my watch.

The second we arrived at Sebastian's home, I leaped out of the car, gave my friend a quick hug and told her I'd see her shortly. Faith must have been used to my kind of crazy because she didn't even bat an eye.

"See you soonish?" she said before greeting Beck and Alice.

I passed Willow on my way inside. "Willow, this way, girly."

The black lab wagged her tail so hard, she damn near fell over. The precious girl trotted behind me as I escaped to my regular guest room and got my laptop ready for my call.

"Morning, Dr. Wozniac."

My therapist smiled and lifted her glasses from where they'd hung around her neck. "Hello, Luna. It's nice to see you. Is that a new room?"

I crossed my legs in the oversized chair in the room, my laptop perched on a stack of books that sat on the side table next to the bed. Willow curled up on the ground in front of me.

"Yes, I'm at a friend's house today."

She lowered her glasses onto the bridge of her nose like she probably had a dozen times already today. The little movement was one I'd come to expect from her in our little time together. "And how do you feel about that latest episode of *Housewives*?"

I chewed the inside of my cheek to keep from laughing. In the initial paperwork I signed with this therapist, she told me that a safe space was conducive to healing. If I ever felt like I wasn't in a safe space but couldn't say so aloud, I was given a safe word of sorts.

"Tamra really shouldn't have thrown that napkin."

With a little nod, Dr. Wozniac's glasses found their rightful place. "Very good. Now tell me about your week so far. How's your body feeling? Any migraines?"

We focused on my physical health first. The brain and the body were connected, and the body often kept the score. It also gave me something easy to focus on—it didn't feel like diving into the deep end without floaties on.

I pulled the fuzzy blanket from the basket next to me and placed it on my lap. "Nope, migraine free. I managed some meditation also and my sleep has been improving." This last bit I said as I broke into a yawn. "So, last night I didn't get too much, actually."

She tapped the notepad with her pen. "Tell me about that."

And I did. I told her everything between Beck and me, forever grateful that Sebastian sprung for soundproof walls in this upstate retreat of his. I could talk and talk without fear that anyone would overhear.

Especially the bit about the blow job. I had to give her credit; Dr. W. didn't even flinch when I mentioned I'd gone down on him.

"Physical intimacy is nothing to be ashamed of, dear." She'd firmly told me during our first session together after I explained the impetus for seeking her out.

"How did you feel when you were with him?"

No other prompting, just an open-ended question without trying to get me to say one way or the other.

"I felt like me. I felt empowered, like I wanted something, and he clearly wanted it too, and so I did it."

"Did you flinch?"

I sat up straighter. "Nope."

She hummed. "Very good. This is a promising step forward, I want you to acknowledge that, Luna. It's important to measure success along the way. It's not just the end goal that matters."

I nodded, understanding why she said that and still not feeling like it was quite enough.

Dr. Wozniac made a face as if sensing my inner monologue, and I wanted to reach through my laptop and pick up that little notepad she always had with her. "And how do you think you'd react if he had wanted to touch you?"

Again, if anyone else had asked me this question other than Faith, I'd flinch or tell them to fuck off, but as it were, Dr. W. created a safe, non-judgmental space that really allowed me to consider things I would have probably kept buried and not addressed. I'd become a pro at that, apparently.

Overachiever.

"Well?" she nudged gently.

I tightened the blanket around me, drawing Willow's attention. The pup lifted her head from her paws to check on me, and when she deemed the all clear, placed that little chin back down with a sigh.

"I've mentioned Beck is handsome, right? Like ridiculously good looking. Like the bad boy who rode a motorcycle to high school and was never seen without his leather jacket, in the body of a grown man with muscles for days—practical muscles, not the ones built by a gym rat, no, it's more like the someone who really earns the muscles, like in his everyday life. And he's protective, so protective it makes my heart ache sometimes because it's been a very long time since anyone was that protective of me. Let's not forget his big hands and we all know what that means, he has a huge—"

My therapist cleared her throat as I cut myself off before I could say "dick" to the nice lady across from me.

She lifted a brow but otherwise remained quiet.

"Right, so I guess what I'm trying to say is that yes, a thousand times yes, I want to sleep with Beck, and I'd like to think that if things were taking a sexy turn, that I wouldn't react the same way I did the first time. That I'd feel ready."

She tilted her head. "What's the plan if you do flinch? If your body does go into fight or flight?"

Honestly, I wasn't sure. I would have to see how I felt in the moment, and I couldn't predict how I might react. That flinch had come out of nowhere.

"You don't have to answer me now, but think about it. That's going to be your homework for the next time we meet. Anticipating your reaction, imagining yourself and how you want to react, that can help give you the tools you need in the moment. It's like soccer practice."

I burst into laughter.

Dr. W. pursed her lips. "Not a great analogy, but you understand the sentiment."

"Practice makes perfect?" I guessed.

"Something like that."

CHAPTER 31

Beck

"YOU LIKE HER, DON'T YOU?"

I checked to see if there were any tiny ears nearby and finding the coast clear, I sent Faith Waters my most dangerous glare. By the twitch of her lips, I could tell that she wasn't shaking in her boots—no, it was quite the opposite, actually.

I combed a hand through my hair and sighed. Would it be bad if I dipped into Sebastian's bar? One glance at the clock confirmed it wasn't an option. Besides, it probably wasn't a good coping mechanism. I could handle a snoopy socialite.

Couldn't I?

Despite myself, I tuned my ears to any noise, any indication that Luna was done with her therapy appointment. I was glad she felt comfortable telling me about it in the first place. Selfishly, I wanted to make sure she spoke to someone about last night—a third party who was going to make sure we hadn't crossed some invisible line that she wasn't mentally or physically prepared to cross yet.

She'd slept in my bed and my body found hers in the middle of the night. At some point, my arm draped over her waist, and I held her tight. She loosed a little sigh of contentment in her sleep and that little sound made me realize what had happened. Luna must have discarded the pillows. So I plucked them from the ground, one by one, and put them between us.

The second time I found myself wrapped around her that night, I gave up and just savored the feel of my arms around her.

Faith waved her hands above her head. "Hello, Earth to Beck? Do you have the hots for my friend?"

I planted my elbows on the table and rubbed at my temples, a headache already forming from the thought of having this conversation. "Do you have some pain meds?"

Faith chuckled over the top of her coffee mug then stood, crossing the kitchen to open a cabinet and pulling out a plastic bottle. She tossed it over to me and I caught it with one hand.

"Are we waiting on the caffeine to hit before you answer my question?" she teased.

I popped open the bottle and took two pills. "I preferred this friendship when I was teasing you about Sebastian."

Faith laughed. "I'm sure Sebastian would disagree."

Footsteps had me turning my head toward the hallway that connected to the kitchen.

Not Luna.

"Don't be so disappointed," my friend said dryly.

I stood and clapped Sebastian on the back. "Jackass. Where were you?"

He shook his head as he dug through the white bag on the table that held the pastries. "The Barnes project is in full swing."

Faith nodded. "He barely comes out of the Batcave."

I nodded in Sebastian's direction. "In his defense, he barely came out of the Batcave before the Barnes deal."

Sebastian covered his mouth as he chewed. "I'm technically still coming out of my office more than I ever had before Faith."

Faith pointed at him. "You didn't call it a Batcave."

"My office is so much more than a Batcave. Besides, I thought I was more Beast than Batman."

Faith chuckled. "True enough."

I'd once asked my friend to explain this whole Beauty and the Beast obsession—all the little remarks I'd caught them volleying between each other—and frankly I still didn't get it. I did, however, understand that my friend smiled more in the presence of Faith than he had with anyone else, so maybe I didn't need to understand it. I just needed to appreciate that my friend was happy.

My attention lingered at the door until Sebastian clapped me on the back. "You've got it bad, bro."

I didn't even bother to deny it. Anyone with working eyes could see that I was completely obsessed with the woman upstairs. "You're late to the party, your girl here already tried to do some digging."

Sebastian pulled Faith into his lap and pressed a kiss to her neck.

I groaned. "Can we not do that here? There's a child present."

Faith and Sebastian laughed in stereo knowing full well Alice was distracted elsewhere.

Then Faith leaned forward, palm planted firmly on the oak table in front of her. "In all seriousness, if you hurt my friend, I'll hurt you."

I held up my hands. "Nobody is hurting anybody." Frankly, it was hard not to be offended that the idea of that ever crossed her mind. "I'd do anything to keep her safe. *Anything.*"

Just then, Alice burst through the door, stealing everyone's attention. "Can we go soon? I want to meet the doggies now."

I pointed toward the sink. "Wash your hands and then finish the ham and cheese breakfast croissant. You need energy if you're going to keep up with all these dogs today."

Alice rolled her eyes, then did as she was told.

Sebastian began to explain the process. How we would go and view the dogs eligible for adoption and how we would play with them to see how comfortable they were with us. It wasn't just about us picking the dog, it was about the dog choosing us in return. Alice nodded, enthralled as her ersatz uncle went into all the details about the current dogs available for adoption. He struck a good balance of explaining the attributes of each dog with an almost scientific precision, eliminating as much bias as he could. That was fine enough for my little girl, but I planned to corner him in the animal shelter to make sure we went home with a good family dog that wouldn't hurt my daughter.

That was my biggest stipulation. I could deal with shedding, slobber, and dog poop, but I would not tolerate an animal that would harm my kiddo.

Sebastian assured me he'd never let that happen.

———

"I want them all," Alice whisper-shouted as she went from kennel to kennel to look at the rescue pups. We'd been there all of ten seconds when she made the bold declaration.

There were rumbled chuckles from me, Luna, and Sebastian as well as the two people on staff who were there to help today. Saturday's were big adoption days, and I knew they planned to take a few of the pups to the local farmer's market since that was a great way to promote the rescue and get folks interested in adoption.

"Let's start with one, Alice. They are a big responsibility. Remember what we talked about? How you're going to need to do some chores if we bring home a dog."

Alice didn't bother to face me. "I know, Dad, we've gone over this. I promise to feed our dog and walk it."

"What about picking up after the dog?"

She shrugged her shoulders. "I can put the dog's toys away when I put mine away. Easy."

"That's not the kind of clean-up I was thinking about…"

Alice squealed again as she approached the last kennel, tucked away in the back.

Harper, the staff person helping us, chimed in. "That's Bruce; he's a beagle-mix, and he's an absolute sweetheart."

Sebastian lifted a finger. "I can confirm this, even though Bruce refuses to jog with me."

"He might not be the most active of our residents, but he loves cuddles and kisses," Harper added.

Alice beamed. "I love those things too."

I placed a hand on Alice's back. "That's true, you do."

Harper unlatched the enclosure. "Let me get Bruce on his leash and we can meet you out in the play yard?"

Sebastian stepped in. "Follow me, I'll show you where the play yard is."

A minute later we found ourselves in a dog's dream house. The play yard had toys and tunnels, mirroring dog parks that I'd driven past and never stopped at. Basically, it was heaven, and Bruce came out with Harper, tail wagging as he sauntered right up to an enthusiastic Alice.

Alice showered Bruce with love and kisses and pets as Harper relayed some basic information about the dog.

Four years old.

Potty trained.

Left behind when its owner passed away suddenly.

Has a sweet temperament.

Has been at the shelter for two months.

I listened to every nugget of info being shared while watching both my daughter and Luna. Luna had taken it upon herself to photograph the interaction between my daughter and Bruce from every angle. I closed in behind her and whispered in her ear, "I think you got the shot."

Luna jumped, and I placed a hand on her lower back. "If

this ends up being the dog, then she'll want some pictures. Trust me."

A cacophony of barks interrupted us. Alice lifted her head as several more dogs made their way into the play area.

"It's morning recess," Harper explained. "Besides, this will allow you to get to know all the dogs we have available."

A little mutt with dark brown hair and a tongue lolling out of its mouth walked right up to Luna and placed a tender paw on her foot. Wiry hair, goofy face, but with the sweetest energy.

I bet that's the dog Sebastian was talking about. Pepper.

Luna immediately bent down and cooed. "Hello, there—" She glanced at the tag on the dog's collar. "Pepper."

The tiny dog graciously accepted pets, immediately lowering itself to the ground to get some good belly rubs in. Then it dashed off, zooming back and forth across the play area before coming back to Luna, nuzzling her legs.

"Careful. I think you may have found your new best friend," I warned.

"I never imagined getting a dog," Luna said wistfully, almost to herself. She poured her love and attention onto Pepper who started running in circles around her.

I shook my head thinking we might not be the only ones getting a dog.

Then my attention drifted back to Alice who continued to be solely focused on Bruce. While I love that she connected instantly with him, she hadn't given the other dogs an opportunity to shoot their shot. "Honey, why don't you greet the other dogs too? Get to know them?"

She wrapped her arms around Bruce's thick body. "But, Daddy, I love him."

Using Taylor Swift lyrics against me...

"Okay, Alice. I know you love him and that's great. We don't want to be rude to all these other dogs that are excited to see you. Like that one." I pointed to a larger dog that had its head tilted to the side. The curious dog sat patiently on the sidelines as if awaiting its turn.

Alice rolled her eyes. "Fine. But I won't change my mind."

My daughter planted a big kiss on the top of Bruce's head before approaching the other dog.

At some point, Luna wandered off, Pepper at her heels, and started chatting with Harper. From the bits of conversation I could hear, it sounded like Luna was requesting all the details about Pepper. The dog continued to stick to her like glue, nuzzling Luna's leg during those rare moments when Luna paused her petting.

While Luna did that, Sebastian ran in circles with some of the larger breeds, clearly trying to get out some of their energy. The man was a running machine and volunteered to take the dogs out on a run at least once a week. Unlike my daughter, the man showed no favoritism, showering all dogs with equal attention.

Luna waved me over, so I joined her on the bench, and we watched Alice together.

"Having fun?" I asked behind the protection of my reflective sunglasses. Luna wore none, so I had front-row access to the myriad of emotions that flitted across her face.

I slid my hand into hers and squeezed. "Do you need me to take you back to the city?"

Luna startled. "What? No. Not until tomorrow at least when you and Alice go back."

I nodded, happy with the answer, while wanting to prod more. We hadn't had a chance to debrief her session with her therapist and I didn't want to bring it up in front of her friends. "Let me know if you change your mind."

She gave me an odd look. "There's nowhere I'd rather be."

That settled my curiosity.

Alice's laughter sliced through the moment. She'd found another dog and while she was trying to give it attention, I could see her head turning toward Bruce who was now flat bellied on the ground, his head nested between his paws, gazing longingly at my daughter.

Luna gestured at Bruce. "Hate to break it to you, but I think you have a winner."

"I know. I imagined getting a dog that was more…what's the word I'm looking for?"

"Active?" Luna supplied, her gaze longingly drifting to Pepper.

"I thought we'd be walking the streets of Brooklyn. I'm not sure Bruce could make it around the block."

Luna whirled back to me. "On the bright side, at least you won't have to feel guilty if you miss a walk or two."

"Facts."

Alice finished her rounds, making sure to say goodbye to each dog before returning to Bruce. And the decision was made. "I know what dog is coming home with me. We can fit two dogs in the car in case you want to bring a special someone home too…"

Luna's smile fell. "I was just talking to Harper about that."

I slid my hands into my pockets. "And?"

She shook her head, shoulders caving in. "There's just too much going on right now to bring home a dog that needs love and attention, and unlike your new dog, will actually require daily walks."

The offer sat on the tip of my tongue. "I could—"

But before I could finish, Luna lifted her hand to stop me. "No."

Despite her firm, one-word answer, I sensed that Luna wanted to say yes. And maybe—*just maybe*—that yes was about more than just the dog.

CHAPTER 32

Luna

"HURRY UP!" Faith shouted at me as I picked at the dress I donned. It was the fifth one I'd tried on this morning and it still wasn't hitting like it should.

I'd come back from my weekend upstate with more problems than I'd left with. All the relaxation from that time away evaporated into thin air the second we crossed the Brooklyn Bridge.

I'd been working like a beast ever since.

Parvati called to let me know that we still weren't getting anywhere close to finalizing the permit sign offs from the city. My blood boiled and my blood pressure shot through the roof (I imagine, I didn't actually check), and sure enough that throbbing between my eyes resumed in full force.

Luckily, Faith agreed to this little shopping adventure in between my morning at the Chateau and my evening at Club Deux. If I didn't find a winner in about ten minutes, I'd be seriously screwed.

The Sexual Assault Survivors Network Gala was just a day away and dammit if I wanted to look good. For me, sure, and because I'd have Beck Bennet on my arm, but also because I wanted to prove to Carter that I was fine and had moved on.

Take that.

And I was starting to become suspicious that she was withholding my permit intentionally. Not only had she ignored my emails, but she'd fully given me bad intel.

Unacceptable and unprofessional. I wanted to channel my inner real *"Housewife"* and call her out on it, but I would hold myself back, become the epitome of decorum and diplomacy.

Work and reality hit like a ton of bricks.

While I'd stepped back in terms of the gala planning, I still garnered a lot of sponsors and items for the silent auction. So when the email came in—again—from Carter reminding me of the details, I wanted to throttle him. Not great considering the cause we were raising money for, so instead of violence I chose a five-minute meditation and when that didn't work, I did a midnight jog with my personal billionaire bodyguard keeping pace next to me.

It didn't help much.

And standing in front of this mirror was only adding to my irritation. I usually stuck to the silhouettes I knew flattered my body and none of them were fancy enough for the event.

"You need to try the emerald gown," Faith insisted. "Like I told you from the beginning."

My eyes found hers in the mirror. "It's too...*demure.*"

Faith cocked her head. "What's wrong with that? You're making demure sound like a four-letter word."

I picked at the dress in question. "Demure isn't exactly my style. I'm more leather and sky-high heels."

Faith jumped up from her chair and picked the dress from the rack. "All the more reason to try something new. Besides, this dress will have Beck drooling all over you."

I ran my fingers over the delicate bodice. "You think?"

"I know."

I peeked at her from beneath my lashes. "I wouldn't mind making that man drool."

She hip-checked me. "Someone will have to walk behind him with a mop."

"Fiinne, I'll try it."

Faith beamed. "You'll thank me later."

———

Someone knocked on my office door, which was just as well because my bleary eyes couldn't review another spreadsheet. I'd double checked the inventory review and read through the recommendations put together by my bar leads.

It told me many things, like what people were ordering, what people asked for that we didn't have in terms of brands, and evaluated if we should change up our buying habits.

This happened monthly to keep my fingers on the pulse of things.

"Come in," I called, shutting my laptop.

"We're ready for you," Monroe said, poking her head through the crack in the door.

I pushed back from the desk. "Let's get to it."

The sober curious movement meant more people were asking for non-alcoholic drinks, which I was all in favor of, so I requested a taste test. Since I couldn't taste test our cocktails, it was a nice change of pace.

My team set up a table for me and I rubbed my hands together as my head mixologist came out from behind the bar with the first drink.

"We need to set up an additional tasting with some key customers." I rattled off a short list of regulars who often ordered mocktails. The mockjito I tried the other day had been fabulous, and I was thrilled to try some more.

Then my phone chimed.

BECK

I had to Google the details for the gala.

I stifled a laugh as the message popped on my screen. Setting my glass down, I considered my reply.

LUNA

Oh, yeah, and did you find the info you were looking for?

BECK

Obviously. But it should have come from you.

LUNA

I told you you're my date.

BECK:

And yet gave me no details.

BECK

You realize I need to get my suit dry cleaned.

LUNA

That seems like a you problem.

BECK

Luna

LUNA

Beck

BECK

You drive me ducking nuts sometimes.

BECK

Ducking not ducking.

BECK

Ducking auto correct.

LUNA

You use that language around Alice? Tsk tsk.

BECK

Luna

LUNA

I'm busy. Talk tomorrow.

I placed my phone face down on the table and ignored it as it chimed and vibrated knowing full well I'd just annoyed the hell out of Beck.

Mission accomplished.

Monroe sank into the seat next to me, clapping her hands. "This is my favorite part of the month."

"Same, girl. Same."

My head bartender came out with a tray of pink drinks. "Here we have the Pink Flamingo. It's a mix of pineapple and lime." They went on to explain where the pink color came from, grenadine, and the lime soda helped give it the feel of alcohol without the booze itself.

Next to us sat a score sheet where we would capture our thoughts. Monroe and I tasted and kept our opinions to ourselves until the end to ensure we weren't accidentally influencing the other person's score.

We snacked on pretzels in between drinks. There'd be five of them, per usual. The mockjito made a reappearance. "I didn't mull it enough when I sent you home with the tester," the bartender insisted.

This time they served it in a gorgeous art déco highball glass. I enjoyed buying glassware for the bar because it made the drink even more special when it came out in a unique glass.

Monroe and I sipped our respective drinks and then looked at each other. I tried to suss out if she felt the same way as me. Sometimes our telepathy was on point.

Then she broke the standoff by pointing to the glass. "That's very good. I'm not even missing the alcohol."

Okay, so we weren't very good at following our own rules.

I tapped my notepad with my pen. "Agreed, and that's exactly what we want to achieve with this menu."

"Sir, the house is closed," Niemand, one of our bouncers, said.

"She's expecting me," the intruder replied in that deep, rumbling voice of his that sent a thrill between my thighs.

The man sauntered in hot as sin in his usual uniform and his hair freshly cut. No doubt in preparation for tomorrow's gala.

He slid into the empty seat next to Monroe and introduced himself. Monroe practically salivated over him, and who could blame her? The man was absolutely drool worthy.

Then his gaze landed on me, and I sat back in my chair as I absorbed the full force of him.

"You know why I'm here."

"Want me to babysit Alice again?" I pretended to search for her in the empty bar.

Beck slipped his arm behind me, and I tried to suppress a shiver. "I'm working."

He ran his fingers through my hair. "And as soon as we solidify a time for us to leave for the gala, I'll head home and have dinner with Alice."

That sounded cozy. Something must have shown on my face because Beck cupped my chin. "I'll save you some spaghetti."

I barely noticed as Monroe sipped on her drink, eyes bulging as she volleyed between the two of us.

Then the bartender arrived, clearing the table and setting down the next round. Beck finally released me from his grip, and I suddenly wished that I didn't have a busy night ahead of me.

Three drinks. They'd brought three drinks.

"He's not staying." I tried handing the drink back, but Beck swept it up out of my fingers.

He took a long sip, and I ignored the tanned column of his neck. "Delicious."

"Mmmhmm," Monroe nodded, blatantly staring at my man.

My man.

Whoa, were we sure those drinks didn't have alcohol in them? I was losing my senses over here.

Beck smacked his lips. "Is that pomegranate I'm tasting? It's refreshing. And the hint of mint adds some dimension. What else is there? There's something else."

Monroe tapped a finger on the guide in front of us. "It's triple sec."

"That's it." He nodded as if it were all clear now. The man really knew how to ham it up.

I put my hands on his shoulder. "I'll meet you in front of our houses at four. I want to arrive before doors open so that I can help out with any final arrangements for the auction items. They need to look good so people will bid."

Beck leaned over and kissed my cheek. "See, that wasn't too hard." He reached out to shake Monroe's hand. "Good to see you, Monroe."

Beck tossed a wink out and Monroe almost fell off her chair. If I hadn't braced myself, I may have too.

"Damn that man is gorgeous. If you don't marry him, I will."

CHAPTER 33

Beck

"BE GOOD FOR MRS. CORBETT," I whispered to Alice as I squeezed her tight.

"I know, Daddy," my daughter said on a laugh before wiggling out of my grip. "Don't forget to tell Luna she looks pretty."

Gotta love getting dating tips from my seven-year-old.

Alice sprinted down the hall to her room where her dinosaurs were battling it out with her Barbies while her new dog watched on. I dared to drag her away to give her kisses and make sure she had what she needed before heading out to the gala. While I knew her nanny had things covered, it was a rare occasion that had me going out when I could be tucking her in.

I adjusted the sleeves of my tux in the hallway mirror, gave one last goodbye, and exited the townhouse, just as my driver opened the door to the limo parked out front.

The driver tipped his hat, and I gestured to the building next door. "Let me just get my date."

I fidgeted as I stood on her stoop, waiting to be let in.

"You're early," said a disembodied voice from the intercom.

I glanced at my watch. "A minute early, tops."

"You're rushing me."

"Luna—"

"Beck."

I leaned in closer so that the camera could capture my expression. "I'd rather not get into it on your stoop while people walk by with their poodles and my driver stares at me like I've lost my mind."

I caught a hint of laughter before the line went quiet.

The front door cracked open, and I entered Luna's house only to catch the laughter in full force.

I stopped in my tracks. There, in the middle of her entry-way, stood Luna in all her glory. A delicate emerald dress poured over her curves, her hair pulled up into an elaborate updo that must have taken hours by a professional to achieve.

A smokey eye and a red lip; it made me want to crawl on my knees and worship her.

My long strides swallowed the space separating us. I slid my hands to her waist and my lips found hers. She kissed me back with abandon before eventually pulling back.

"If you fucked up my lipstick, I'll never forgive you," she chided as she palmed my freshly shaven cheek. "I like you better with a little scruff."

I chuckled. "You really know how to make a guy feel special."

Her words held little bite and if anything, from the expression on her face, my Luna wasn't completely unim-pressed with me. Her fingers went to my lapels, straightening them out of any invisible wrinkles that our kiss may have caused.

Then she drifted to the hallway mirror for a quick touch up.

Like a moth to flame, I trailed behind her, wanting to touch her in a million little ways. Our eyes collided in the mirror. Luna's teeth sank into her bottom lip.

I grabbed her chin, and her breathing hitched. "We don't want you ruining that lipstick, now do we?"

With our bodies this close, I wondered what it would be like if I were to just lift her dress and have my way with her while we stared into each other's eyes?

I pushed away from the side table. We weren't about to find out. I cleared my throat. "My driver is out front."

"Let me grab my purse."

"I'll get it." I snagged it from the bottom stair before holding out my arm for her.

She slid in and her arm wrapped around mine. "What a gentleman."

"Only sometimes." My thoughts about the woman on my arm were anything but. Whenever I showered I gripped myself while thinking of her, replaying that blow job over and over like a movie imprinted on my brain.

I'd woken up this morning with my dick straining for release. I'd dreamed of her smell and her hair falling over her shoulders. I'd remembered our night together all those years ago and the brief kisses we'd shared since.

Fuck. I discreetly adjusted myself as I held the car door open for Luna.

She slid onto the leather seats. "How's being a doggy daddy treating you?"

"For fuck's sake, Marks. Don't call me a doggy daddy." Although it did seem to quell the rising desire that had been building between us as I slid into the car.

She toyed with my collar again as the driver took off. "But it's funny."

I crossed my leg at the knee. "Alice loves him."

"I knew she would. It was practically love at first sight." Just briefly, she looked wistfully out the window, and I wondered if she was thinking about Pepper.

I set a hand down on her silky thigh. "You would know all about that."

Her eyes blazed as they found mine. "I think you have that the wrong way around."

I brought her lips to mine, then whispered behind her ear. "Maybe I do."

"Beck—"

"Luna—"

Before we could banter more, the limo lurched to a stop.

"Sorry, sir. Ma'am," the driver said through the intercom. "We've arrived."

CHAPTER 34

Luna

THE VENUE DAZZLED. Clearly the planning committee knew what they were doing when they chose to rent out the New York Public Library's main branch and transform it for a night of good food, dancing, and raising a hell of a lot of money for a good cause.

Upon arrival, I towed Beck to the auction area where all the goodies the gala volunteers spent the afternoon preparing were regally presented to lure in prospective bidders. I adjusted table skirts as I inspected the setup, pleased with what I had found.

Then I dragged us over to the bar area, which I'd sponsored, where we had a healthy mix of cocktail and mocktail options. Kiera, one of our best bartenders from the club, was working, so I said hello to her and made sure that she had what she needed. The woman had it handled.

Finally, I approached Khelani, the executive director of the foundation. She'd established it after enduring sexual assault at the hands of the man she should have been able to trust the most—her husband. She'd been lucky in that she got out and had the funds to start a new life. She recognized not everyone was that lucky and decided to create a space for victims of all forms of assault.

The second I made my first penny from Club Deux, I committed to the foundation. A portion of my funds went there every month. Not only did the foundation help survivors, but it also tried to change policies to prevent assault in the first place.

I hugged Khelani and then turned toward my date. "Khelani, I want to introduce you to Beck Bennet."

They shook hands, and I smothered a smile with my sparkling water as I watched her size him up.

Beck wrapped an arm low around my waist. "It's a pleasure to meet you. I'm glad Luna let me come with her. The work you do is incredible."

Her brows raised. "How much do you know about the work we do?"

It was a test, and I found myself holding my breath to see how he'd respond.

"I did my research after Luna told me she was involved, and I have to say the work you're doing in congress is impressive. Not to mention the individual supports you provide. I work with a lot of veterans and try to do the same with them, making sure they have the housing and financial supports are foundational, alongside making sure they have access to mental health services."

This piqued Khelani's interest. She immediately dovetailed into one of her many efforts around universal mental health screenings and linkage to care and Beck animatedly reacted and offered ideas. They were mid-conversation when something drew my attention from across the room.

Carter and Delaney were there, the woman strutting like a supermodel with her attention fully on me, while Carter waved and chatted with people they passed by.

"She's obsessed with me," I murmured, only half-joking.

Beck gripped me a little tighter, the only indication that he heard me.

Meanwhile, someone tapped on Khelani's shoulder and whispered in her ear. "You'll have to excuse me; duty calls," she said while pointing at Beck. "I want your contact information to see how we can combine some of our efforts."

He saluted her, bringing his full attention back to me. "You look beautiful tonight. This is amazing work you're dedicating yourself to."

My cheeks warmed, so I buried my face in his chest, carefully not to ruin my makeup.

Beck kissed my flaming cheeks before whispering, "We've got company."

I suppressed a groan, twirling to greet the incoming couple. Hopefully the smile plastered to my face was halfway convincing.

"Carter, Delaney. It's nice to see you both." I leaned in for an air kiss. Not usually my thing but it seemed like the right move considering we were wearing gowns and tuxedos.

Beck greeted them with a handshake before tucking me close to him again. The possessive move had me ready to tug him into the nearest coat room.

While Carter appeared genuinely happy to see me and meet Beck, Delaney's face told a different story. But then maybe I was reading too much into it.

"I have a feeling we will raise a lot of money tonight," Carter said to me glancing around the room.

"I hope so," I said, keeping it friendly.

Carter gestured to the room. "The planning committee put so much time and effort into this thing. These last couple weeks I'd spent nearly every evening on some sort of call."

I nodded. Despite my reduced role in the planning this year, I still received the meeting notes and supported however I could. Carter meant well but I couldn't shake the irritation that his statements implied. It felt like he was telling me I should have done more.

Delaney kept touching Carter's shirt, a claiming in her own right. "I practically had to beg him to come back to bed."

I nodded, struggling to maintain the smile plastered on my face.

The music faded, and Khelani called the room to attention, inviting folks to find their seats.

I nearly sobbed in relief. The last thing I wanted to do was make awkward conversation with my ex. I'd rather talk to Beck, dance when it was time, and sneak off the second the auction ended.

We waved goodbye and Beck's hand found its favorite place on the small of my back, guiding us to table two. Beck scooted his chair closer to mine, and threaded my hand in his, listening attentively as Khelani welcomed everyone and gave us an overview of the evening.

Beck occasionally glanced at me, surveying me as if to check on my wellbeing before returning his focus to the host. When the announcements completed, Beck began introducing himself to the other folks seated at our table, practically oozing charm like he was completely in his element.

Finally, our food arrived, and we returned to our little bubble, just the two of us.

Beck kissed my temple before lifting his fork. "Carter keeps looking over here at you and his date notices every single time he does. From the frown on her face, I'd venture to say she's less than amused by that."

"Where are they even sitting?" As casually as possible, I glanced over my shoulder.

Beck brushed non-existent lint from his shoulder. "They're just out of my direct line of sight. I can feel them."

"They're looking that much?" Rather than take a peek myself, I glanced at his face, trying to decipher what he was really getting at.

"Delaney is."

"Huh. I wonder why. More importantly, what do I do with that information considering she's a roadblock for my project?"

Beck played with my hair. "Do you want to talk to her here?"

I considered it. While I'd love to nip this all in the bud, I didn't think this was the time to do that. "If it comes up, then I'm more than prepared to talk to her. If not, I'll meet with her next week. I don't want to muddy the waters between the foundation work and the Chateau. There's a time and place for everything."

He nodded, as if satisfied with my answer. We chatted as we ate.

When the dishes were being cleared by the catering staff, he leaned over and whispered in my ear, "Dinner was good, but I personally can't wait for dessert."

Someone tapped on a microphone.

"Now we will hear a few words from our amazing auction item lead, Luna Marks."

I blinked. Beck grinned.

I squeezed his thigh as I stood, making my way to the corner of the room that held the high-ticket items, straightening my dress as I did.

Then Khelani called Carter's name too.

We locked eyes as he approached the auction area.

"I want to give special thanks to Carter and Luna for their tremendous work getting auction items for tonight's event. They've truly outdone themselves and I'm sure you'll be very pleased with the offerings. They don't know this yet, but I'm putting them to work. They will be walking around answering any questions you have about the items for the silent auction. As soon as you're ready, I invite you to start perusing, and bidding." She raised her eyebrows, and the room chuckled.

Small talk ensued and Carter immediately drew closer. "Did you know Khelani was going to do this?"

I shrugged. "I had no idea, but I should have figured she was up to something."

"Right? Remember last year when she made some of the committee do a choreographed dance?"

I feigned a shiver. "At least it's not that."

Folks were slowly making their way over although nobody approached us with questions.

Carter gave what I could only describe as a wistful smile. "I can't help but compare this year's event with last year's."

Fuck.

I held up a hand. "Carter, this isn't about us."

He pinched his eyes closed. "I know that. Trust me. It's just, I still remember that night, getting to know this amazing woman and feeling hopeful."

I swallowed. I didn't want to hurt him. Carter was a good person, just not good for me.

There's no comparison in my mind and yet I still don't want to hurt this man.

He clutched the back of his neck. "I don't want to make this awkward, Luna."

Too late.

"I just want to know that you're happy," he said with the earnestness of a golden retriever. "That's all, then I'll never bring up our past again. I promise."

My eyes searched the room, immediately finding Beck. He tilted his head, a silent *Are you okay? Because you know I have no qualms about making sure this man knows you aren't his.*

I shook my head at Beck, just a small movement to call him off. My heart thudded in my chest thinking about how much I adore him. I know standing down was against his baser instincts and yet he did it because he knew I could handle it.

I reached over and grabbed Carter's forearm. "I love

Beck," and I probably should tell him that myself. "He's my person."

Carter flinched, and then tried to cover it up with a smile that didn't quite meet his eyes. "I'm happy for you."

I gently knocked him in the shoulder. "I'm happy for me, too. Tell me about your lady friend. You like her?"

He smiled. "Delaney is great."

Carter segued easily into sharing about how they met and as he did, my shoulders loosened up. I finally felt like we were honestly putting it behind us. We were occasionally interrupted by folks asking us questions. Eventually the interruptions made it impossible to chat, so we went our separate ways.

It wasn't until later, when Beck was helping me with my coat, when I realized I hadn't seen Carter anymore that night.

I needed to stop by the ladies room, so Beck and I walked hand in hand down a hallway when I heard a raised voice.

"You talked to her for *twenty minutes*, Carter. Twenty *full* minutes. What on Earth could you possibly talk about for that long?" Delaney hissed.

"I swear to you, there's nothing going on between Luna and I. That's over."

Delaney scoffed. "You actually think I'm going to believe that?"

"She's in love with Beck," Carter insisted.

"But are you in love with her?"

Carter sighed. "There's nothing going on between us. Trust me on this."

I kept a hand on Beck's chest, despite my bladder screaming at me to find a restroom. They were still talking, so I started shifting on my feet to get some relief.

Unfortunately for me, the library custodian did an excellent job polishing the floors.

The screech created by my heel twisting on the highly

polished floor immediately shut down the convo between Carter and Delaney.

I winced and pushed forward around the corner pretending like I was just walking by. With a small smile plastered on my face, I waved and headed straight for the bathroom leaving Beck in the hallway on his own.

A second later, the bathroom door opened again. "You don't need to come in after me. I'll be just fine without my bodyguard."

I started pushing on a stall door.

"He's still in love with you, you know," Delaney said from behind me.

What the actual fuck?

I held the stall door open, doing a double take as my brain caught up. My bladder didn't appreciate the ambush and threatened to mutiny.

Delaney waved a pink painted finger in my direction. "He's in love with you. Watching you like a little puppy dog."

I held up my hands. "The feeling is not mutual. Which I've explained to Carter. He's well aware."

Delaney's heels clicked on the tile as she closed the distance between us.

Was this really happening right now?

She pointed at her chest. "He's with me."

I held up my hands. "I know."

Her hands found her hips. Her head tilted. "Are you messing with me?"

My head started to pound. I hated everything about this. Absolutely everything.

"I'm not trying to steal your boyfriend. I'm very happy with Beck. And if you love Carter and want to be with him, then I'm so happy for you. Honestly. There's no competition here."

Delaney heaved a sigh and shoved her hair behind her ears. "Damn. I think I believe you."

My bladder was on the verge of full rebellion. I rushed into the stall. "I know this is the worst timing, but I really don't want to pee my pants while we hash this out."

My whole body tensed before my bladder finally released. "Oh thank God."

"Sorry. I guess I should have figured you needed to use the restroom."

I waved, not that she could see me. "It's fine."

The automatic towel dispenser buzzed, and I heard sniffles as I finished up.

When I exited to wash my hands, I sidled up to the vanity. We stood side by side, Delaney dabbing her eyes while I washed my hands.

I leaned my hip against the counter while I dried my hands. "I hope you believe me. I'm madly in love with Beck Bennet, although I won't tell him that to his face. Not yet anyway."

Delaney managed a small smile, before wiping it clear from her face, a look of horror replacing it. "I can't believe I stormed in here to accuse you of liking my boyfriend. What is wrong with me?"

I waited patiently as she worked it out on her own.

"How insecure am I over this man? I need to check that," she said, and it felt rhetorical but still...

"We've all been there," I assured her because it was the truth.

Annoyance and appreciation battled in her eyes. "In high school, maybe. I'm a grown woman."

I shrugged. "We're all entitled to make mistakes."

She rushed me, pulling me in for a hug that nearly knocked me off my feet. "Thank you."

We left the bathroom together, to find Carter and Beck on opposite sides of the hallway, Carter on his phone and Beck surveilling the room around him.

Delaney flashed me one last smile before catching up with Carter who boasted a confused look on his face.

When there was a safe distance between us and them, I discreetly pinched Beck's ass. "You let her follow me into that bathroom."

He pushed off the wall. "I figured I'd come in if I heard shouting."

"Ppft. Some bodyguard you are."

He threaded a hand in mine and kissed me gently on my cheek. "A true bodyguard knows when to step in and when to let things be."

"That's a really annoying and noble trait you have there."

"Don't I know it."

I gripped his hand tighter. "And if it had been Carter to follow me into that bathroom?"

He gave a sharp shake of his head. "I'd never allow that to happen."

Beck squeezed my hand reassuringly and didn't let go even as we entered the limo for the short ride home. The car rocked back and forth as our driver navigated the city streets. There was a quiet comfort between us, our hands still threaded together. Without second guessing myself, I placed my head on his shoulder, enjoying the comfort he was offering me. The adrenaline from the bathroom situation ran its course and yet my body buzzed from the proximity.

When we pulled up in front of our townhouses, he placed a kiss on the top of my head. "We're home."

Without so much as a discussion, Beck led me up the stairs of my town house.

I punched the code, and the door opened with a click. Beck held it open for me as I entered, immediately kicking off my heels. My feet finally had a chance to breathe.

"Do you want some water or anything to drink?" I asked as I removed my earrings and set them on the hallway console.

Beck shook his head, his eyes darkening as he took me in. "I have an idea."

My eyes flitted down to where the outline of his cock was threatening to rip his pants. I sank into my hip. "Is that so?"

He licked his lips and began stalking toward me. On instinct, I backed up, my ass hitting the console and sending it rocking.

Beck stalked closer, staring at me as electricity bounced between us.

My core ached.

God, I want this man.

I wanted him desperately.

Beck pulled something silver from the pocket inside his suit jacket.

My jaw dropped to the floor. "Handcuffs?"

Don't get me wrong, I'd tried them before, but it had been a while.

Beck gently encircled my wrist, turning my hand up and placing the metal bands into my palm. "You're going to tie me up and do whatever the fuck you want with me."

I gulped. A little thrill zinged between my legs as I examined the handcuffs.

The man was serving himself up on a silver platter.

My heart thumped in my chest. The anxiety that had arisen the last time we tried to have sex was nowhere to be seen.

"Yes," I said, nearly breathless. Rather than cower, I threw my shoulders back feeling more myself.

I tugged him toward the bedroom, and he let me push him onto the bed.

I tossed the handcuffs from one hand to another deciding what I was going to do with him. "Scoot back and put your hands on the bedposts."

Beck's dick twitched. He was just as into this as I was.

The glint in his eyes remained as I grabbed his hand and

locked him to the bedpost. Painfully slow, I crawled over him, rather than walking around the bed.

He hissed. "You're a fucking tease."

I nipped at his ear as my hands clicked the other cuff into place. "You love it."

The cuffs rattled as he pulled against them, testing them. "I think we're good."

I sank back onto my heels. Beck had a devious smile on his face as if he couldn't wait to get started.

"I'm all yours," he said, his voice like gravel.

My dress pooled around me. Unfortunately, I couldn't get the zipper without his assistance. But there was something that I could do. I got out of bed and slowly bent over, giving Beck a view of my ass while my hands slid under my dress, removing my barely there thong. He might as well enjoy the show.

Beck inhaled sharply, his gaze locked on the wisp of fabric.

I stood up, capturing his complete attention. "Want this?" I twirled the thing before dragging it up his chest and flicking it away.

"Told you you were a tease," he said with a smirk.

Like me, he was woefully overdressed. I climbed back on the bed, lifting my dress to make it easier to straddle him.

The cuffs rattled.

I wagged a finger at him. "Naughty, naughty."

"Your naked cunt is on my waist, and as much as I love it, I'd love it more if my hands were on your waist while I piston into you, so I could watch those gorgeous tits bounce as I make you come."

Fuck if that filthy mouth of his didn't make me even slicker.

My hands found the hard planes of his chest. Then I began unbuttoning his dress shirt. He'd shucked his coat off earlier and now he was there, his olive skin beneath my hands. He was mine for the taking.

Beck looked like he should be on the cover of a romance novel. His muscles flexed under my fingers and his cock twitched beneath me.

My nails pressed lightly into his skin. "Patience, Bennet."

"It's hard to be patient while you're touching my body, Marks," Beck grumbled.

"I'm taking my time, and you'll have to deal with it."

My hands explored more, venturing further south.

I palmed his length through his dress pants, and Beck emitted a hiss.

The sound of him wanting me drove me onward. Had I ever been so nervous *and* excited?

Blood pumped through my veins as I released the metal buckle of his leather belt. The button came next, and then down went the zipper.

It had been dark when I'd gone down on him the other night and I was desperate to see him again. I stood mesmerized as his cock sprang free of the confines of his pants.

Fuck. He was glorious. Hard, thick, and straining. I would need a warm up first.

I licked my palm before wrapping a hand around his length and pumping it slowly, teasing him.

"Christ, Luna. You have no fucking idea how good that feels." His eyes fluttered shut as I added a second hand, my grip tightening.

Then I stopped.

Beck's eyes flew open. "What the—"

"My turn."

Beck relaxed. "Fuck, yes."

"I want to feel good, Bennet."

He nodded. "Let me make you feel good."

I suppressed a smirk. "I was thinking…"

"Whatever you want. Name it."

"I want your mouth on me."

He nodded, eyes darkening. "Come sit on my face. I can't wait to taste you again."

My heart pounded a little harder. I climbed up his chest, feeling sexy and powerful as I hovered over him. My knees on either side of his face.

Beck wasted no time. He took his wide tongue and dragged it slowly across my seam. I quivered, barely keeping myself upright.

"Careful," he warned. "Come closer. Sit on my face."

My legs wavered, the strain of trying to hold myself up. "I can't actually sit on your face."

"Do it."

I rolled my eyes, leaning into him as his tongue ran along my lips before plunging into me.

I tilted my head to my chest. "Fuck."

He licked and sucked like his life depended on it. Until my legs were shaking and the orgasm I so desperately wanted was on the horizon.

Then I shattered.

I trembled as waves of pleasure roiled through my body. Not until every wave passed, did I sit back, giving Beck room to breathe.

The evidence of my arousal sat on his lips. He nodded. "You going to take care of that?"

I reached behind me to find him even harder than before. With my body relaxed and still ready for more, I eagerly climbed backward, hoisting myself up so I hovered right above the tip of him.

"Do it."

I felt the blunt head of his penis searching for purchase.

I hesitated. "We don't have a condom."

His stormy eyes swept down my body. "Are you on the pill?"

I nodded. "IUD. And I'm clean."

"So am I, get the fuck on—"

I sank onto him. Despite his size, my body was ready for him. My hands found his chest again as I shifted my hips, adjusting and savoring the feeling of him inside me.

It had been years since I'd been like this. Since *we'd* been like this.

My eager hips began to rock.

Beck hissed. "Fuck, yes. Use my cock, Luna. It's all for you."

I picked up my pace, lifting higher and slamming down on him. My nails dragged against Beck's bare skin.

I threw my head back, so close to another orgasm I could hardly stand it.

"You take me so good." He'd let me take the lead but as I slowed down, he took over, pistoning into me. The angle was just right, and I found it impossible to catch my breath.

This man. This man.

I fell forward to kiss him as he took over the hard part, his cock hitting exactly where I needed him. I chased my second orgasm of the night just as he reached his.

My muscles finally gave in, and I laid flat out across Beck.

The cuffs rattled. "You have no idea how much I want to hold you right now."

I began drawing circles on his chest. "Wow. Just wow."

His muscles relaxed underneath me, his cock still semi hard. "You're wow."

I pushed back my damp hair. "Next time, we'll try it without the cuffs."

Beck shrugged as if he really would do it this way all the time if that's all I had to offer him. If that's all I would ever be ready for. "Ladies choice."

CHAPTER 35

Luna

PARVATI

> The city processed the permit. Whatever magic you worked sealed the deal.

I PLACED the phone face down on my lap, replaying the ugly scene in the bathroom from the other night.

I'd barely even remembered it since the after party in my bedroom had been a delicious distraction.

Now, with the text in black and white, all I could do was shake my head. Delaney was withholding the permit because of me and my past relationship with her boyfriend who she was convinced still wanted me.

That solved that mystery.

But, *damn.* And all because of a man I didn't even want.

I inhaled deeply, counting slowly to eight as I released my breath through my mouth.

At least that was over. I wanted to roll my eyes, but I decided to take the win with as much grace as I could muster.

"Can we stop at a coffee shop on the way to the club?," I asked as we drove. "The Coffee Library is around the corner."

"Yes, ma'am." Darnell put on his blinker.

It had been two days since the gala. Two days since Beck let me use his body, handing over the control on a silver platter. I couldn't quite believe that I'd finally broken the seal. I'd finally had sex after so many years of celibacy, of playing it safe. Of protecting my body and my soul.

And of course I'd broken that spell with *him*. My body still ached from our joining. It had been a shock to the system and my system was still trying to figure out how it felt.

If I closed my eyes, I could still feel him inside me. Could feel him throbbing, aching, and releasing inside me.

To see his cum slide down my thigh afterward... I don't think I'll forget that anytime soon.

Eventually, I released him from the cuffs, gently kissing the angry red marks circling his wrists.

Beck had made it very clear he didn't give two shits about his wrists.

Like magnets, our bodies found each other in the middle of the night. Beck finally gave up on the ruse of trying to build a wall between us.

I woke up with my hand on his cock. His very hard, long, girthy cock. My kitty clenched, wanting more. Wanting all of him. I was fucking ready to go.

Beck hesitated, still treating me with kid gloves despite our evening activities. Then he slipped out at the crack of dawn, placing a quick kiss on my lips and darting back to his place before Alice got up.

The next night we spent at his house, just holding each other. He didn't want to push it and while my body craved his, we didn't have a repeat performance.

It was almost as if we both knew that we needed to have deeper discussions before that happened.

PARVATI

Did you get the latest designs for the restaurant?

Ahh, work. Where I needed to focus my attention.

LUNA

Not yet. I'll review them ASAP.

PARVATI

Faith helped a lot. I just glanced at them and the mock up is a huge improvement over last time.

LUNA

Thanks for flagging.

Parvati sent a photo of the construction site. These daily pictures quelled my nerves, alleviating some of the pressure on my shoulders. At this point the changes were significant.

I closed my eyes, took some deep, centering breaths and realized that I felt good.

No migraine on the horizon. No increased heart rate associated with my tremendous workload. The only flutter I detected was courtesy of one Beck Bennet.

BECK

Want to have dinner with Alice and I today? She's requested Hawaiian pizza.

LUNA

I thought I taught her that pineapple wasn't the best topping for pizza.

BECK

Turns out kids like what they like. In fact, sometimes they dig their heels in even deeper when you suggest they like something.

I smiled.

LUNA

Ahh, that's where I went wrong. I didn't play it cool enough. I made too big of a deal of her liking pineapple on her pizza.

BECK

Exactly. Now it's bound to remain her favorite and I'll forever need to order a second pizza with toppings I like.

LUNA

Seems like a you problem

BECK

So, dinner? We plan to eat at six.

I opened my calendar. Tonight was college night at the club, which meant we didn't have a lot of VIPs that required my attention. It did mean that I wanted to sweep to check out the floor and make sure our safety procedures were on lock, but that didn't require me until way past dinner time.

LUNA

Count me in.

BECK

Alice can't wait to see you.

LUNA

And what about Alice's father?

BECK

I'll have to ask him.

LUNA

BECK

I'd be happier if YOU were dinner.

An image from the other night popped in my head. Beck devouring me like a starved man. I could only imagine what he would have been like had I granted him full use of his hands. He'd probably crush me to him, kneading my ass as he held me against his tongue.

I found myself instantly slick. If I touched my cheeks, I'm sure I'd find them flushed. Not great timing, considering I was on my way to work and had no way of alleviating the ache.

LUNA

If you're good, you can have me for dessert.

BECK

Is that a promise?

LUNA

Only if you make it worth my while.

Rather than a responding text, my phone began to ring with Beck's name flashing across the screen.

I answered on the first ring. "Well, hello."

Beck grunted. "You're sleeping in my bed tonight. Don't think I didn't notice that you left in the middle of the night."

I slunk down in my seat, as Darnell pulled up to The Coffee Library. He exited the car to give me some privacy.

"And here I thought you were calling to explain how you were going to make it worth my while."

"If you want to wake up with my head between your thighs, you're going to need to stay the night. I changed my mind. I don't just want you for dessert, I want you for breakfast too."

I tugged on my silk blouse. "You drive a hard bargain, Bennet."

"That's not the only thing that's hard," he said, his voice low.

I frowned. "Where are you?"

He chuckled. "The office stairwell. You were teasing me in the middle of a meeting. I had to excuse myself."

I tucked a piece of hair behind my ear. "You're obsessed with me."

"I am," he said with a seriousness that hadn't been in his voice just a few seconds earlier.

I unbuckled myself and sat forward, hand on the passenger seat in front of me. "You really like me, don't you?"

"I think it's a little deeper than that," he confided, his voice serious.

My throat constricted. "For me too."

It was the closest we'd come to saying I love you. The words were on the tip of my tongue. I definitely didn't want to say them for the first time on the phone.

No, those words should be shared in person. They were precious. And I'd never said them to a partner. Ever.

For the first time ever, I wanted to. But in person. Not over the phone.

Beck cleared his throat. "Alice keeps asking me if we're together."

That warmed my heart. I loved that pineapple-pizza-loving kiddo. "And what do you tell her?"

He sighed. "I tell her I need to talk to you."

This man. This bossy, annoying man who thinks he knows what's best for me drew the line here because he knew it was important to me.

I pretended to scoff. "You don't just make up an answer? I'm shocked, Beck Bennet."

He hummed, like he could see through my bullshit. "And what, exactly, would you have me say?"

Playful banter. We fell back into our playful banter despite the heaviness in the air. A raw and real conversation that needed to be had.

I couldn't do this now. Not over the phone.

So I hung up on him. Oops.

CHAPTER 36

Beck

MY NEW CELEBRITY CLIENT, Tyler James, turned out to be a real asshole.

It happened. More often than I'd like to admit. Luckily, I knew how to handle it, and I taught my team the same thing. We were not there to be "yes" people. To jump and take care of all the wants and wishes of our clients.

No. We were there to protect. Not to be a glorified assistant.

We were there to protect our clients at all costs. That level of commitment demanded respect.

Tyler balked at the idea of Margot as part of his detail. And if he didn't get on board and show her some respect, then I would refuse to work with him. I had no capacity for bullshit.

I explained all of this very clearly up front with any new client, and sometimes it bears repeating. If it continued, I could preemptively end our contract and have them pay me out for breaching our agreement.

Usually that little threat cleared things up real nice. I took the integrity of my business seriously and nobody would want to work for me if they thought clients could get away with their bullshit.

"Beck, you have your next client here to see you," my assistant announced.

"Send them in." I scrubbed a hand down my face. It was going to be one of those days. I hadn't even had my second cup of coffee yet and shit was already hitting the fan.

I'd slept like shit after Luna snuck out of my bed in the middle of the night.

I watched her from my bedroom window as she went out the back door and crossed into her house using that connecting gate. The one she hated with a passion of a thousand suns and yet made her little early morning escape route extra easy and made me worry just a little less.

Someone knocked on my open door.

I stood, expecting to see my ten o'clock. It was just Sebastian.

"What the hell are you doing here?" I got up and shook his hand, bringing him in for a quick pat on the back.

"Do you have a minute?"

I lifted a finger. "Let me just che—"

"Your meeting got moved to next week. You're free," my assistant yelled from just outside my office.

"Well that clears that up." I shut the door. "Tell me what brings you here. Is everything okay with Faith?"

Sebastian revealed a small smile. "She's great. I'm actually here to invite you to her next show."

I lifted a brow. "You want me to go to an art show? Is there another security threat?"

I mentally flipped through my list of staff who might be able to make it happen depending on when the event took place. It wasn't ideal, but in a pinch I could step in.

Sebastian held up his hands. "Nothing like that. Things have settled down now with the press. Turns out, it's not very exciting to report on Faith now that she's busy upstate painting and being a dog mom."

I settled back in my chair, happy to hear that. More importantly, I was glad my friend was letting up a little. He took his partner's safety so seriously that I worried for them at times.

Not that I'd ever say that to his face.

If caring for Luna had taught me anything, it's that loving someone can make you do crazy things.

Like right now I was running through my mind all the ways I could convince her to move in with me and Alice.

I stood. "Let's get coffee."

Sebastian gave me an odd look. "Sure."

When we got to the street, I shoved my hands in my pockets.

Sebastian glanced at me curiously. "You're quiet. You're never quiet."

We headed toward the nearest coffee shop, and I ordered two cold brews without bothering to ask Sebastian for his order since he usually drank the same thing as me.

I dropped into a chair at the only remaining table and Sebastian raised a brow. "What the hell is going on with you? I've never seen you like this."

My elbows hit the tabletop. "I slept with Luna."

Sebastian choked on his drink.

"I'm in love with her." It felt good to share this with my friend. Cathartic even.

Sebastian nabbed a napkin from the holder in the center of the table and started cleaning up the mess he made. "I don't understand."

I lifted my head. "I thought I was very clear."

Sebastian crumpled up the coffee-soaked napkin. "I'm not sure why you think this is big news. Everyone knows you're in love with Luna Marks."

I frowned. "Everyone?"

He nodded emphatically. "Everyone."

"What about Dominic and Daisy?" I hadn't spent much time with them recently.

Sebastian tilted his head.

"Fuck, really?"

Sebastian laughed as he sipped his drink. "You guys have been bickering like a married couple since you reconnected."

"We barely bicker anymore."

My friend shook his head. "Not true. Last time we were all together you were going back and forth. I hadn't realized I'd purchased tickets to a tennis match."

"We're neighbors."

Sebastian stared at me like I'd grown a second head. "Again, I know this."

"I bought that house because I wanted to be near her."

Sebastian waved his hand. "Again, you're just stating the obvious."

I leaned forward. "Is that not a little crazy?"

"Why are you second guessing this now? I've never heard you unsure of anything. You're the surest person I've ever met. It's annoying really."

I ignored that last little comment. "We slept together. It's more real now. I'd completely put that part of me on pause after Alice was born. I hadn't so much as looked at anyone else. Then she reappears in my life—"

"And you do everything you can to be near her." Sebastian stated the obvious.

"Be near her. Antagonize her," I countered.

But he plowed right ahead. "*Protect* her. *Care* for her."

We sat in silence for a few long seconds.

"What if I'm not enough?" I asked quietly.

Sebastian fully glared at me. "You can't be serious?"

I waved a hand in the air. "I have a child."

Sebastian blinked. "And has Luna ever given any indication that she has a problem with you being a single dad? That she doesn't like Alice?"

I almost flinched. "Hell, no. She's great with Alice, even if she doesn't think she is. My daughter adores her."

"Then what the fuck is the problem? Luna is a grown woman, with a life and a career. She doesn't do anything half assed, and she's one of my best friends. I'm going to let you have whatever the fuck this is, this doubt for just a second, and then I need you snap the fuck out of it. This is Luna we're talking about. The woman you never forgot about. The woman of your literal dreams."

I scrubbed a hand down my face. "You're right. It's just the sex. It made it real. It made it—"

"You won't lose her again, Beck. As long as you treat her well, and be patient with her, just like you already are, you'll be just fine. I promise."

My heart thudded painfully in my chest. The idea of living another day without Luna would physically pain me. The idea of losing her forever would be unfathomable. "How can you be so sure?"

He shrugged. "Because Faith can tell, and I trust her. And because I've seen you and Luna together."

His confident response immediately dissolved the panic.

I hadn't experienced this level of uncertainty since Alice was born and I was left with a newborn and no clue how to take care of her. I now had a second chance with the woman I loved, and I would do everything in my power not to fuck it up.

"She's coming over for dinner tonight with me and Alice."

Sebastian shrugged. "You've had dinner with her before."

"This feels different."

He clapped me on the back. "Do yourself a favor, and don't overthink it. Just spend time with her, enjoy it, and see what happens."

"I want to marry her," I said just as Sebastian was taking a sip of his drink.

He spat it out all over me.

I snagged some napkins from the center of the table and began wiping away the worst of it. Well, there goes my white shirt. "What the fuck, man?"

Sebastian wiped his face. "Sorry about that. I know you've been in love with Luna for all these years, I just wasn't expecting marriage yet. Took me by surprise."

"You're not the only one who wants marriage, my friend." Sebastian would have put a ring on Faith's finger months ago if she'd have let him.

"We've never talked about it."

Sebastian tilted his head as if he was carefully considering my words. "To be fair, you're just getting to know each other again."

"I feel like I know her, and I like what I know."

Sebastian released a rare laugh. "Then take care of her, wait for her, and everything will be alright."

CHAPTER 37

Luna

NOTHING WAS GOING RIGHT.

Parvati rang to tell me there was an actual shipping issue with the materials for the restaurant. We hopped on a quick call with the designer to figure out a workaround.

Then I got caught in an ungodly amount of traffic. Traffic in Manhattan was usually terrible and just doubly worse today for no apparent reason.

To make matters worse, I was about to take my therapy session from the back of the town car because I hadn't made it home in time.

Just wonderful.

"Could you maybe pretend you aren't listening to the conversation I'm about to have?" He'd already overheard so many things over the last two years, I doubted this would be any worse.

Rather than reply, Darnell just kept his face neutral as he stared ahead.

I'll take that as a yes…

I took a few deep, steadying breaths and pressed the *join* button.

I had emailed my therapist earlier asking if they had time

to fit me into today and within minutes her office manager sent over the calendar item with the meeting link.

The second my doctor appeared on the screen I spat out, "I slept with him."

I hadn't even bothered with the usual safe word to kick off the meeting.

Dr. Wozniac blinked twice. "Tell me more."

And where Faith would make it all lascivious, my therapist said it with a level of curiosity and a clinical need to understand that made it easy for me to spill all the beans.

When I finished, I huffed a breath, gasping like I'd run a marathon.

Her lips twitched, and I just knew she was trying to squash any semblance of a smile. "You need some water?"

I waved her off. "I'm good. Just happy to get that off my chest. I've been holding onto it for a few days."

She nodded and wrote something down on that infamous notepad of hers.

What I'd give to get a peek at that journal.

"Now that you've had some space from the encounter, how are you feeling?"

My brows almost flew off my forehead. "Are we calling it *the encounter* now? I love that for us. Sounds fun and sexy and also a little mysterious."

My doctor cleared her throat.

"Right...I'm feeling good. Like I want to do it again."

"And when you imagine doing it again, are there handcuffs?"

"Kinky," I teased, because the truth was I didn't have an answer right away.

She frowned.

Tough crowd.

I closed my eyes, trying to envision us going at it again. This time Beck's hands were on me, holding my hips, cupping my ass, holding my face. I sighed, imagining him threading his hands behind my head as he kissed me.

"Alright, save the full visualization for *after* our session."

My eyes flew open. "*Riiight.*"

Then I glanced around my laptop to check out the expression on Darnell's face.

Still neutral, no look of horror or amusement gracing his face. I made a mental note to double his holiday bonus.

"I'm glad you're open to Beck. It seems like you've made incredible progress. The thing about progress is that it isn't always a straight line. I want you to consider this as you move forward together. It might feel like one step forward..."

"Two steps back." I nodded. "I get it. I'll keep my expectations in check."

Her head tilted to the side. "I want you to be brave and I want you to protect your heart and mind. That's your homework."

I exhaled, letting her words wash over me. It made me feel both lighter and happier. Like I was in control. That feeling of control allowed a calmness to settle over me.

Someone knocked on the car window, making me jump and sending my laptop crashing to the floor.

"Fuck," I swore as I twisted to catch the culprit.

Alice was on the other side of the glass, her broad, gap-toothed smile greeting me. "Hurry up, the pizza's here!" Then she darted up the short set of stairs leading to her brownstone.

"Well, that's one way to end a call." Sure enough, the sudden laptop closure ended my call with Dr. Wozniac. I shot her a quick message on my phone letting her know I was just fine using my safe phrase, then tucked the phone back in my bag.

I collected my things and got out. "Thanks, Darnell. I'll see you in the morning."

"Night, Luna. You take care now."

My body automatically has me moving towards my brownstone, although a small part of me wants to go directly next door. I decided to drop off my things and make my way next door through our secret passage in the backyard.

Alice must have known I would do that because the second I crossed over into their backyard, she popped her head out the French doors of their house and waved at me. "Hurry. Daddy said it's getting cold."

Daddy.

Beck Bennet. Despite all the time we'd spent together, the man still made me feel like there were tiny acrobats performing in my belly.

I was a badass at business and needed to channel that energy into telling Beck I wanted him and only him.

In fact, it has always been him.

I wiped my hands down the front of my skirt which was a bad idea seeing that it was leather.

Then Bruce slowly sidled up to me. The dog might not be old, but he gave wise old pooch energy.

"Hi, sweetheart," I cooed as I patted the top of his head. I made a mental note to call Harper to see how Pepper was doing. I couldn't stop thinking about that pup.

Alice patted the top of his head. "He wants pizza."

My eyes met hers. "Are you saying Bruce is trying to butter me up?"

She nodded in agreement, but her facial expression made it clear she didn't know the idiom. "It means he's being extra nice so that I give him pizza."

Alice smiled. "Oh, yeah, then he's definitely buttering you up."

My lips twitched and my gaze found Beck's and he held it, sharing that small moment.

"Can we *please* eat now?" Alice asked, exasperated.

Beck tilted his head. "Wash your hands. Pizza's on the table."

"Yes!" She ran down the hall and I heard a faucet turn on.

"She's excited," I said on a laugh.

Beck put a hand out and lifted me to my feet, tugging me into his chest. Our bodies met.

"I'm excited too," he said, leaning in close before planting a kiss behind my ear.

I sighed.

As Alice bounded back into the room, I stepped back, unsure where exactly Beck and I stood with our relationship. Those three little words I still needed to say were caught in my throat.

We sat together, the three of us, enjoying the pizza, as Alice talked about the new girl in her class who just moved from California and how fun it would be if she lived in California because that's where Disneyland is.

"We can go to Disneyland for spring break next year. How does that sound?" he asked his daughter while I watched, enamored with the two of them.

Alice shot out of her chair to hug her dad, forcing him to drop the pepperoni pizza he was about to take a bite of, the red sauce splattering everywhere.

I tossed a napkin at him, watching as he attempted to clean up the mess.

"How about you, Marks? Are you in for a trip to the happiest place on Earth?"

I choked on my pizza. The hacking and coughing lasted an exponentially long time, so long that Beck's grin slid off his face and he started clapping me on the back. "You okay? Alice, get her some water, please."

Alice reluctantly set down her slice and got me a glass of water.

"Thanks," I said with a cough.

Alice and Beck remained waiting for my response. The little girl even started patting my back. "You should come with us. It will be way more fun than with just Daddy."

Beck's eyes were tuned to me as I mulled over the invite. To be invited to something so far in the future, it could only mean one thing.

It meant…

Well, it meant everything. It meant this wasn't temporary and since I'd only lived and thrived in the temporary, I wasn't quite sure how to handle it.

He must have picked up on my internal turmoil because he didn't press me in the moment.

Instead, Beck reached over and began tickling his daughter. "What am I, chopped liver?"

Alice giggled. "You're fine, Daddy."

Beck gave an exaggerated gasp. "Just fine?"

She squirmed out of Beck's grasp and ran around the table. "Daddy no tickling at the dinner table. Someone could get hurt."

He held up his hands in capitulation. "You're right, no more tickles….for now."

Alice side-eyed her dad, as I worked through some shit methodically chewing each bite of pizza I was putting in my mouth not because I was hungry but because I wanted to keep busy.

Beck continued to eat, asking Alice questions about her day, effectively moving us onto the next topic of conversation. The way his gaze kept drifting back to mine, I knew he would ask about it later.

I just hoped I'd have an answer for him.

———

"She's finally asleep," Beck said, as he plopped down on the couch next to me.

I turned to face him, lifting my legs to put them in his lap. He began absently rubbing my calves which were hurting from my most recent run. I groaned as his strong hands worked the muscles. "Please don't stop doing what you're doing."

His deep chuckle settled over me, so I closed my eyes and leaned back against the edge of the couch, adjusting the pillow behind me for maximum comfort. "Does Alice usually require two dozen books before bed?"

I'd gone upstairs to help with the bedtime routine at Alice's insistence. It had been the kind of domestic activity I'd never taken part of, and I found myself enjoying every minute of it. But I hadn't been prepared for it, that was for sure. Parents deserved gold medals for surviving the bedtime routine on a nightly basis. It certainly wasn't for the faint of heart.

"It goes in waves but yes, lately it's about squeezing as many books out of me as possible. Until her lids are so heavy that she passes out mid story."

"That's my kind of girl. I need to work on my reading stamina. I was on the verge of losing my voice after thirty minutes of reading aloud. Besides, my bladder was screaming at me." I'd gone to the bathroom and peeked back into the room to find Beck cuddled up with Alice, struggling to keep her eyes open as her dad read the same book for the third time in a row.

I'd been very tempted to crawl into bed with them, but I thought better of it. It was their bubble, and I didn't want to break it. Besides, I wanted a minute to myself to think about Beck's offer to go to Disneyland. To travel with them and make future plans with them. I just needed a minute to consider all of it.

He continued to massage my calves. "In the future, you should use the bathroom *before* we start story time..."

In the future. Did he know how that statement squeezed my heart?

Beck shook his head. "Pitiful. How do I know you even needed to use the restroom? You could have been faking it."

I playfully pushed him. "Oh, please. You're just jealous you didn't think of it sooner."

His hands stopped. "That's probably it."

"Aha, I knew it," I said smugly. "It's hard to have both beauty and brains, you know."

"Now you're just pushing it," he said as his hands wandered higher.

I swallowed. "I'll have to buy her some *Little House on the Prairie* books. I loved those when I was her age. Well, maybe a little older. I wonder where my copies are."

Beck hummed. "Chapter books are a good idea."

His strong hands kneaded my thighs, working their way up from my knee to the juncture between my thighs. They grazed, teasing and taunting. I tossed my head back, closing my eyes to feel the sensations. To have them overwhelm my good senses.

All thought of books poofed from my brain like some fairy had come and waved them away with a wand.

All that mattered was Beck and his fingers which were occasionally grazing my clit, igniting my nerve endings.

"Definitely keep doing that." My knees draped open. The more access I could give him, the better. Not that he needed any help on that front. The man knew how to play my body like it was his own personal instrument.

I only had to let him. And I *was* going to let him.

"Beck," I moaned, loving the feel of his strong hands that were so confident in their movements. So assured.

When his thumb brushed over that bundle of nerves I shifted, trying to recreate the movement because once wasn't enough. After so many years of getting pleasure only from myself, my body finally let someone else do the hard work.

I licked my lips as Beck's hand dipped beneath the band of my tights. My breath hitched. In fact, I'm pretty sure I stopped breathing, waiting to see what happened next.

His broad hand pushed past the tight elastic, dragging

along my pelvis until he was cupping me. I mewled, the excitement building inside me as he adjusted himself. With my eyelids shut I could still sense him moving between my legs, his body facing mine.

I pouted when his hands slipped out, leaving me wanting more. Luckily, I didn't have to wait long before his hands found my hips, tugging the sides of my tights. "Let's get these fucking things off you."

"Yes, please," I whispered breathlessly.

I wriggled, helping Beck shuck off the offending fabric.

"I officially have a love-hate relationship with leggings and tights. How pissed would you be if I ripped these off?"

If they hadn't been my most comfortable and most expensive pair, I'd give him carte blanche. But these were a special pair of tights and despite trying to chase an orgasm, I couldn't throw them away for the sake of some temporary pleasure.

"I'll handle it." I grabbed them myself and pulled them the rest of the way off, tossing them haphazardly off the side of the couch.

By the time we successfully removed the tights, the two of us were panting like we'd run the NYC marathon.

Our eyes collided, and I watched as Beck's lip twitched.

A laugh burst from my chest and in return Beck's lip twitch escalated into raucous laughter. Then we glanced down at the black tights on the ground, and back at each other.

The laughing continued, Beck dipping his head to meet mine. "Those fucking tights."

Finally, the laughter died when Beck's lips claimed mine.

CHAPTER 38

Beck

I STARTED SMALL. One kiss, then two, my tongue exploring her mouth just like it was going to explore her pussy in a few minutes.

Her hands roamed over my shoulders, drawing me closer. With us lying on the couch like this, I was careful not to hurt her, my size never more apparent than when there was little room for me to go.

And under normal circumstances I'd throw her over my shoulder and carry her to my bedroom, but I didn't want to break our spell. I selfishly couldn't wait to taste her again.

Luna went for the hem of my shirt, lifting it as high as she could without breaking the kiss. When she started struggling, I pulled away to finish the job, tossing the black tee on top of her tights.

It's then I got a better glance of her underwear. Not that you could call them that. Underwear suggested that something was covered. That wasn't the case here, not with the wisp of fabric that stood between me and Luna's cunt.

"Fuck, Marks," I hissed, pushing back so I could get a better look at her. She let a leg fall to the ground, not a hint of reticence or fear or anything that might make me second guess my next action.

I bent down and dragged my tongue along the wisp of lace. "These are pretty. Are they for me?"

Through hooded lids, Luna nodded.

I pushed the offending fabric to the side so I could get a better look. Then I watched as she bit down on her plum-stained lips, and my cock instantly hardened.

Once again her head fell back, her red hair swaying in the most beautiful way.

"Come here, gorgeous." I dragged her toward me and began to feast on her. She tasted better than I remembered. I sucked on her clit as I plunged two fingers inside of her. Luna's hips lifted, as if seeking more.

All those years apart, and it was her I thought of when I closed my eyes and fisted myself. Now I had her again, all to myself.

She whimpered, grinding herself against my mouth, chasing her own pleasure. It made me harder than I thought was possible.

"Beck, I need you. All of you. *Now*."

I peeled back. "Luna—"

"Beck—" Her voice was firm. "I need your cock."

Her hips were desperately shifting as I pulled back, taking my pants off. My cock sprung to life and Luna's hungry eyes only served to make it harder.

I hovered over her, ready to take her. "If you want me to stop—"

Her eyes softened, but her words challenged me. "Not this again."

"Yes, this again. I feel your body react to mine and you know I always want you, always crave you. And if you're not feeling the same way, consciously or if your body is telling you otherwise, then we stop. No questions. No awkwardness."

Luna's eyes roamed my torso, and her fingers trailed the grooves on my abs before her gaze cut back to mine. "Let me make this crystal clear. I want you to fuck me, Beck Bennet."

The invisible leash broke. I pulled her on me, so she was sitting pretty in my lap, hair mussed, and writhing on top of me.

"You still get control. I just get to hold you while you take the reins," I told her.

Her arms dropped over my shoulders as I ran a finger through her pussy, testing to see how ready she was for me and pleased to find her drenched. "You're dripping all over me, Marks."

My dick twitched beneath her.

"Then why don't you do something about it?" she taunted.

Without thinking twice, I gave my dick a few slow tugs, watching Luna's mesmerized face.

"Ride me," I commanded.

She bit her lips, nodding as if in a trance, then shifted her hips, dragging the head of my dick through her lips, achingly slow. Her hands found purchase on my shoulders, her fingers digging in, claiming me.

I reached between us, aligning myself with her entrance. And when she plunged down on me, I hissed, my hands grabbing the flair of her hips.

My eyes were glued to her breasts as she started to rise and fall, finding her rhythm. I pulled her tight to me as her hips picked up speed. Luna burrowed her face in my neck, her little noises driving me damn near over the edge.

Suddenly, I couldn't take it anymore, and I fully took over, my hips speeding up to meet her thrust for thrust, my hand sliding between us to stroke her clit as I started pulsing inside her. My orgasm triggered her own.

When our bodies finally calmed down, I noticed each of us had a sleek sheen of sweat.

"That wa—-" Luna shook her head.

I nipped at her lips. "Incredible."

She sighed. "It was okay."

I chuckled at her audacity. I lifted her up and smacked her ass for her sass. She squealed as I lifted her over my shoulder in a fireman's hold and crossed the room.

She slapped my ass back. "And where the hell do you think you're taking me, sir?"

I palmed her ass and thought of all the little things I wanted to do to it. "Don't sir me if you want to get any rest tonight. And you're a dirty little thing; you need a shower."

Her hands flattened against my back holding her steady as I carefully took the stairs. "Don't threaten me with a good time."

We both quieted as we passed Alice's room, but once I closed my door, it was fair game.

"You can put me down, you know," Luna teased as we passed the bed.

I shook my head before remembering she couldn't see my face. "Not a chance."

With the flick of the light switch the bathroom illuminated, the settings programmed for low lighting given the time of day—or night—in this case.

I turned on the shower and finally decided to put down my captive. Luna's palms found my torso once again, and she leaned in. "You might want to take off your socks."

Then she patted my cheek and entered through the glass door separating us from the rainfall showerhead.

In a few swift movements, my socks were off, and I joined her. My hands found her body wet and wanting.

Luna handed over a bar of soap. "If you're going to put your hands on me, you might as well make yourself useful."

"Gladly," I said, eager for any excuse to keep my hands on her. I lathered the bar and dragged my hands over her body, starting with her breasts, kneading them as I did. Luna groaned and leaned back into my touch, her head against my chest and eyes closed as I played with her, moving one hand down the flat plane of her stomach to touch the sensitive flesh between her legs.

She squirmed against me as I dragged a finger through her flesh.

"I'm still sore," she whispered loud enough for me to hear her over the sound of the water pouring over us.

I nipped her ear. "Want me to stop?"

Her hand banded around my wrist. "Don't stop."

I didn't stop until after she screamed my name, as if it were a prayer on her lips.

CHAPTER 39
Luna

WE SWEPT past the security guard and into the gallery in SoHo. In the last few months, it had become the place for up-and-coming artists, Faith Waters included. From what Beck relayed to me, it was quite the madhouse the first time Faith showed here. Thankfully, this time there weren't any paparazzi stalking my best friend outside.

I bounced on my heels. "I can't wait to find Faith. She's been a nervous wreck all week even though she has no reason to be."

Her work was stunning, and she had a wait-list a mile long. And she knew it.

I expected everything to go off without a hitch, but even someone as talented as Faith could get nervous before a big launch. Especially when the unveil was something as personal and vulnerable as art.

My phone buzzed in the pocket of my skirt. I winced but looked at the screen anyway.

PARVATI

You've been missing out on the progress this week. We have some decisions to make, and I want you here in person for them.

LUNA

I'll be there in the morning. Darnell assured me the car is gassed up and ready to go.

PARVATI

Tell D I'm going to have a coffee ready for him.

LUNA

D???

Since when do YOU call Darnell D?

How did I miss this?

PARVATI

Since you decided to go above and beyond schmoozing all the inspectors after their last visit. D and I had a good chat while you were preoccupied.

LUNA

Is there something going on between you and "D"?

Because I'm fully supportive if that's the case.

Darnell was a young widower. He was steadfast, dependable, and just the nicest guy.

PARVATI

No comment.

LUNA

OMG now I really need to know. I'm 100% grilling you on this when I see you tomorrow. Consider yourself warned.

Then I stashed my phone away and reached for Beck's hand. He was there in an instant, his grip firm in mine.

Not realizing I even had tension there, my shoulders relaxed at his touch as I searched the packed room for Faith.

A crowd gave away her position.

"This way." I tugged on Beck's hand, and he let me tow him over to where Faith was enchanting a group of art enthusiasts. Giving her space to connect with her fans, we sidled up to Sebastian, both of us greeting him with a hug.

"Your girl is popular," Beck said with a nod.

With a look of pure adoration, Sebastian smiled. "She is."

"And for good reason," I chimed in, feeling left out. The gallery walls were covered with Faith's latest collection. A literal urban jungle. "Actually this might be fun for my office at Club Deux."

"Good luck with that," Sebastian said. "She's already sold everything in the room and the people surrounding her are begging to get on a wait-list."

Maybe I should throw my name in the ring too.

Sebastian asked Beck how Alice was adjusting to life with Bruce, asking to stop by for a visit. My friend might be grumpy with people but was a veritable Squishmallow around dogs.

I turned, looking for a place to get drinks when I spotted a familiar face.

She must have felt my attention because her head turned in my direction.

Paige.

My stomach dropped, and I swayed on my feet.

Beck was there with a steadying hand. "Whoa there."

The man immediately began scanning the room. No doubt he recognized her too. I had no doubt my billionaire bodyguard had done a full search on Paige once I revealed my past with her.

Without looking at him, I reached back to pat his arm. "I'll be right back."

"Do you need me to come with you?" he asked, and I could hear the hint of worry in his tone.

"I've got this," I assured him.

"Okay." He nodded, still assessing the situation in that way of his. "I'm here if you need me."

I dropped my grip. My focus was across the room, completely on the woman I hadn't seen for nearly eight years.

All my usual badassery flew right out the window. Still, I found a kernel of something deep within me to pull my shoulder back and swallow the space between us.

Paige stood there, unmoving, as if trying not to spook me. All I could think was how good it was to see her. Despite my nerves, despite the small lines I could see on her face, the little signs that time had marked us in our years apart, she still looked like the girl I once knew.

I came to a stop just in front of her.

"Hi," she said, her eyes misting.

"Hey." I swallowed.

A silence fell between us, and it was as if the rest of the world had disappeared. Like we were the only two people in the room. There was no time for nerves or fear of what to say. It was just the two of us and for just a second it had felt like no time had passed between us. That comforted me, transporting me back to a place where we'd trusted each other and shared our lives with each other.

"You're still in the city," I commented, not sure where to start.

Paige smiled. "I'm just visiting. I moved back to Connecticut a few years ago and got married. We come to the city every other month for a date night."

My jaw dropped. "Married? Wow!"

An invisible pain lanced through me, and I blinked rapidly, pushing back the tears that threatened to spill. How many times had Paige and I stayed up late talking while she talked about all the things she'd do for her wedding? It had never been a thing I dreamed about, but for her, it was the goal. To date around, have some fun, and then meet her forever person.

She did that, and I wasn't a part of it. Wasn't her maid of honor like we'd talked about all those long nights. Not that I had any right to be after cutting her out so thoroughly.

Paige lifted her left hand, showing off the ring. "His name's Gabe and he loves art. Hence—" she waved her hand around. It reminded me that we were in a public place and what a small world it was to run into her this night of all nights.

"It's beautiful. I'm happy for you." And sorry I wasn't there for you.

She gave me a reserved smile, probably protecting her heart just like I had protected mine.

Like a dam bursting, I spewed out, "I'm sorry."

Paige startled, and on instinct I reached out to her, hands grasping her forearms. "I was a real asshole to you, Paige, and I'm so, so sorry I cut you out like that. You didn't deserve that. You didn't deserve to be punished for something you didn't do."

She shook her head, her short raven hair swishing across her shoulders. "You have nothing to apologize for."

My laugh was borderline maniacal. "I actually do."

Someone bumped into me, and I fell forward. Paige braced me.

The world around me resurfaced. Sure enough we were in the middle of an event. Unlike the *Real Housewives* who always say this isn't the time or place, I worried that this might be my only chance to clear the air. "Can we go somewhere quieter?"

Paige was already scanning the room. "Maybe there's an office we could pop into."

"Let's go look." It didn't take long for us to find a back-room. Paige shut the door behind her and the sudden quiet felt oppressive.

I pointed to a small couch. "I'm going to sit for this."

Paige followed my lead.

My hands were clasped in my lap. If I weren't wearing a tight latex skirt, I'd sit crisscross applesauce and really relax.

Although in this scenario, even the coziest getup probably wouldn't make this conversation easier.

"I'm sorry," we both blurted out in unison.

We devolved into giggles.

I swiped at a rogue tear. "I'm sorry. That night..." I pinched my eyes shut. "That night left a scar so deep that I measured my life in everything that came before it and every-thing that happened after."

Paige nodded solemnly.

"You came *before*. You, and alcohol. I quit both after that night. It completely changed my priorities and how I wanted to walk through this world. I put safety at the forefront and ditched anything I deemed unsafe."

She swallowed, taking in my words. "And I was unsafe for you. I invited him to my apartment and left you alone with him."

My heartbeat kicked into overdrive and my throat was as dry as the Sahara. This conversation activated everything in me.

So I took a deep inhale through my nose and exhaled through my mouth. I didn't worry about how I must have looked to Paige. I'd pull out every tool in my toolbox to work through this moment. Those sessions with Dr. W. weren't all for naught, they were for now, for exactly this moment.

Not just to mentally prepare me for intimacy, but also to have me conquer the inner demons that had left their imprint eight years ago.

I licked my lips and wished for a bottle of water. When

one didn't magically appear, I proceeded on my own. "I did blame you all those years ago, and in the spirit of outrageous honesty, I still blamed you up until last year." I took a steadying breath and continued. "But that was wrong of me. I should've never placed my blame on you. We both went out that night. Neither one of us should have had to worry about what that piece of shit did to me. That was all on him. You couldn't have known that he'd drug me and try to force himself on me. That's on *him*." My arm struck out into the air as if the perpetrator was in the room with us. "It should have never gotten between us and I'm so sorry I misplaced my anger. You were collateral damage."

Tears carved a path down my former best friend's face. She swiped them away. "Damn. I came to this show looking for art and am leaving with a much-needed therapy session."

I dabbed away my tears. "I'd kill for tissue."

"Right? My husband's going to be so worried when he sees me."

"My boyfriend too." The words slid off my tongue like they belonged there.

Paige's eyebrows flew up. "Ohhh, boyfriend. Tell me everything. Do we like him?"

And just like that we fell back into our easy cadence. One conversation didn't solve years of hurt and confusing feelings. It did, however, feel like a heavy weight had been lifted from my shoulders.

We chatted like that for God knows how long. Eventually, a knock on the door interrupted us.

I'm unison, we turned toward the door. In walked Beck and another man who was clearly relieved to see Paige. Her husband, I presume.

No mullet in sight, I couldn't help but notice.

"The event is wrapping up. The host has invited everyone to leave," Beck explained. His expression was neutral, the same one he sometimes takes when talking business. But behind his eyes I could sense the hint of curiosity dashed with concern.

No doubt the man already knew this was Paige. He didn't own a security company for nothing, and he probably did a full background check on every person I'd ever mentioned.

"Right, we should get going then," I said, turning to Paige. Part of me didn't want to leave, but another stronger part of me felt depleted. Like an emotional hangover was already setting in.

"Can I see you again?" Paige asked. "We leave first thing in the morning to go back to Connecticut, but we will be back soon. I'd love to get coffee. Catch up more." She hesitated, her attention drifting towards her husband before coming back to me. "If that's okay with you."

I swiped at another rogue tear. If I didn't stop crying, I'd get another migraine. "Yes, please."

We swapped numbers and hugged. Introductions were exchanged, and I waved goodbye on the sidewalk in front of the gallery while Beck slung an arm around my waist.

I placed a hand over my chest. "My heart is beating a mile a minute."

Beck kissed the top of my head. "I'm proud of you."

I leaned into him, his presence steadying. "I honestly might pass out. That was not how I planned this evening to go."

The conversation, though productive, proved emotionally and physically taxing.

I was thinking about my mushy brain when I stopped in my tracks. Horror rushed through my veins. "Oh my God, I forgot about Faith."

My sudden stop sent Beck barreling forward before he caught himself.

"Everything's fine. We're meeting Faith, Sebastian, and Faith's brother at the after party. Sebastian rented a room because apparently Faith requested tacos," he reassured me.

I nodded absently. "That makes sense. It is Tuesday."

And I couldn't help but feel like I'd just betrayed my best friend with my former best friend.

Beck pulled me tight against him, the maneuver doing its best to reassure me. "Trust me. She won't be mad at you. It's Faith. She'll be so happy you connected with Paige and will probably insist the three of you go out together or visit her upstate. Probably with Dominic's wife too. Total world domination."

A small smile teased my lips. "You're probably right."

"I *am* right. You saw how busy she was. Faith didn't have time for her friends or family at the showing. She was too busy having customers and potential customers fight for the right to get on her waiting list."

I appreciated him trying to make me feel better about this. "As she should be."

While I still wasn't thrilled I hadn't been there for my friend, I decided I would make it up to her someway. Maybe a girl's weekend or I could set her and Sebastian up with a private booth at Club Deux or maybe send a private chef to their apartment the next time they were in town.

Beck tucked me close, his fingers splayed across my abdomen as we walked to our destination.

"I assume you know where we're going?" I asked, keeping in step with him.

Beck pointed right, a silent indication for us to turn at the corner. "Yep, Sebastian sent me the details while you were talking with Paige."

I nodded. "That's good."

"Do you want to talk about it?" His brows were knitted in concern.

I considered it. "Yes, but not now."

"When you're ready, I'm ready to listen."

I loved this man. So I did the other thing that I wanted to do at that moment—I pulled him in for the kiss.

CHAPTER 40

Beck

"THAT DOESN'T LOOK GOOD," Alice complained from where she stood two feet away from the planter.

As soon as Alice had come home from school an hour ago, Luna stopped by with a bag full of goodies declaring it time to build the fairy garden.

Alice squealed so loud my ears were still ringing. She immediately changed out of her school clothes and into something more "garden appropriate"—her words, not mine—before grabbing a bag from Luna and running next door.

I observed from afar as my daughter proceeded to unpack all the items from their packaging and began laying things out in Luna's yard like she owned it. Luna kept throwing me looks of pure amusement after each new delightful demand from my daughter.

"This is my first fairy garden, so I'm trusting you to make it look good," Luna had told Alice who was taking that comment and running with it.

Luna moved the fairy door for the fifth time. "How about this?"

My daughter clicked her tongue. "The door is the centerpiece; it needs to be perfect."

Luna stood up, dusting off the jeans that sinfully wrapped around her legs. "Maybe you can move it?" she suggested.

With an eye roll, my daughter bent down and started adjusting the bright yellow door that would sit at the base of the large tree that ensconced the backyard.

When she finally found the exact spot she wanted, Alice did her best Vanna White impression. "See? So much better."

Luna and I nodded in unison. I for one, couldn't tell Alice had adjusted it at all, but I was smart enough to keep my mouth shut.

Alice impatiently waved at Luna. "Come on, we gotta finish the cobblestone path leading to the swimming pond."

Luna crouched back down, whispering with Alice while she worked. Alice wore a perpetual smile as they worked together. The indomitable team.

I managed a few emails while they continued until the alarm on Luna's phone went off.

She stood, brushing off the debris from her shins. "I'm sorry, Alice, but I need to head to work."

My daughter immediately abandoned her spot to protest. "But I was hoping you could do movie night with us."

Alice glanced back at me as if looking for backup. "Al, she has to go to work." Then my eyes found Luna's. "But maybe we can find another night this week to watch a movie together."

Luna squeezed my daughter. "I would love that, as long as we can be *extra* cozy."

Alice straightened her arms to get a better look at Luna. "I like being cozy."

Luna grinned. "Who doesn't?"

"And can we get pizza and ice cream?" Alice asked Luna before quickly facing me, hoping for an answer.

I stood and pocketed my phone. "I'll order whatever food you decide on."

Alice launched into Luna again, throwing her off balance. I stepped in to brace them both before anyone crashed.

Luna mouthed a silent "thank you" before saying good night to Alice and heading inside.

When all I wanted her to do was stay.

———

Alice and I were cuddled on the couch watching *Encanto* for the millionth time after Luna left for work.

We were munching on popcorn and singing every chance we got. I loved this time with her. Friday nights were for us. At the end of the long week, I insisted on picking her up from school, making her dinner, and then doing an activity of her choosing. More often than not it entailed movie nights, which suited me just fine.

The unexpected visit from Luna was a bonus. Icing on top of the cake.

During one of the sadder songs, I got up and poured myself a scotch then checked my phone for notifications from Luna. She'd left for Club Deux hours ago and things were probably quiet at the club since it was only eight.

Once I refilled Alice's water, I sat back down, and she immediately crawled next to me, cuddling close. Sometimes she was still my little baby, and I knew any day now she'd be too cool to spend Friday nights with her dad.

"Did you check on Luna yet?" Alice asked, not bothering to take her eyes off the television.

"Huh?"

"Luna. I know you worry more when she's gone."

When did my daughter get so observant?

"She's busy working," I explained.

"Otherwise, she'd be here with us, right, Dad?"

I absently rubbed the spot on my chest over my heart.

"Yes, sweetheart. If she wasn't working tonight, I would invite her over."

Alice finished chewing. "That's good."

I turned to face her. "Is it? Do you like it when Luna's here?"

Finally, Alice peeled her attention away from the TV. "I like her, Daddy. She's nice, and she has the coolest outfits."

I suppressed a laugh. "You like Luna because of her clothes..."

My seven-year-old rolled her eyes. "That's not the only reason."

"Then tell me the other reasons," I prodded.

"I like Luna because you smile more when she's around," Alice said with the confidence and knowing of someone thrice her age. "Except when you guys are fighting. But part of me thinks you like that. It must be some weird grown-up thing."

I chuckled. "You certainly have that right."

Alice reached for the remote and paused the movie. "Are you going to marry her?"

My heart caught in my throat. I'd been dragging my heels on talking to Luna and maybe it was because I needed to have this conversation first.

"If you marry her, will she become my mom?" Alice's face filled with hope.

I swallowed. "If that's what you want and what she wants. But I haven't talked to her about that yet. I would never talk to her about marriage without talking to you about it first."

Alice raised a brow. "That's why we're talking about it now, duh."

I went in for a tactical tickle. "Let's not use the word duh, it's not nice."

She squealed. "No tickles."

I stopped immediately. "No tickles and no 'duhs,' got it?"

She sighed as if this was a major concession. "Fine."

"But seriously, would you be okay if I asked Luna to move in with us?"

"She already lives next door, and she's here most nights."

I dragged a hand through my hair. "That's true."

"If she wants to live with us, she should." Then Alice grabbed another handful of the buttery popcorn and turned the movie back on.

My jaw dropped. "So, I guess we're done talking now."

"Shhh, Dad. The movie's on."

I stifled a laugh and shut my mouth.

————

I fell asleep on the couch after putting Alice to bed, waking frequently to make sure I didn't miss any notifications from Luna. I wanted to make sure she got home safe.

When I hadn't heard from her by two, my willpower ran out, so I texted her.

BECK

> I miss you. Is Darnell driving you home from the club tonight?

While I waited for a reply, I cleaned up the kitchen and put some water in the electric kettle so that Luna could have a cup of herbal tea when she came over tonight.

I assumed she planned to come over.

BECK

> The kettle is hot. The tea bag is in the cup.

LUNA

> I'm really hoping that's a euphemism for something.

I smiled, happy to get a response.

BECK

Let's explore that.

LUNA

You figure it out while I finish up here. Just making one more loop to check on the team.

LUNA

I think Monroe likes the responsibility. She's trying to kick me out.

BECK

That's good. You've talked about her a lot. She's helping to hold down the fort when you're at The Chateau.

LUNA

It's been nice having her to lean on.

Luna's migraines had reduced significantly when she leaned into good supports. I'd like to count myself as one of them.

Between Monroe, Parvati, and Faith, Luna had built quite the support system.

LUNA

And yes, Darnell is on standby. I'll see you at home.

BECK

I'll make sure to reheat the kettle.

———

The alert woke me up.

Luna was *finally* home.

I'd tossed and turned the last couple of hours, jolting myself awake like I was about to miss an early morning flight.

With heavy feet, I padded down the stairs and restarted

the kettle, leaning against the counter top, eyes trained on the door to the backyard.

When the kettle whistled, I lifted it off the stand and poured Luna her chamomile tea. Just then, movement drew my attention.

In slipped Luna wearing her quintessential silk robe. My body relaxed now that she was *here*, at *home*, with *me*.

Exactly where she should be.

I quickly swallowed the distance between us, threading my hands through her hair so I could draw her close. Our lips met in an instant.

Her hungry tongue flicked out, seeking mine, claiming me as much as I claimed her.

Desperate for more, I walked forward until her back was pressed against the wall.

On instinct, she jumped into my arms, legs wrapping around my waist.

With one hand behind her back, I let my other hand wander under the bottom of her robe and hissed. "You don't have anything underneath."

My cock twitched in excitement.

"I didn't want anything to get in the way of this," she said, with a hand caressing the stubble of my jaw between kisses.

I swiped a finger through her sex, sliding in easily. "Are you ready for me, baby? You feel fucking ready."

"Yes," she said breathlessly. "Please, Beck. I've been counting the minutes to get home to you. Don't make me wait any longer."

I withdrew my finger from her sex and pulled my dick out of my loose sweatpants.

My broad tip rested against her entrance, the feeling of her slickness sending me dangerously close to finishing before I even entered her.

The power this woman held over me.

Luna wiggled in frustration before reaching between us

and driving me home. I slid in easily and watched Luna hold her breath as she adjusted to my size.

Our foreheads met.

"You okay there?" I asked.

She nodded, a hand wandering to my ass. Her nails dug in, encouraging me to move.

I met her demand. Thrusting hard to hit her in the place I know she liked so much, the one that would put her over the edge.

We were fast, hurried, and I loved every second of it. It wasn't long until her breathing changed, and her grip tightened. The second the orgasm began to rock Luna, I lost any semblance of holding it together. I immediately came, filling her with my cum.

Once we milked the last of our orgasms, I pulled out of her, and slowly let her feet drop to the floor.

"My feet are wobbly. There's a good chance I'll need you to carry—"

I swept her into my arms before she could even finish her sentence. She laid her head in the crook of my neck. "Now I'm sleepy."

"Let's get you cleaned up and then I'll bring up your tea."

Luna yawned. "Sounds lovely."

She nestled there and was asleep before I laid her on my bed.

With a warm towel, I cleaned her up and pulled the comforter over her lithe body. Then I climbed in after her and fell asleep, Luna's tea long forgotten.

———

I awakened to fingers stroking my back. Luna must have stayed. I stretched, letting her fingers work their magic, and I suppressed a shiver.

"I know you're awake," she said, her warm breath on the

back of my ear. She began planting kisses there and hitched a leg over my body.

"I could get used to you being Big Spoon."

Luna chuckled sleepily. "You wish. Special circumstances."

She was right, and I took a minute to appreciate it. "You stayed the whole night."

Luna nipped at my earlobe. "I did. By the way, you need to put a shirt on before you go downstairs. I may have been a *little* aggressive with these long fingernails while you were having your way with me last night."

I turned around, so we faced each other, completely unbothered that she'd marked me up. I proudly took the claiming. *Still*. "Have my way with you? What is this, some regency romance?"

"God, I wish. You know I love me some Captain Wentworth."

I tucked a stray strand of hair behind her ear. "A second-chance romance. That does sound like something you'd appreciate."

She gaped. "You know *Persuasion*?"

I shrugged. "It's only my favorite Austen novel."

"Since when do you know Austen?"

I loved that I could surprise her. "In the Marines, we didn't have a lot of books in the library. We did, however, have pristine copies of Austen's novels. I must have read them each a half a dozen times."

She shook her head into the pillow. "Wow, you really should have led with this information. I'd have slept over much sooner."

I lifted her pillow out from under her.

She gasped in mock indignation. "No, you didn't."

I propped myself up on my elbow. "Seems like I just did."

Her mouth fell open, and her eyes lit with unfiltered joy as she, quick as a whip, grabbed my pillow out from underneath me and whacked me with it.

"No," I cried, holding my hands up to block the second hit.

"Daddy?" Alice asked from the hall.

Luna and I both halted our movements mid-air. Her pillow fell to the floor, and she immediately reached for the tie on her robe as if Alice would just burst through the door at any second.

Which, *fair*. She was still naked under that thing.

"Meet me downstairs, Alice, and I'll start breakfast."

"Can I watch cartoons?" Alice asked eagerly.

I smiled. "Sure."

"And is Luna joining?" my daughter asked.

Luna looked terrified. I went over to give her a hug. "If she wants to, and I hope she does."

Luna melted in my arms.

"I do," she said.

And for a quick second my mind didn't compute the question, just the response and the spark of hope it ignited for our future.

I heard footsteps leading away from my room.

It was just the two of us again, with Luna looking curiously at me.

My hands found her lower back, and I pulled her close. "I love you."

CHAPTER 41

Luna

I BLINKED SEVERAL TIMES. "Did you just tell me that you love me?"

A smile played on Beck's lips. "Are you suggesting I shouldn't?"

"N—"

"No, I shouldn't love you?" he teased.

I ran my hands up the firm planes of his chest, trying to keep them from shaking. Carter said he loved me, but I'd never felt that feeling in return. The idea that the man in front of me could love me. It struck me senseless.

Even though I felt the same. Even though the words had been on the tip of my tongue several times now.

So I relied on humor. "Oh, please. You barely know me."

He captured my hands in his, his grip firm, centering. "I've known you for eight years."

I tilted my head. "Well, that's not true."

"I met you eight years ago and fell for you harder than I've ever fallen for anyone."

I gulped.

"Since we reconnected—"

"You mean since I ran into you when you were with Sebastian," I clarified.

His heated gaze met mine. "Yes, that. I was so startled to see you. So fucking furious with you for giving me the wrong number."

I lifted a solitary finger. "Let the record state that I didn't actually give you the wrong number."

Beck roughly dragged a hand through his hair. "Yes, I fucked up the number. That's on me and I'll never be able to get those years back."

I traced Beck's pecs paying close attention to a name written there. *Alice.*

"Then you wouldn't have Alice," I said. "And we need Alice."

Pure love and adoration. That was the look Beck blessed me with.

"Yes, we definitely need Alice," Beck confirmed.

He lowered his forehead to mine and said those three little words again. "I love you."

I beamed. "I kind of love you too."

———

"Dr. Wozniac is going to be so excited I had sex standing up."

Beck choked on his coffee.

Alice had gone up to her room to get dressed for the day. When we told her our plan to take her to the Brooklyn Zoo, she immediately bolted upstairs to get ready. I wasn't about to tell her I still needed to shower and so did her dad.

"I'm glad you're going to your therapist about it," Beck said. While other men may have been uncomfortable or embarrassed, Beck held no such judgment. He was genuinely glad I had someone to talk to.

"She gave me two gold stars for the convo with Paige," I said, chest puffed with pride.

Beck finished chewing his scrambled eggs. "As she should. How are you feeling about the run in?"

I sank back in my chair and thought about it for a second. "Is it weird to say I feel great? Like I'm glad I didn't have time to think about it or get nervous about meeting with her. Like the universe knew it needed to happen and didn't give me a chance to second guess myself."

Beck nodded. "You didn't have time to be in your head."

I pointed my fork at him. "Exactly."

We chatted about our plans for the day. I would have to go into work later, but the morning was for us. I'd probably have to sneak in a nap between our activities and the going into the office because I wasn't used to keeping the schedule of a seven-year-old, not that I was complaining.

"Can I take the last of the coffee?" I asked with the warming carafe already poised over my ceramic mug.

Beck smiled. "Sure."

"I appreciate the green light, but I have to be honest, I was going to take that coffee no matter what."

"I figured," he said, dragging a thumb across his bottom lip as I brought my drink to my lips. "So when are you going to move in?"

It was my turn for a spit take. "Excuse me?"

His sly grin sent a vibration across my skin.

Beck stood. "Just letting you know I plan to ask you to move in for real soon."

I pointed to the wall that separated his place from mine. "I literally live next door. Why do we have to move in together?"

He tilted his head over mine in that slow torturous hover, then glanced over his shoulder. "You think we should just make some sort of passage between the two places? Because honestly, Alice would love that."

I coughed on my saliva.

Beck smirked and his kiss brushed my cheekbone. "Consider yourself warned."

Epilogue

ONE YEAR LATER

Luna

"I think I'm going to be sick," I said as Beck zipped me up. We were in my dedicated suite in The Chateau, and it was officially opening night, which meant I was going to razzle and dazzle my first customers.

All my friends were here for the official ribbon cutting, as were some celebrity clients Beck and Faith rounded up. They wanted this place to be as much of a success as I did which meant they may have twisted a few arms and called in a few favors to make sure we had the jet set crowd here.

I also invited every media outlet within a two-hundred-mile radius and even a few west coast outlets that might drum excitement from people across the country.

After years of work and planning and setbacks my dream was about to become a reality and all I could think of was the over/under on my throwing up tonight.

"Do you need a Dramamine or something?" Paige asked. She and Faith were buzzing around like my fairy godmothers directing my glam squad.

I'd hired a director of marketing who was in the room next door waiting for me to come do a few quick interviews before heading down to the Casino floor where the major festivities would take place.

Monroe, who had stepped into her general manager role at Club Deux, had the place on lock just as she had for the last several months while my attention was here in Atlantic City.

The makeup artist was putting the final touches on my lipstick. When she finished, Faith stepped in, placing her hands on my shoulders, our eyes locking in the mirror. "You got this. You're the fiercest boss lady I know."

"I still think we should get something for her stomach," Paige said to Faith. The two were conspiring like I wasn't sitting here, and I kinda loved it.

Paige and I had met up several times since Faith's art show. Those meetups evolved into texting which quickly escalated to sending Austen memes to each other on Instagram.

Then when Paige met Faith, they formed an instant bond too.

My phone beeped.

BECK

Sebastian's mom sent a photo of Bruce and Pepper. They are living their best lives upstate with all that space to run around. Apparently, Willow has adopted them.

I released a breath I didn't know I was holding, a smile stretching across my face as the image came through. Sure enough, the three dogs looked inseparable.

Oh yeah, you didn't think I wasn't going to get Pepper, right?

BECK

You'll do great tonight. Everything is handled down here. Can't wait to see you.

LUNA

You're my sexy security detail; you better be watching my body tonight.

BECK

I'm always watching your body, baby. You should know this by now.

"She's smiling now. Must be Beck," Faith whispered to Paige.

"I can hear you guys. I *am* in the room with you."

They shared a guilty glance as Parvati entered the room. She'd become a vital part of my business management and there was no way I could do this without her now that things were just getting started.

Parvati tapped her clipboard. "It's time to go."

———

The ribbon cutting was a huge success, I made nice with everyone, including some reporters who were more interested in my love life than my business. I easily batted away their irrelevant questions, giving them just enough to keep them on my good side while protecting what I had with Beck and Alice.

Because they were absolutely mine to protect.

Finally, I spotted Beck where he stood talking to Sebastian, Faith, Paige, and her husband Gabe, at a highboy at my favorite bar in the Chateau.

I savored having them all here to support me. My friends who waited up just to be able to congratulate me in person, navigating through all chaos and hoopla without a complaint. I'd been looking forward to this all night. The moment my official duties were finally complete, and I could spend time with my favorite people in the world.

"Hi, baby." Beck enveloped me the second I stepped into

his reach. The hug was deliciously long and grounding. I inhaled his scent and instantly felt more at peace.

"You're incredible and this place you've created is incredible," Beck whispered in my ear.

"Thank you," I said before quickly kissing him.

"Get a room," Paige heckled.

Faith laughed and nudged my old friend. "Hey, I was going to say that."

We moved so that I was standing in front of Beck with my back to his chest. I could lean against him this way while also being able to see my friends.

Then a bartender swooped in with my favorite mockjito.

"Thank you," I mouthed, making a mental note to give them kudos the next time I saw them.

My friends were chatting about the bowling alley when I twisted in place.

"How's Alice?" I asked Beck.

"Having the time of her life," Beck said. Alice spent the evening in the kids club area. She was the inspiration for it to begin with, so it only made sense she christened the space too by eating pizza—still Hawaiian—and playing with other kiddos her own age while being watched by childcare experts who had been highly screened and vetted. "I'll probably have to drag her out of there."

"Well the kids club was too good of an idea. Honestly, cruise ships have them, and I don't know why casinos don't. Parents are going to be more likely to come here if they know they can have fun while their kids are safe and sound."

Beck kissed the corner of my lips. "You're brilliant."

"And Alice can spend all the time she wants at the kids club when you guys are visiting."

We'd talked about this a lot. With The Chateau opening, I needed to spend lots of time overseeing things. I'd spent more time here than in Brooklyn these days which proved challenging at times, but then Beck insisted I get a helicopter.

That had turned out to be an amazing idea because I could shuttle high rollers in from the city and cut my commute time. Making it home most nights because Beck and Alice were my home, and I didn't want to waste a minute not being with them.

Darnell got to work in Atlantic City more, which made him happy since he and Parvati were definitely dating. Not that either of them would admit it.

"We should do something fun to celebrate," Beck said into my ear for only me to hear.

I held his arms around my waist like a belt. "What do you have in mind?"

"We should go to France," he whispered in my ear.

I must have misheard him. "I'm sorry, I thought you said we should go to France."

He nuzzled me. "You heard me correctly."

I frowned. "I just opened a business. I can't fly to France."

His hands splayed in my waist, a thumb coming dangerously close to my breast. Not that I would ask him to move it. "Not right now, you can't. December. Christmas. You, me, and Alice."

"What would we even do there?" Was this man out of his mind?

Beck's thumb kept up its ministrations. "I was thinking we could get engaged."

I spun around so fast I nearly missed my stop. "You want to get engaged?"

The table went silent.

Beck lifted an amused brow. "Yes."

"And you're telling me now. Most women like a little element of surprise," I choked out.

"You aren't most women. And I'd never want to surprise you with a big ask. I want you to feel completely in control."

My face softened. "You're a good man, Beck Bennet. A fine bodyguard and the nosiest next-door neighbor."

"Hey, watch it," he said in mock offense.

"And I love you for it," I said, draping my arms across his shoulders.

He smiled. "You better."

Then the man kissed me like his life depended on it. Like I was his life preserver.

And, well, that was a good thing, because tonight I planned to ask *him* to marry *me*.

The end. Sort of.

Bonus Epilogue

Beck

My woman deserved the world. So, I said no when she proposed. Luna pouted, of course, but I stayed firm in my decision.

Besides, her ring wasn't ready yet.

The End.

Want more of Luna and Beck's love story? Perhaps see how he proposed?

Visit my BookFunnel to read the bonus epilogue:
https://dl.bookfunnel.com/hktcy7g6vc

Also by Erika Lynn

If you're looking for something on the steamier side…

Kiss Cam

Beauty and the Billionaire

Saucy Neighbor

This Thing Between Us

———

If you're looking for something on the sweeter side…

Check out my Christmas Cove novellas. They will leave you with all the Hallmark-Christmas feels.

Christmas Cove Series

Christmas at the Coffee Shoppe

The Christmas Checklist

Saving the Christmas Tree Farm

The Christmas Games

Trigger warning

This book makes reference to a date rape drug and attempted sexual assault. These themes might not be suitable for some readers.

If you want to continue reading, you can jump back to the beginning.

www.ingramcontent.com/pod-product-compliance
Lightning Source LLC
Chambersburg PA
CBHW050025120726
47903CB00006B/1909